The
CRAFTERNOON
— Sewcial Club —
#3

SHOWDOWN

By
JC Williams

You can subscribe to J C Williams' mailing list and view all of his other books at:
www.authorjcwilliams.com

Copyright © 2023 J C Williams

All rights reserved. No part of this book may be reproduced in any manner without written permission except in the case of brief quotations included in critical articles and reviews. For information, please contact the author.

All characters appearing in this work are fictitious. Any resemblance to real persons, living or dead, is purely coincidental.

Cover design by J C Williams

Interior formatting and proofreading & editing by Dave Scott

ISBN: 9798367916386

First printing January 2023

Books by JC Williams

The Flip of a Coin

The Lonely Heart Attack Club

The Lonely Heart Attack Club: Wrinkly Olympics

The Lonely Heart Attack Club: Project VIP

The Seaside Detective Agency

The Seaside Detective Agency: The Case of the Brazen Burglar

Frank 'n' Stan's Bucket List #1: TT Races

Frank 'n' Stan's Bucket List #2: TT Races

Frank 'n' Stan's Bucket List #3: Isle 'Le Mans' TT

Frank 'n' Stan's Bucket List #4: Bride of Frank 'n' Stan

Frank 'n' Stan's Bucket List #5: Isle of Man TT Aces

The Bookshop by the Beach

The Crafternoon Sewcial Club

The Crafternoon Sewcial Club: Sewing Bee

The Crafternoon Sewcial Club: Showdown

Life's a Pitch

———

Cabbage Von Dagel

Hamish McScabbard

Deputy Gabe Rashford: Showdown at Buzzards Creek

Luke 'n' Conor's Hundred-to-One Club

Chapter One

The previously sunny mood shifted in an instant. Gone was the carefree laughter, replaced instead with a grimace and an impending sense of dread.

"Where are we going?" Larry enquired, offering slight resistance to the forward momentum being applied to each of his arms. "Ahem," he said, looking first to his left and then to his right. "I asked where we're going?" he pressed, while attempting to adjust his trajectory with an increased level of resistance. But his efforts were in vain, as he was promptly pulled back on his original course in short order.

He stared intently at a passing lady, trying to convey the severity of his situation, hoping she'd somehow intervene and rescue him from his dire fate. But his attempted telepathic communication went unanswered by the distracted lady, her attention taken by her toddler, who was having something of a hissy fit, bawling and making a terrible racket, and with the young one even throwing herself unceremoniously to the floor to continue her tantrum. Indeed, it was a tactic Larry himself briefly considered adopting if it would offer him any sort of way to halt his progress.

"I didn't sign up for this!" Larry protested as the vicelike grip on each arm intensified. "You promised me a nice pot of Earl Grey and a freshly baked scone!" he reminded his captors standing on either side of him like bouncers ejecting a drunk at closing time.

"Oh, you'll be fine, Larry," Beryl insisted, using her free hand to stroke his arm tenderly, as if she were petting a cat, though

Larry failed to find this action reassuring given his present circumstance.

"Besides," Beryl said, looking across to her friend Joyce positioned on the opposite side. "We both needed a second opinion, Larry, and we value your input. So you should take it as a compliment that you've got your finger on the pulse of high fashion."

Larry looked down to the fingers of both hands, which were dangling helplessly in the air just now, and thus not on the pulse of anything at all right at the moment. "You're just trying to butter me up," he said, currently offering no resistance, resigned now to what was written in the stars for him as, sadly, resistance appeared to be very much futile.

"No we're not," Joyce entered in, using her most soothing tone. "We just wanted a man's opinion, and then we'll head upstairs to the café and treat you to that Earl Grey and delicious scone you were promised."

"That's right," Beryl added. "We're just going to pick out a few bits and bobs, see what you think, and maybe try a couple of things on. It's nothing to be afraid of, Larry. Ten minutes, max."

Larry looked up to the heavens, rolling his eyes. "That's what you told me the last time you dragged me here, and I can guarantee you it wasn't *ten minutes, max*," he said. "It felt like a flippin' eternity."

Without further struggle, Larry was ushered into the Marks & Spencer underwear department, already blushing and doing his best to avoid direct eye contact with the two scantily clad mannequins positioned on either side of the entrance modelling their smalls.

"Whaddya think?" Beryl asked, releasing her grip on Larry. "Do you think Joyce and I could carry off this lacey little number?" she asked with a cackle, striking a pose next to one of the mannequins Larry was trying so earnestly not to look at.

"It's a bit revealing," Joyce observed, moving in for a slightly closer look. "I don't want the boys down at the bingo thinking

I'm a sure thing, now do I, if they caught a glimpse of this?" she mused.

"But if I know you, you'd make certain they caught a glimpse, wouldn't you?" Beryl commented.

"Ha! That's true enough. You've got me there," Joyce heartily agreed, with the two of them laughing boisterously.

Larry shook his head in response to this exchange. "Have you two been getting stuck into that hip flask?" he asked, narrowing his eyes. "Because you're awfully giddy this afternoon."

"Not a drop has crossed our lips," Beryl replied on their behalf. "Clothes shopping is a serious affair that requires a clear head. Doesn't it, Joyce?"

"A clear head," Joyce echoed. "Besides, we're saving the contents of our hip flask to Irish up our coffee later," she added.

Larry followed the two ladies around the underwear department, shoulders sagging, giving the impression that he'd rather be elsewhere. Anywhere, in fact. But fortunately, it wasn't too long before Joyce and Beryl had several bathing suits shortlisted and draped over their arm for further consideration. Indeed, Larry couldn't resist a brief smile, watching his two companions virtually skipping between the aisles, such was their excitement. "You'd think you two were twenty-somethings going to Majorca on holiday by the way you're carrying on," he remarked.

But it wasn't Majorca they were going to, and it was likely some time since either of them had been referred to as twenty-somethings. With a combined age equal to a very respectable score in a game of darts, Joyce and Beryl were, in fact, shopping for suitable swimwear for their highly anticipated visit in a few short weeks to Center Parcs. Ever since Calum extended them an invite to the holiday lodge he'd booked, the two of them had been like excitable schoolgirls, counting down the days until the off.

In truth, neither of them had known precisely what Center Parcs was. But young Stanley went to great lengths explaining all of the outdoor activities that'd be on offer, having provided a detailed description of the lodge Calum had booked, and offering chapter and verse about the hot tub that was sure to soothe their weary bones after their first solid day of new adventures. And according to Stan, there was a generously sized indoor pool to be had as well. As compelling as all of this sounded, Joyce and Beryl were just pleased to be spending time with good friends. And the fact that the venue also boasted several on-site pubs? Well, that had absolutely no bearing at all on their elevated state of enthusiasm (or that was their story, at least, and they were sticking to it).

In addition to Beryl and Joyce, occupying the remaining rooms in their six-bedroomed accommodation were: Stanley and a friend (the friend not selected as yet, with Stanley still struggling to narrow it down), Bonnie and her friend and fellow Crafternooner Abigail, Sam and Mollie, Calum and Charlotte and, finally, Larry occupying the only single room. Although, for a time, Larry was concerned if he'd be able to join the gang on the trip owing to his previous fall.[1] Still, his ankle injury had been healing up nicely, and his doctor had no objections, going so far as to suggest it might be good for Larry to relax on holiday, although armed with instructions not to overdo things. Instructions Charlotte additionally advised to Stanley for good measure, as Stanley was often the chief instigator in the art of overdoing things.

"Surely you're not buying all of those bikinis?" a weary Larry eventually asked, having trailed Joyce and Beryl around for what seemed like an age. "Need I remind you we're only going away for three days?" he reminded them, looking over towards the cashier's desk, where his misery, he hoped, would soon conclude.

Beryl glanced down at the colourful garments she'd selected, draped over her arm. "Of course not," she said, admiring Joyce's equally bright and plentiful bounty as well. "We're going to the changing room to try some on and narrow down the selection."

Larry released a pained sigh, suspecting he'd be waiting a while longer for his scone and cuppa. "I didn't think you were

---

[1] See THE CRAFTERNOON SEWCIAL CLUB: SEWING BEE for details!

permitted to try articles such as that on?" he asked. "You know, items of such an intimate nature?"

"*Pfft*," Beryl said, unconcerned by this comment and forging ahead to the changing room, leaving Larry in her wake. "How am I supposed to know if they're comfortable if I don't try them on?" she said over her shoulder. "Come along, Joyce," she added, calling after her friendly co-conspirator. "I can't wait to see you in that pretty yellow number you picked out."

"Wait!" Larry said, panic evident in his voice. "You're both going in at the same time?" he asked. "What about me? You can't leave me all on my own, hanging about outside in the underwear department! What will people think?"

"You could come in with us," Joyce cheekily suggested. "But I'm not sure your blood pressure would cope."

"We'll only be a few minutes, Larry," Beryl assured him. "Why don't you have a wander around the shop, or just take a seat?" she advised, directing him towards the sofa positioned outside the changing rooms for similarly fatigued people in the situation poor Larry found himself in.

With both options left open, Beryl and Joyce entered the dressing room, leaving Larry rooted to the spot. Surrounded by lacey underwear, vibrant bikinis, and scantily clad mannequins in every direction, Larry pivoted round uneasily, unsure of what exactly to do next. He knew his panic was likely irrational, but he was of a particular vintage where seeing ladies' bloomers on display wasn't the done thing for a gentleman. As such, he was like a rabbit caught in the headlights, uncertain if he should take a seat outside the ladies' changing room as Beryl suggested or wander through the lingerie department towards the exit, unescorted. Neither option was particularly appealing to him.

However, Larry's contemplation was disrupted by a young shop assistant who would have likely noted his indecisive body language. "Can I help, sir?" she asked, presenting herself before him. "Or are you just looking?" she added, flashing him a courteous smile.

"What?" a startled Larry replied, offering the helpful assistant a nervous laugh. "Looking?" he said as his cheeks turned a shade of crimson. "No, I'm definitely not looking!" he assured her, lowering his head, suddenly very interested for a moment in the condition of his polished shoes.

"Ah," the young lady said, her pleasant, accommodating expression indicating she was familiar with this sort of situation and willing to render the required assistance.

But before she could continue, Larry reached out his right hand, extending his index finger. "I'm only just waiting for my friends," he explained, his head bowed again as he pointed in the general direction of the changing rooms. Unfortunately, because he wasn't looking at what he was doing, Larry's extended finger promptly came into contact with the pert chest of one of the store mannequins which was proudly displaying the shop's wares. This, of course, made him even more horrified and embarrassed than he'd been previously.

The shop assistant couldn't resist an amused smile. "It's fine, sir. We often have gentlemen waiting for their lady friends," she said, hoping to put Larry at ease. "If you like, there's a waiting area next door in the men's clothing department. Perhaps you'd be more comfortable there, and I could let your companions know where you are when they're finished? And, as it's not too busy at the moment, I could swing by the staff canteen and fetch you a nice cup of tea as well?"

"That would be most wonderful," said an immensely relieved Larry. "That's a very kind offer and one I'd be delighted to take you up on, young lady."

After a lovely cup of tea and a detailed review of the day's newspaper (both items supplied by Shannon, the helpful sales assistant), Larry was finally starting to enjoy his unscheduled shopping experience.

"Ah, there he is," Joyce announced a few minutes later, flashing the seated Larry a toothy grin.

"Would you just look at that," Beryl added in. "Lord Muck relaxing over there like he owns the place," she remarked. "Anyway, you'll be pleased to know that's us all finished," she advised, raising her shopping bags to confirm that point. "The young lady said we'd find you here, and so here is where we are."

Larry folded the newspaper, placing it on the arm of the sofa. "So that's you both swimming-pool ready?" he enquired, pushing himself into a standing position, and happy he never had to watch the ladies model their purchases after all, as they'd originally suggested (his finger being on the pulse of fashion, and all that rubbish).

Joyce linked her arm through his. "We're ready for action, Larry," she was pleased to confirm. "Now, I believe we owe you a scone and a cup of Earl Grey for being so patient with us?"

"Yes, that's the least you can do," Larry offered with a scowl, although he wasn't being serious in his displeasure.

"Hang on, before we leave," Beryl said, directing their attention towards a metallic display stand that had caught her eye, one which offered up an array of gentlemen's swimwear options. "Do you need to pick something out for yourself while we're here?" she asked with a grin. "There are some terrific-looking budgie smugglers, and they're only half-price," she noted.

Larry shook his head in the negative. "My swimwear drawer is already amply stocked, thank you very much," he asserted. "And besides, I'm not sure the smugglers you speak of would leave too much to the imagination," he added with a raised eyebrow. "Would I be correct?"

"If they're good enough for that new Sean Connery replacement, Daniel Craig..." Joyce considered aloud, drifting away for a moment to imagine, in her mind, the thought of a dripping-wet James Bond emerging from the sea.

"Come on, Miss Moneypenny," Larry said, giving Joyce's arm a gentle tug. "Let's get you out of here before you end up all hot and bothered. Also, there's a scone in the café which has already waited long enough to meet me, I should think."

Chapter Two

"Yes, this is Charlotte Newman," Charlotte confirmed to the caller on her mobile phone. "How can I help?" she asked, sounding somewhat sceptical, having not recognised the caller's number, nor the man's voice.

Charlotte listened to what the fellow had to say, pacing slowly back and forth past the shelving unit in Joan's Wools & Crafts crammed tightly with balls of wool. "Right," she offered after a minute or so, removing the phone from her ear to check once again the number displayed on the screen. "George, is that you putting on a silly voice?" she asked, once the phone was pressed back against her ear. "Because if that is you, then you should know that I'm on a *very* critical business appointment," she advised, reaching out and extracting a ball of sunflower-yellow wool that she reckoned would be perfect for her latest cardigan.

But it wasn't her ex-husband on the phone. At least according to the assurances being offered her way. "Wait, you're actually being serious?" she asked, walking to the shop counter and placing the ball of wool she'd selected next to several others she'd previously placed there. "You're not teasing me?" she said, her frown emerging into a smile. "Oh, well, in that case, I'm sorry for saying you had a silly voice, Chris," she added, holding up an apologetic hand, which of course Chris, on the other end of the call, couldn't see.

Charlotte reached into her handmade bag, removing a notepad and pen and then furiously jotting down the details provided by Chris. "That shouldn't be a problem at all," Charlotte declared, once finished, drawing in a happy little smiley face at the foot of her notes. "Yes," she said brightly. "I'll look forward to seeing you all then."

Charlotte placed the phone back in her pocket, grinning like a fool.

"Well?" asked Laura, from the business side of the counter. "Not that I was being nosey," she said, fibbing. "But the look on your face tells me that was an interesting call?"

Charlotte gnawed away on the inside of her cheek, staring dreamily into the distance, reflecting on her conversation with Chris moments before.

"Earth to Charlotte," Laura said, waving her hand slowly. "Is there anybody at home?" she added, but with no response. "Free wool for today only!" she shouted, hoping that might do the trick.

"What? Oh, sorry," Charlotte offered, shaken from her reveries. "And you *were* being nosey," she teased. "But that's okay. That phone call was from a BBC researcher called Chris," Charlotte revealed, reeling in her bait ever so slightly, enticingly, now she had a little nibble on the end of her line and the fish was showing some interest, so to speak.

Laura placed her elbows on the countertop, leaning in closer. "And...?" she said, eager to hear more. "Spill it, Charlotte."

"Well," Charlotte said, giving her rod a gentle jiggle. "Apparently, word of our crafting-related initiatives has reached the ear of BBC North West. And they're keen to hear more about the Crafternoon Sewcial Club, Make It Sew, and also the work on the school uniform recycling programme."

"And they want to interview you?" Laura ventured, putting two and two together.

"Yes!" Charlotte confirmed, clapping the tips of her fingers together while dancing a happy little dance. "They've asked if they can send a camera crew to one of our Crafternoon sessions to record a feature for the evening news. And who knows? This could mean other people getting involved and rolling out similar programmes of their own across the UK. That would be fantastic, right?"

"Ah, that's wonderful news, Charlotte. And your sparkling personality will be absolutely brilliant in front of the camera."

"Oh, but..." Charlotte began.

"But? You're not nervous, are you, Charlotte? Because I'm sure you'll—"

"Me? No, I'll be absolutely fine. Well, I think I will. It was the guys at Crafternoon I was thinking about, actually."

"Ah, I'm sure the nerves won't get the better of them."

"No, it's not that," Charlotte advised. "Most of the time, you can never shut them up. So I don't imagine there'll be any problem there," she added with a fond smile. "No, I'm just wondering how on earth we'd narrow down which of them should be interviewed, if the need should arise. Because I expect all of them to be vying for the microphone, given half the chance!"

"That's a nice problem to have," Laura said with a chuckle. "And if, during your own interview process, you wanted to drop in a little mention of your favourite craft shop..." Laura hinted, stuffing Charlotte's multiple purchases into a bag after ringing them through the till. "That's twenty pounds and fifteen pence, if you'd be so kind?"

But instead of reaching for her purse, Charlotte narrowed her eyes, staring across the counter with the steely resolve of Clint Eastwood in an old Sergio Leone Spaghetti Western, the only thing missing being the distinctive Ennio Morricone score. In fact, from the looks of things, Laura was afraid she might even spit out a bit of chewing tobacco.

"Uhm, everything, okay?" Laura asked, briefly maintaining eye contact for as long as she was comfortable. "You've not forgotten something, have you?"

"No," Charlotte said, squinting her eyes even squintier now. "But I think *you* have?"

"I have?"

"Sure. I'm fairly certain you mentioned 'free wool for today only' not two minutes ago."

"Did I? How odd. That doesn't sound like something I'd say...?" Laura offered, a sudden case of amnesia overtaking her. "It must have been the shock of that phone call from the BBC," she put forth. "You know, making you hear things?"

"Hmm," Charlotte said, reaching for her purse. "Shock does do funny things to you, I suppose."

"It does indeed," Laura agreed. "But you know what I *can* do for you before you go, Charlotte?"

"Oh, what's that?"

"Make my favourite customer a nice cuppa, and we can talk about how you can drop the name of the shop into your interview," Laura said with a playful wink.

"If you throw in a biscuit, Laura, you've got yourself a deal."

❊ ❊ ❊

No matter how hectic or jam-packed Charlotte's diary was with crafting-related commitments, she made sure she was available to drop young Stanley to school and fetch him again at chucking-out time. It was a highlight of her day and an opportunity she relished, made possible by the flexible nature of her workload. More often than not, she'd leave the car at home (as they lived relatively close), making the journey on foot. And with no technological distractions on Stanley's part — such as Minecraft or YouTube on his computer or what have you — she'd have the full attention of her walking companion twice daily. And whilst their conversations were often inconsequential, nattering on about this thing or that, it didn't matter as it was quality time with her boy and an opportunity she knew that many parents didn't get a chance to enjoy.

But she knew it wasn't going to be forever, and that realisation, on occasion, left her a bit glum. With Stanley getting older, his time at primary school wouldn't last forever, and he'd soon be promoted to 'Big Boy School' — where having his mum walk him to and from probably wasn't going to be on top of his 'cool' agenda. There was a time when Stanley, not so long ago, was glued to her side, gripping onto her hand for dear life. But that was starting to feel like a distant memory. Now, he was morphing from being a child onto his journey to being a young man, and Charlotte often wanted to hit the pause button on life just to keep hold of her little boy for as long as she could. Still, it was as if Stanley had a sixth sense for matters involving his mum's fragile emotions, bless his heart. While he wasn't overly generous with his public displays of affection (at least in front of his mates), he seemed to know just when his mum needed a gentle hand squeeze, a peck on the cheek, or to be wrapped up in her arms for a nice cuddle (again, as long as his mates weren't in the vicinity, of course, and within viewing distance).

Charlotte had experienced the same type of conflicting emotions throughout young Stanley's life, such as when he was leaving nursery school, his first day at primary school, and his first trip off-island without her, for example. Because of this, she knew it was all just another part of life's rich tapestry and would form the next chapter in his grand adventure, and she was delighted to be there, with him, along for the ride.

Today, coming from Joan's, she had driven the way to school. And soon enough, the school bell chimed, signalling the conclusion of another day of ostensible learning. Milliseconds later, a swarm of children spilt onto the playground, a sea of red jumpers filled with ecstatic youngsters thrilled to break free of their academic shackles.

"You've been to Joan's," Stanley remarked a short time later, having successfully navigated a path through the throng to his mother's location.

"And it's lovely to see you, too," Charlotte said with a laugh, running her hand through his mop of hair. And then, with his words registering, "Wait, how do you know that?" she asked, confused, as she had no bags about her person at present.

"Ah," Stanley said, raising a finger in response. "First," he said, glancing briefly down to her feet, "you're not wearing your comfortable walking shoes today. Which must mean you've come by car, rather than on foot, correct?"

Charlotte nodded along, pressing out her lower lip, amazed by his sudden powers of observation. "Correct. But how does—"

"Ah," Stanley cut in, one step ahead, it would appear. "You only ever drive here if you've done some shopping along the way, or if it's raining cats and frogs," he explained, pointing to the clear blue sky without a raincloud visible, illustrating that there were no such cats and frogs on this fine day.

Charlotte overlooked the 'frogs' reference, not bothering to correct him, as his charming malapropism always made her smile. "Okay, but I might just as easily have been to Tesco, not Joan's," she offered up as an alternative. "So there's that," she said, folding her arms across her chest in a *how-do-you-like-that* manner.

Stanley went quiet. However, it wasn't the sort of quiet indicating he was stumped, but rather that he already knew the answer and just wanted to build tension. (Although, in truth, he was still working out the solution.) He cradled his jaw between thumb and forefinger, caressing his still-hairless chin as he looked his mum up and down. "Aha!" he announced shortly thereafter, like a seafront magician pulling a rabbit out of his top hat. "Because if you'd been to Tesco, you probably wouldn't have a cloth *measuring tape* hanging out of your trouser pocket," he suggested, pointing to the offending article.

Charlotte was distracted for a moment, glancing over her shoulder to see if the traffic in the carpark had started to ease. "Yeah, but," she said, giving her full attention to Stanley once again. "But that doesn't necessarily mean—"

"Right. Well what about that?" Stanley cut in once more, extending his hand towards her jumper. "This looks like a strand of yellow wool that very much doesn't belong on a cream-coloured jumper," he observed, removing the errant item. "May I present Exhibit A for your consideration?"

Charlotte laughed in response, caught bang to rights as she was. "All right, guilty as charged," she said, holding up her hands in surrender. "That was some very impressive deductive reasoning, Stanley," she offered. "Although I think maybe you've been watching a few too many episodes of *Sherlock* over at your dad's house, am I right?"

"Guilty as charged," Stanley confessed, echoing his mum's words, and raising his own hands in surrender.

"Come on, then, Hercule Poirot," Charlotte suggested, switching between fictional detectives and leading him towards their parked vehicle. "The carpark is starting to clear, so let's get you home, yeah?"

Once underway, Stanley unzipped the school rucksack sitting atop his knees, staring lovingly at the contents held therein.

"You can't wait to start your homework, kiddo?" Charlotte joked after losing her son's attention for a moment and figuring it wasn't his textbooks that were so captivating. "Stanley?" she added a moment later, with no response offered. "I said..." she went on to say, but experience taught her that he'd drifted off to another place and that it was best to just wait a moment or two and eventually he'd come back to the present.

"Do you want a KitKat?" Stanley asked, after dipping his hand inside his rucksack. "Or a Mars Bar?" he added as an alternative, removing one of each for his mum's consideration.

Charlotte flicked her eyes over to her son before returning them to the road ahead. "What's with all the chocolate, Stan?" she asked. "How much have you got in there? Have you robbed the school tuck shop or something?"

"No," Stanley replied, removing several other sugary delights from his bag. "I just have *very* generous friends," he suggested and then, changing the apparent direction of the conversation, "Mum, when do you need to know which one of my mates is coming to Center Parcs with us? I mean, what's the absolute last date?"

Charlotte was about to reply, when the significance of this seemingly unrelated question suddenly registered, producing a raised eyebrow as it did. "Stanley..." she said, stopping before the red traffic light ahead.

"Yeah, Mum?"

"Stanley, are you being bribed by your mates so they can come to Center Parcs with you?" she asked, shifting her attention towards the passenger seat. "Is that why your rucksack is currently like a vending machine?"

"Bribed?" replied Stanley, blinking innocently, as if he didn't know what the word meant.

"Yes. Are your mates each giving you sweets, so that you'll select them to come on holiday with you?" Charlotte asked, breaking it down for the young fella.

"Oh. *Bribed*," Stanley answered, as if the meaning of the word had suddenly become clear. "I suppose. Yeah," he said nonchalantly. And then, "Can we go to Disneyland next year?" he asked. "Because if we did, I reckon I could request cash, rather than sweets. Although sweets are also good."

Charlotte laughed. She wasn't quite sure what she thought of this little bribery scheme but figured if Stanley's mates were willing to part with their chocolate, then it was at least doing their teeth a favour. "I suppose I should be honoured," Charlotte suggested, having given the matter some consideration, until the light turned green at least.

"Eh, why?"

"Well, coming away with us crafting oldies must be the hottest ticket in the playground, if your mates are so keen on joining us, no?"

Stanley squirmed in his seat, returning the various chocolate bars to the safety of his bag. "Ehm... yeah. I suppose so, Mum."

"Wait, you've not told them, have you?"

"Of course I have, Mum," Stanley shot back. "I've told them all about Larry, Joyce, and Beryl, and what you all get up to with your, you know, knitting needles and stuff."

"And they're still wanting to come?" Charlotte asked, feeling rather proud about this revelation. "Ooh," she added, "perhaps I could give your friend some crafting instruction on the journey over? I mean, if your friends are that excited about it?"

"Sounds like a plan," Stanley offered, giving her a thumbs-up. "Mum...?" he added as an afterthought. "Mum, I don't suppose there are any theme parks near where we're going, are there?"

"I don't think so, Stan," Charlotte answered, somewhat puzzled as to why he would ask such a thing. "I mean, I could ask Calum, as he's visited the area previously, when..."

"Yes? When what?" Stanley asked, confused as to why his mum had trailed off, never finishing her thought.

"Stanley Newman!" said Charlotte.

"That's my name?" Stanley replied.

"Have you told your mates you're taking the most generous one of them to a theme park when we're on holiday? Is that why you've got a rucksack full of chocolate?"

"Well... pretty much," Stanley confessed with a shrug. "I may have also accidentally mentioned that there might be a firework factory in the area where you can make your own and set them off," he added. "I don't suppose there is, is there?" he asked, more in hope than in expectation.

"No, Stan. I'm fairly certain there won't be a firework factory," she said, unsure if she should be annoyed with her son or commend him on his entrepreneurial spirit (even if he'd been a bit more than liberal with the truth to his friends). "Anyway," she said, moving the conversation along to something else, "I have important news to share."

"I'm not having a brother or sister, am I?" Stanley asked. "Because Charlie in my class now has to share his bedroom for that reason. And I don't mind a brother or sister, but I'm not sure how I'd feel about sharing my room."

"What!?" Charlotte said, taken aback that her being pregnant was Stanley's immediate assumption. "No, you're most certainly *not* having a new brother or sister," she insisted. And then, under her breath, "At least I flippin' hope not."

"Ah," a relieved Stanley said, pleased he'd continue to have his room all to himself for the foreseeable. "So...?"

"Well, young man," Charlotte said, pulling up outside their cottage. "Your mum is going to be appearing on *BBC News*!" she informed him, hoping for an enthusiastic reaction such as the announcement warranted.

Stanley, however, groaned in response. "Oh," he said, pushing his head back into the seat. "Is this because you stole that aubergine from Tesco last week? If so, this will be so embar—"

"I didn't *steal* the aubergine from Tesco," Charlotte shot back, looking all around to make sure she wasn't heard through the open car windows. "I missed it in the bottom of the shopping trolley, and I completely forgot it was there," she said, lowering her voice. "Besides, I went in and paid for it the next day," she reminded him.

"So you're not going to jail?"

"Of *course* I'm not going to jail, Stan. Not for an aubergine," she assured him, before explaining the actual, real reason for her upcoming appearance on the Beeb.

And to give him his due, young Stanley listened intently to everything she had to say, and secretly wondered if he might possibly make an appearance on the telly alongside her as well. "Way to go, Mum!" Stan offered once he was entirely up to speed on the situation. "You know," he added, "as far as mums go, you're pretty cool. And if you should happen to go to jail, I just want to say, I'm fairly certain you could look after yourself in there."

"Oh, thanks!" Charlotte said, happy to accept whatever compliments she could get. "And am I cool enough for a peck on the cheek?" she asked, manoeuvring her head into position so as to receive said peck.

"Yeah, go on," Stan said, puckering up. "Oh, and Mum?" he said, once the requested kiss was duly dispatched. "When we get inside, can we double-check that there isn't a firework factory anywhere near where we're going on holiday? You know, just to be sure?"

Chapter Three

It wasn't that the Crafternoon Sewcial Club attendees were ordinarily shabbily dressed, necessarily. But on this particular Thursday, every arrival at the Union Mills Methodist Church hall was impeccably turned out, sporting their finest attire and looking for all the world like they were attending a swanky red-carpet movie premiere. Congregating on the freshly cut lawn outside the church hall, the members chatted happily amongst themselves, enjoying a nice cup of tea in the pleasant afternoon sun.

"Raise your hand if you need a refill," Larry called out from the steps leading up to the church entrance. "I said raise your hand if you need a refill!" Larry shouted a little louder, scanning the crowd like an auctioneer looking for bids. "Ah, there we go, Stan," Larry said, directing his able assistant towards the far side of the grass. "The minister and his wife need a top-up."

"On it," Stanley confirmed, carefully negotiating down the steps, armed with his teapot, and continuing onward. But before he'd travelled too far, another group out on the lawn spotted him approaching, their china cups raised for his immediate attention. The minister and his wife would have to wait for a refill a moment longer, it would appear.

The arrival of the BBC camera crew on the island was meant to be a fairly simple, straightforward affair, at least according to the researcher Charlotte had spoken to, an opportunity, mainly, for the production team to record a three-minute feature showcasing Charlotte in action alongside her carefree Crafternooners, and then a short interview where she could highlight her recent crafting and school uniform initiatives as well. The hope for Charlotte was that there would be a ripple effect once the feature aired, inspiring others to organise similar events across the UK and beyond.

However, as the recently landed BBC team quickly realised, this was anything *but* an informal affair if the sizeable group enjoying refreshments al fresco was anything to go by. Packed into the church grounds were most of the Crafternooners, a number of the representatives from Make It Sew, and a good number of those who'd been involved with Square If You Care and ReCyCool as well.

For Charlotte, organising a little afternoon shindig was her way of showing appreciation to those who without their support and enthusiasm none of the ideas in her head would have come to fruition. And one of the benefits of being involved in the island's crafting scene was that when the call went out for volunteers to help cater the bash, Charlotte was soon drowning in egg sandwiches, mushroom vol-au-vents, and an extraordinary selection of freshly baked cakes, amongst other things, as many of her fine members loved to cook and bake as much as they loved to craft!

"What are you three up to?" Charlotte asked, walking over to Joyce, Beryl, and Mabel, who were all presently standing motionless like statues. "Everything okay, ladies?" she enquired, wondering why three of the most sociable people she knew were lined up and not saying a word to each other. "I said..." Charlotte started to say, until she followed the direction of their eye line, realising what (or *who*, as it should happen) had currently taken their attention. "Ah," Charlotte said with a smirk. "I'm guessing you three are fans of the BBC roving reporter, Darren Shipley?"

"He can interview me any day of the week," Joyce advised, fanning her face with her fingertips.

"He's worth the TV licence fee all on his own," Beryl added.

"So why don't you go and talk to him instead of hiding over here gawping?" Charlotte suggested. "He's lovely, and I'm sure he won't bite."

"Pfft," Mabel chipped in. "These two..." she said, motioning to her mates. "These two haven't left the poor bloke alone since he arrived. Why do you think he's carrying around a plate with several too many pieces of cake on it? Bloody stalkers, the pair of them, and likely ruined any chance I might have had with him with their pestering ways."

"Oh, he's walking over," Charlotte observed, but as the others were already zeroed in on him, eyes unblinking, this was a fact the three women were likely already aware of.

"Charlotte!" Darren called out, carrying his weighty, cake-laden plate. "Hello, ladies," he added politely upon arrival, resulting in a schoolgirl titter from his blushing cheerleading section. "I think I'm going to struggle to finish all of this cake you've given me," he said, giving his tum a gentle pat, which only served to release another round of titters.

"Darren, you're sure you don't mind us hijacking you and your cameraman for our little get-together here, before we get down to business inside?" Charlotte asked, tilting her head with a concerned look.

Darren shook his head in the negative. "No, not at all," he assured her. "I'm delighted to be here. After all, I am a community reporter, so it's a pleasure to spend time in the community. In fact, I wish I'd more time before our return flight to enjoy the island a bit more. But at least we've yet to record another piece, that one being with a farmer in Ramsey laying claim to growing the world's largest turnip. So there's that."

"Wow," Charlotte offered, unsure what else to say on that topic. "Impressive."

"I know," Darren said with a flicker of a smile. "But I suppose it beats reporting on murders, muggings, and armed robbery on a daily basis. Plus, these feel-good community stories mean my cameraman and I get to visit your charming little island on occasion, periodically affording us the chance to meet the wonderful locals."

"Oh, stop it," Joyce interjected, waving away the compliment, as she assumed the latter part was intended specifically for her benefit. "Can I get you some more cake?" she asked, overlooking the bounty of slices already occupying Darren's plate. "Or you could have a good slurp from my hip flask if you'd prefer?"

"No, but thanks," Darren offered cordially, glancing down at his watch. "Charlotte, perhaps we should..."

"Ah, yes. Of course. The tables are set up and ready for crafting action in the church hall," Charlotte advised. "So all we need now are some crafters to man the guns, so to speak."

Darren and his cameraman headed indoors to prepare what needed preparing from their side, leaving Charlotte to round up her crew. Ordinarily, the Crafternooners were practically breaking through the church door, desperate to start scratching their crafting itch. But when there was cake, conversation, tea, or a glass of fizz on offer, gathering the team could prove as challenging as herding cats. Apart from Joyce, Beryl, and Mabel, that is, who trotted along smartly, following after Darren like lovesick teenagers.

Charlotte took up a position on top of the church steps, clearing her throat to make herself heard. But before she called out, she used her elevated view to cast an affectionate eye over those congregated on the church lawn engaged in conversation, many with new friends they'd made through their collective appreciation of crafting. For a brief moment, Charlotte's mind wandered back to her very first Crafternoon Sewcial Club. She enjoyed a nostalgic smile, recalling how nervous she had felt, worrying if anybody would actually show up. Similar to her Make It Sew class, however, what started out with humble beginnings slowly evolved, building in numbers week on week to what they were now.

But she certainly wasn't resting on her laurels. She'd experienced firsthand the impact of community initiatives and directly witnessed the positive outcomes. Whether it was new parents desperate for adult company, lonely pensioners looking for friendship, or even those in school hoping to learn a new skill, these clubs and those similar played an essential role in building communities, forging friendships, and offered, for many, a reason to climb out of bed each day and leave the house. Each smile, each laugh, each completed crochet square and each dropped stitch all motivated Charlotte, convincing her she was involved in something fabulous and spurring her forward to spread the positive message to anybody willing to listen (and sometimes to those who weren't!).

"Ahem, ladies and gentlemen," Charlotte eventually offered, politely raising her hand. "Ladies and gentlemen," she repeated a moment later, having garnered zero reaction with her first attempt. But unfortunately, her second attempt wasn't having too much success either. "Excuse me, if you could—"

"Right, let's be having your attention!" Larry's gruff voice bellowed out from behind Charlotte, accompanied by him banging a metal serving spoon against the sturdy plastic tray he was carrying. It was crude but effective, as dozens of heads turned in their direction.

"Thanks, Larry," Charlotte offered over her shoulder.

"No problem, skipper."

"Sorry to interrupt the festivities," Charlotte announced, with all eyes now on her, "but the BBC team are eager to get started. So if we could have some crafting bums on seats in the church hall, that'd be marvellous."

"Drain your drinks, consume your cake, and let's get going!" Larry chipped in, hooking a thumb over his shoulder in the direction of where they should be heading.

"Yeah, thanks, Larry, I think they've got the message now," Charlotte said, turning to him with an affectionate smile. "Now let's get you inside and into position for your own small-screen debut."

"Ah, well, it's not actually my debut," Larry advised, feeling a gentle guiding hand placed between his shoulder blades. "You see, there was this one time back in the sixties, nineteen-sixty-eight, to be precise, when I answered an ad to be cast as an extra in a series of..."

After the rest of Larry's story, and soon enough and without too much further cajoling required, every seat inside the church hall was occupied with Crafternooners and representatives from Make It Sew, all dutifully busying themselves with their latest crafting project and trying their best not to look in the direction of the camera, as instructed.

"Susie?" Charlotte whispered to the table closest. "Susie, dear, you're holding your knitting needles upside down," she pointed out.

"What? Oh, sorry. Nerves," Susie whispered back, along with a chuckle, adjusting her needles accordingly.

"Just be yourself, and you'll be fine," Charlotte suggested, a moment before the interior of the church hall was flooded with additional, artificial light emanating from the camera equipment.

"Ready, Brian?" Darren asked of his cameraman, receiving a firm nod and a raised thumb as confirmation. Darren glanced over to Charlotte, indicating he was about to start, before then pressing the microphone to his lips and proceeding.

"Many of our regular viewers will know that I'm partial to craftwork, having made and modelled my own Hawaiian shirt during our Children In Need fundraiser this year," Darren began, while adopting his finest camera-ready voice. "And so it's an enormous pleasure to be on the Isle of Man today, surrounded by crafters who know what they're doing. The brainchild of dedicated local crafter Charlotte Newman, Make It Sew and the Crafternoon Sewcial Club are just two of the initiatives drawing the community together with a collective passion for all things crafting, and—"

"Hang on... Cut," Brian the cameraman interjected, temporarily peeling himself away from behind the viewfinder. "Right. There's a chap in the background of the shot, standing stiff as a board and staring directly at the camera," he advised, motioning towards the particular culprit.

"Everything okay, Larry?" Charlotte stepped in, identifying where the cameraman's index finger was directed.

In response, Larry continued to stand like a tree, his gaze unwavering, his face sporting a somewhat constipated expression.

"I'm posing for the camera," he said through clenched teeth and pursed lips, talking like a ventriloquist. "Looking at the camera, as ordered, and waiting for the instruction to smile."

Darren laughed, but not in an unkind way. "I think you've possibly misunderstood," he said. "Why don't you relax, maybe have a seat, and it's probably best if you *don't* look directly at the camera while we're filming," he explained. "Oh, and don't worry, this isn't going out live."

"I thought you'd done this before!" Joyce called over with a cackle. "The way you were carrying on earlier, we thought you'd spent more time in front of the bloody cameras than David Attenborough!"

"But I thought we were taking a photograph?" Larry asked, looking around for answers. "I could've sworn I heard we were taking a photograph first, for some reason," he added, laughing happily away to himself.

"Get yourself over here, you," Joyce instructed, sliding up the bench she was sitting on to open up a space for her pal. "Thought it was a photograph indeed."

Darren glanced over to his cameraman. "Do I need to start from the top, or can we…?"

"Pick it up where you left it," Brian advised, returning his attention to the viewfinder.

"Each week," Darren continued, effortlessly resuming right where he'd left off, "the various crafting clubs attract over one-hundred creative people of all ages and abilities." Darren drew up alongside one of the busy tables, offering a reassuring smile. "Can you tell me what brings you along each week?" he asked of Carole, one of the newer Crafternooners, who was stitching the arm on a cardigan she was working on.

"Oh, ehm…" Carole offered timidly, somewhat startled to have a microphone unexpectedly thrust in her direction. "Well, I've only been coming in for several weeks, you see…" she indicated, trailing off and lowering her head, as if she'd already reached the conclusion of whatever she was going to say.

"Right, well..." Darren replied, sounding uncertain if Carole was still considering her response, or if that was indeed the end of it. He slowly retracted his microphone so that he could move his attention elsewhere.

"But it's the people!" Carole blurted out, suddenly raising her head again. "I mean, that's the reason."

"Ah. The people?" Darren enquired, sounding like he was open to hearing more.

"They care," Carole advised, looking to those seated on either side of her. "I didn't really get out much after my Alan passed away," she explained. "But I saw a video online with Charlotte and the others being interviewed after their school uniform recycling thingy. And I thought they looked like a fun bunch."

"And they are?" Darren prompted.

"Oh, yes," Carole said, nodding in complete agreement. "It feels like being part of a huge family where everybody looks out for each other, plus you get help in learning how to make some lovely new things," she said, proudly holding up her partially completed cardigan towards the camera.

"I'll leave you to your creation, then," Darren warmly suggested, continuing on with his tour around the church hall, giving Brian, behind the camera, the opportunity to capture more of the industrious crafters, all with their heads buried in their work and, unlike Larry and his initial faux pas, doing their very best to avoid eye contact as directed. And once Brian had recorded enough content and was happy with what they'd got, he signalled towards Darren.

And, taking his cue, Darren then presented himself before Charlotte, standing with the crafting tables as her backdrop. "And that brings us nicely on to the architect of the crafting clubs, the designer, if you will, Charlotte Newman. Charlotte, how important are these initiatives to the community?"

In response, Charlotte's face immediately lit up. "Oh, they're vital, in my opinion," Charlotte advised. "And we're blessed to have a membership ranging in ages from fifteen all the way to ninety-two."

THE CRAFTERNOON SEWCIAL CLUB: SHOWDOWN

"Ninety-three!" Joyce called over, out of camera shot.

"Sorry, ninety-three," Charlotte said with a grin, happy to be corrected. "But that's why I adore crafting so much, as it doesn't discriminate against age or ability. So anybody can give it a go, is what I'm saying. Everyone is welcome."

"Even me?" Darren asked.

"Of course," Charlotte answered. "Just look at how expert you were at crafting that Hawaiian shirt!" she joked. "But seriously, what started with a bunch of amazing people taking a crafting class in a nursing home has spread across the island, as you can see today."

"So what would you say to someone who's never crafted before and wanted to come along?"

"I'd say feel free to join us! The more the merrier!" Charlotte insisted. "Honestly, we just have the most wonderful time. And while the crafting might get somewhat involved, depending on your project, equally important is just making new friends, socialising, and having fun."

"I can certainly see you've been having fun today," Darren responded, sounding like he was wrapping things up. "Well, I want to thank you all for the cake, and the—"

"Can I just...?" Charlotte cut in, raising her finger like a pupil asking the teacher a question.

"Yes, of course."

"Thank you, Darren," Charlotte answered, appearing somewhat apologetic about interrupting. "I just wanted to appeal to your viewers to look around their community. And if there aren't any crafting clubs or similar happening in your town, I promise you that being involved in setting one up is one of the most rewarding things you can ever do. So, make an effort, and it'll be one of the best decisions you've ever made."

"Charlotte Newman, thank you for your time," Darren concluded, as he turned towards the camera. "After a creative day on the Isle of Man, this is Darren Shipley, with the Crafternoon Sewcial Club!"

"Right. That's us clear," Brian announced, popping up from his home behind the viewfinder. "Oh," he added with a gentle laugh, directed towards Charlotte, while flicking his eyes over to one of the crafting tables. "You might want to tell the old boy that we've finished filming, as he's still grinning that widely his teeth will be in danger of drying out."

"Oh," Charlotte said, looking over as indicated. "Larry, my love," she then said. "Larry, we're all finished with the filming."

"In that case, I'll go and fire up the tea urn," Larry suggested, relaxing his jaw.

"So," Charlotte said, returning her attention to Darren once more. "You've got what you need?"

"Absolutely. If we can get the footage to the editing team today, the story will hopefully air on tomorrow night's news bulletin," he cheerfully advised. Then, looking distracted for a moment, he opened his mouth as if he was going to say something else, but then stopped himself.

"Everything okay?" Charlotte asked.

"Before I go, I just wanted to ask you something...?"

"Sure. Go right ahead."

"Well, it's just... that is, you see... well, Charlotte, I wanted to ask you something delicate. I'm visiting the island often enough as part of my job, and I just wondered—"

Charlotte's cheeks flushed. "Oh, Darren," she politely cut in, looking towards her feet. "Darren, I've got a boyfriend," she told him. "A boyfriend called Calum," she added, even though there was no real need to specify his name. "Plus," she went on with a nervous laugh, "those three would skin me alive," she joked, pointing over to Joyce and company. "They've all got the hots for you, and I reckon they'd be the jealous type."

Once again, Darren opened his mouth as if to speak, but no words came out. Then, after a long, awkward pause, "Ehm, yes. Charlotte, I'm pleased you have a boyfriend called Calum. But I was only going to ask if you'd have time to perhaps give me a sewing lesson the next time I'm on the island?"

"Oh," Charlotte answered, her cheeks now scarlet upon realisation of how much of a plum she'd just made of herself. "Oh, I see. And, yes. Yes, of course. Absolutely not a problem. But, hang on... I thought you could already sew?"

"What, the Hawaiian shirt, you mean?" Darren whispered. "My mum made it for me," he revealed, still whispering. "And I ended up taking the credit for it. So that's the reason I think I should *actually* learn to sew, before my little fib is uncovered."

"I see. Well, in that case, let me know when you're next on the island, and I'd be delighted to teach you a thing or two," she said brightly. "About sewing, I mean," Charlotte was quick to clarify. "I'd teach you a thing or two about sewing."

"Then it's a date," Darren said, holding out his hand to seal the deal. "Oh, and mum's the word," he said, tapping his nose conspiratorially. "You know. About my mum making the shirt."

"Darren, we need to get going," Brian advised, wandering over with his eyes fixed on his mobile phone display. "The farmer in Ramsey has just texted me. He says he and his wife are anxious to cut their turnip up for dinner, and they can't wait around for us forever."

"Ah, the glamorous life of a roving BBC reporter," Darren said with a shrug, to no one in particular. "In that case, we'd best be off," he told Charlotte. And then, shifting his attention to address the seated crafters, "Thank you all for having us!" he offered, along with an appreciative wave. "Brian and I have both had an absolute blast!"

"You're not going already, are you, Darren?" a heartbroken Joyce answered. "I've got a spare pork chop in the fridge, and I was going to invite you back to mine to cook it up for you real nice. Amongst other things..."

Chapter Four

In the days following the Crafternooners' appearance on the telly, Charlotte was quite the celebrity around the village of Laxey, with at least three autograph requests and one confused chap even mistaking her for a presenter from *Countryfile*. He was rather insistent about her apparent career change in his confusion, in fact, and so Charlotte simply went with it, even posing for a photo that he insisted would take pride of place on his sideboard.

Those in the know were already aware of Charlotte's various crafting initiatives, of course. But the news feature would, she hoped, showcase their collective efforts to a broader audience, both locally and across the water. So she was delighted to have already received several emails from BBC viewers, inspired by her story, planning to implement similar projects in their own communities. Charlotte's vision — or dream, if you will — was to see something of a ripple effect, with Crafternoon Sewcial Clubs springing up in towns and villages across the UK. However, there was no financial incentive on Charlotte's part. Rather, like other volunteers, she happily devoted hours of her time, motivated by the overriding desire to help others. Charlotte often imagined other clubs springing up, each with its own Joyce, Larry, Beryl, Bonnie, and others. All who would likely never have had the pleasure of meeting if it weren't for the benefit of the Crafternoon Sewcial Club.

In the kitchen of her Laxey cottage-cum-workshop, Charlotte was, as usual, drowning in a sea of fabric, thread, toy stuffing, and various other items, along with several pairs of curtains as well that she'd recently agreed to alter in a moment of sheer weakness. So in other words, the few days away from work ahead wasn't ideal. Although it's not as if she wasn't looking forward to their upcoming trip off-island, because she totally couldn't wait. But as was often the case, Charlotte simply had more work on her plate than the hours available during the day. As such, she was currently burning the candle at both ends, trying to make a dent in her lengthy 'to-do' list. With most of her time taken by the crafting classes, fitting in her various commissions — such as memory bears, blankets, and what have you — was proving challenging, though something she otherwise adored. Plus, the extra income these projects brought in was certainly not to be sneezed at.

"Aww, new baby smell," Charlotte remarked, holding a pink babygrow to her face, giving it a lingering sniff. "I'm so sorry," she said, before laying it down on the kitchen table and reaching for her crafting shears. "But if it's any consolation, you'll soon be a crucial part of a beautiful unicorn cuddly toy for your former occupant," she added, along with an apologetic expression.

However, the baby onesie was offered an unexpected stay of execution, at least for the time being, courtesy of a rata-tat-tat on her front door.

Charlotte pushed her chair back, offering the wall-mounted clock a cursory glance. "Oh, I know who this could be," she said to the partially constructed unicorn before her. With a spring in her step, she headed through the hallway before then opening her front door. "Yes!" she said with a broad smile. "It's Harry, my favourite postman!" she announced, greeting the cheery face staring back at her.

"Good morning, Miss Charlotte!" Harry offered, along with a friendly salute as he often did. "And need I remind you that I am in fact your *only* postman? Be that as it may, how is the lovely Crafting Queen of..." he started to say, but Charlotte no longer appeared to be looking directly at him. "Erm... hello?" he said, waving his hand to attract her attention. "Hello, Lotti? Are you still with me?"

"What? Oh, sorry, Harry. I was just—"

"More interested in looking to see if I've any boxes of crafting supplies for you today?" Harry surmised, with only a small stack of envelopes for her in his possession, Charlotte was sorry to see.

"Am I that easy to read?"

Harry nodded, setting his chubby cheeks wobbling. "Yes, but not to worry, Lotti. Us posties are subjected to extensive training so we don't take such things too personally. And it's a circumstance we regularly encounter."

"Harry, you know seeing you most mornings is one of the highlights of my day," Charlotte said, flashing him a smile. "It's just that I was hopeful you might have a fabric delivery," she explained. "You see, I'm wanting to make a new dress for our holiday and, unfortunately, time is currently my enemy."

"Alas, no boxes of any cloths or fabrics today, Lotti," Harry reported. "But if you like, I'll attempt to track down the culprits for the delay and have them raked over the coals for their tardiness," he advised with a playful grin. "Or perhaps keel-hauled over a rash of some particularly painful barnacles?"

Charlotte pressed out her lower lip and appeared in complete agreement with this suggested course of action. "Quite right, Harry. Standards must be maintained," she concurred, sharing what she sincerely hoped was a joke on Harry's part.

Harry held the envelopes in his hand up to his face, fanning himself like they were a pile of cash he'd just won at the casino. "I may not have fabric," Harry teased. "But, if I'm not mistaken, I might have something you might appreciate even *more* than a fabric delivery."

Charlotte gave him a sideways look, appearing unconvinced. "Oh?" she said. "That's a bold claim, Harry. Besides, what you've got there looks more like bank statements or bills to me than anything else. Neither of which usually make for compelling reading, really."

"What if I told you one of them was..." Harry began, pausing for maximum dramatic effect.

"Yes?" said Charlotte, easing a mite closer, her interest now piqued.

"Fan mail, Lotti!" Harry said, fit to burst like he'd been waiting all day for the big reveal. "Or at least I think it is."

"Because, em, because you're fanning your face with them...?" Charlotte replied, trying to work out what he was on about and thinking this to be perhaps just a simple pun on Harry's part.

"What? Oh! Oh, splendid, I didn't even realise I'd made a joke just now," Harry answered, not appreciating how clever he'd been until right then, but proud of himself nonetheless. "No, no. I meant actual fan mail."

"All of that's fan mail? For me?" Charlotte asked, feasting her eyes on the wad of envelopes in Harry's hand.

"Well, no... Not all. At least I don't think so," Harry said, managing Charlotte's expectations. "As you said, some appear to be bank statements or bills, but not *this* one," he went on, plucking one out of the stack like a magician extracting an Ace of Spades from a deck of cards.

"How do you know it's—"

"It's all in our training and decades of experience," Harry suggested playfully, handing it over for Charlotte's inspection. "It's not like we steam open our customers' envelopes back at HQ or anything like that," he was eager to point out.

Charlotte couldn't contain her excitement, running her eyes over the handwriting before reading it out loud: "Charlotte the Crafting Lady, care of Crafternooners, Isle of Man."

"Certainly looks like fan mail, if I'm not mistaken?" Harry suggested. "And it's an international delivery, if you look at the stamp."

"Ooh," Charlotte said, doing just that. "Canada," she added, telling Harry what he most likely already knew. "But how on earth did this letter arrive safely without a complete address?" she wondered aloud.

"Us posties are a tenacious breed," Harry insisted, proudly puffing out his chest and giving his imaginary medals a quick polish. "We like nothing more than a challenge such as this, leaving no stone unturned in our relentless quest to ensure no piece of mail ever goes undelivered, and..."

But Charlotte had already moved on, more intrigued by the envelope's contents than the efficiency of the global postal service, it would seem. "Oh my," she said, flicking her eyes up to Harry and then back to the handwritten note she'd by now removed.

"Well...?"

"It is fan mail, of sorts," Charlotte was happy to confirm.

Harry offered a *what-did-I-tell-you* kind of shrug, wanting to move in for a bit of a closer look, but conscious of overstepping the boundaries of his postal training.

"It's from a lovely woman by the name of Freya, who resides in Ottawa, Ontario," Charlotte revealed, with a sparkle evident in her eyes. "Apparently, she's watched our BBC news story over the internet."

"Impressive, Miss Lotti," Harry offered. "Is she asking for an autograph, then?"

Charlotte folded over the letter before returning it safely to the envelope. "No," Charlotte said with a happy sigh, the corners of her mouth curling up into a contented smile. "It's even better than that, Harry."

Harry raised an inquisitive eyebrow. "And?" he pressed, eager to hear more.

"Freya is a crafting addict," Charlotte revealed, although there was no negative connotation implied when she used the word *addict* in this instance, and in fact just the opposite. "She enjoyed learning all about our club and has now been inspired to set up her own in her local area, with several members already signed on. Freya was asking in her letter if she could use the Crafternoon Sewcial Club name for her new venture."

"Ah, I see. Should I assume she can?"

"Of course," Charlotte confirmed, embracing the letter like a cherished childhood dolly. "Anyway, have you time for a cuppa?" she asked, moving the conversation along. "I've whipped up a batch of those apple turnovers you like."

Harry glanced at his watch like he had somewhere else to be (which in fact he did, as there was other mail to deliver), but the tongue running over his top lip suggested he already knew what answer he was going to give to Charlotte's question. "With fresh cream?" he asked.

"The freshest of fresh," Charlotte said, stepping to one side and encouraging her guest to enter.

"You know what this means, Miss Lotti?" Harry said, moving through the front doorway. "The Crafternoon Sewcial Club now has its very first international branch," he declared. "Hmm, and with your international fame, you might soon need an agent," he added, thinking out loud.

Charlotte danced a jig as she skipped down her modest hallway. "An international branch, how cool is that?" she said. And then, glancing ahead, into the kitchen, "Oh, Harry, we'll need to have our elevenses in the living room, as the kitchen table currently has a unicorn sprawled all over it with half its guts hanging out," she added.

Harry took the slight detour, as directed. "You know, coming from anybody else, a statement like that would have me worried and heading back out the way I came," he joked.

"And it wasn't just the Crafternoon Club that Freya was a fan of," Charlotte continued, talking half to herself and oblivious to Harry's humorous comment. "I'll need to let my friend Larry know he's got his first international admirer over there in Canada," she said, holding the letter aloft and waving it in the air.

Harry carefully parked himself on the sofa, taking care not to disturb the partially completed knitting project already resting there like a napping pet. "Oh?" he said, looking up.

"Yeah, Freya mentioned in her letter how she'd love to one day meet the distinguished older gentleman with the handsome, toothy smile," she continued. "At least I assume she must mean Larry, because he was the only man in the news video grinning like a Cheshire Cat."

"Is there no end to your talents, Charlotte? Not only are you the Isle of Man's Crafting Queen, but you're now an international matchmaker as well?"

Charlotte swatted away the compliment. "Oh, I don't know about all that," she said coyly. "Still, my talents don't stop there, Harry."

"They don't?"

"Nope," Charlotte advised. "Just you wait until you taste these apple turnovers!" she said, heading towards the kitchen.

Harry rubbed his hands together in delight. "Splendid," he said, now offering his rumbling tum a few pats to settle it down while he waited. "I'll tell you what, Lotti," Harry called out from his place on the sofa. "It'll be quiet around these parts when you go on your holidays, but I reckon my expanding waistline could use a short break from your delicious baking!" he joked, giving his belly another gentle pat like an anxious mum-to-be.

Chapter Five

Young Stanley rarely refused a visit to Auntie Mollie's farm shop with his mum. Mollie liked to say it was because she was so cool, hip, and down with the kids. But, in reality, she knew it was likely due to her always-overstuffed biscuit tin, amongst other things, and the fact that the farmer on the shop's adjoining farm property was always willing to accommodate an inquisitive ten-year-old following him around like a duckling showering him with a hundred or more questions an hour. And today…

"Auntie Mollie!" Stanley excitedly called out, darting through the front door of the shop. "You didn't tell me that Farmer Phil had two llamas delivered recently!" he said, glancing about. "Erm, hello? Auntie Mollie? Mum?"

With no customers present and the place seemingly all to himself, Stanley wondered if the two grown-ups were currently in hiding, ready to jump out unexpectedly and scare the bejesus out of him — a pastime he was often eager to partake in himself, but it was more fun, of course, when he wasn't on the receiving end of such an endeavour.

"Mum?" Stanley called out, cautiously creeping forward while scanning the shop for any possible places for them to hide. "I know where you are," he said, lying, wondering if they were concealed behind a wooden display case packed with assorted jars of local Manx jam. "Gotcha!" he shouted, leaping forward, hoping to catch the two of them. But there was no one there.

He tried other likely hiding spots as well, including behind the counter towards the rear of the shop. But with nobody skulking back there, or anywhere that he could see, Stanley's anxiety levels began to rise. Where were they? His mum's car was still outside, so he knew she should be here someplace. And yet the shop was eerily quiet, like a tomb. Had Mollie and his mum been kidnapped? Abducted by aliens? Stanley's mind raced with the possibilities. If this was a joke, it wasn't funny. He didn't like being the victim for a change, and he made a conscious decision to never intentionally frighten his mum like that again.

Still hopeful they were merely hiding somewhere, he stepped back gingerly, taking several paces in reverse, while inspecting the shop for any signs of life. "You can come out now..." he offered, along with a nervous laugh. But it was at this moment that his bottom made contact with something solid, solid and yet somewhat giving, like... like a pile of dead bodies. "Arrrgh!" he yelled, as something gave way beneath him.

But it was just a handful of potatoes, tumbling free from the open burlap sack at the top of the pile he'd just sat on. Only potatoes. "Stupid spuds," Stanley said, scolding them. Nerves still raw and on the verge of tears, Stanley instinctively kicked out at one of them, sending it skittering across the tiled floor, where it eventually came to a halt after an abrupt meeting with a sturdy stone wall, leaving the poor tortured tuber battered and bruised. "Uhm... whoops," Stanley said, realising what he'd just done, and grateful now that there was no one there to witness it. "Stupid spuds!" he said again. Because obviously it was the tatties' own fault for this infraction, not his.

"Stan, is that you shouting?" his mum's familiar voice called out, from somewhere behind the stockroom door.

Stanley breathed a sigh of relief. "Yeah, it's me," he replied, playing it completely cool, as if he no longer needed to change his underpants. "Are you two playing hide and seek or something?" he asked, casual-as-you-like. "What are you and Auntie Mollie doing back there?"

Charlotte opened the door just a smidge, peering through the narrow opening. "We're just coming out, Stan," she told him. "Is the shop still empty?" she said with a giggle.

Stan looked over both of his shoulders to confirm, and then gave a nod of the head. "Yep. Why?" he asked.

In response, the door of the stockroom slowly creaked open, accompanied by a further round of laughter, before finally revealing its two occupants. Instinctively, Stanley recoiled, uncertain of what he was looking at and unable to trust his eyes. First, he worried they'd been snatched by aliens. Now, it appeared to be even worse than that— his mum and his Auntie Mollie had not only been abducted by extraterrestrials, but looked to have been the victim of some crazy experiment by the mad devils in which the hapless women had somehow been transformed into two obscenely large root vegetables.

"Mum...? Mum, is that you...?" he asked of one of the strange, orange-hued figures standing before him.

"Whaddya think?" Charlotte managed to ask between fits of giggles. "Don't I look fantastic?"

"I think my makeup is starting to run," Mollie chipped in, wiping tears of laughter away from her cheek. "Do we look delicious enough to eat?" she asked of Stanley, receiving a blank expression in return.

For reasons unknown to Stanley, his mum and Mollie were presented before him dressed in orange costumes, with their faces and exposed limbs covered in matching orange body paint.

With the complete movement of her legs restricted by the bulky costume, Charlotte shuffled forward like a participant in a three-legged race. "Do we look like carrots?" she asked of her son. "What I mean is, would you look at us and think, oh, there's a couple of carrots?"

"I only left you for ten minutes," Stanley said, looking the two of them over with mild disdain. "And I come back to... to this."

"But do we look like carrots?" Mollie pressed, pushing her shoulders back as best she could and striking a pose.

"I s'pose," Stanley offered, along with a shrug. "The green hat thingies that look like something leafy or sprouty are a nice touch, I guess. And, well, you *are* both big and orange like a—"

"Like a big carrot?" Charlotte cut in, now imitating the proud stance of her fellow root vegetable. "You know, Mollie, I reckon I could've whipped us up a couple of costumes and saved you buying them," she pondered aloud.

"Ah, they were only cheap," Mollie pointed out.

"You don't say?" Stanley scoffed.

Charlotte curled one of her orange hands into a ball. "Cheeky monkey," she said, playfully shaking her fist. "Anyway, in case you were wondering," she explained, "Auntie Mollie was hoping to promote the farm shop's online social media presence."

"Which is why we're dressed like this," Mollie entered in. "I've arranged for a photographer to come along."

"Uhm, yeah, I kinda figured that one out, Auntie Mollie. But why didn't you warn me that you were..." Stanley started to ask, until his attention was drawn towards a long piece of fabric dangling from his mum's hand, a hand that had formerly been hidden behind her back. "What's that?" he asked, squinting his eyes to get a better look. But when his mum moved her hand back out of view again, he suspected he wasn't going to like the answer. "Mum, what's going on?"

Charlotte lowered her head like the naughty carrot that she was. "Stanley, do you remember me saying that Auntie Mollie had plans for a pick-your-own strawberry field?"

"Yeah, Farmer Phil was talking about it before," Stanley advised, a moment before his shoulders sagged. "Please don't tell me... Is that thing in your hand a strawberry costume...? Please don't say it is," Stanley begged.

Charlotte cleared her throat, looking over at her partner in crime. "We just thought it'd be an ideal opportunity to showcase Mollie's upcoming plans."

"And that strawberry costume is for me, then, isn't it?" Stanley asked, mortified.

Mollie nodded her head enthusiastically. "You'll look *adorable* in it, Stan, simply adorable, I promise."

Stanley knew the two of them well enough to know there was little chance of escape. So, resigned to his fate, he reluctantly held out a hand so he could inspect his fruit-based attire. "Most of my friends don't have Facebook anyway," he advised, thinking of one small positive aspect of this overall miserable situation. "So at least they won't see me looking like a prize plum."

"It's actually a strawberry," his mum gently corrected, although it wasn't obvious if she was being serious in chiding him or not. "Although..." she began, about to say something else.

"Although?" Stanley enquired. "Although, what?" he asked, when his mum never finished her thought.

Charlotte shuffled back by a few baby steps, leaving Mollie out in front to handle this one.

"The thing is," Mollie chipped in. "The thing is, Stan, the photos won't *just* be on the farm shop's Facebook page. They're also going to be in the local newspaper."

"Aww," Stan moaned, rolling his head back until he was staring at the ceiling. "But you'll have plenty of red makeup to disguise me...?" he pleaded.

Mollie gave a hearty thumbs-up in confirmation. "Stanley, we'll need a roller for all of the paint I'm going to apply to your cute little face!"

※ ※ ※

An hour or so later and the photographer had come and gone, having successfully captured Stanley Strawberry & The Carrot Twins in a plethora of poses both in and around the shop, all designed to showcase the business to the great Manx public. And those customers arriving during the photoshoot, many of whom were regulars, were most amused to witness the proceedings. Even Stanley entered into the spirit of things eventually, confident he could unleash his expressive side without being recognised and ridiculed by his mates in the playground.

"Oh, Moll, that was so much fun," a breathless Charlotte declared, puckering her lips, pretending as though she'd just spotted another camera trained on her person. "Honestly, I think I'd probably enjoy a career as a catwalk model."

"Catwalk model?" replied a sceptical Mollie. "More like allotment model," she suggested with a smirk. "Anyway, now I really need to get this off, though," she said, peeling back the portion of the costume covering her head like a motorcycle helmet. "I don't know what material this headpiece is made out of, but it's not breathable at all, and I think it's given my hair a weird, musty smell like dirty socks or something," she added.

"Ooh, it has," Charlotte confirmed, after moving in for a quick sniff, and agreeing a little too readily for Mollie's pleasure. "Oh wait, I suppose that probably means mine does, too," Charlotte suddenly realised. "And there I was, about to suggest wearing these costumes for the entirety of the day, but, ehm, now I'm not quite so sure."

"Yeah, perhaps it's best not to," Mollie commented. "But before we go and get changed out of these, Lotti, I just wanted to thank the pair of you for participating today."

"And miss the opportunity to get all glammed up? Are you kidding?" Charlotte said with a laugh, running a hand over the cheap polyester outfit that felt as though it'd be a clear liability around a naked flame.

"Sam and Calum are two lucky men, aren't they?" Mollie replied with a chuckle. "But seriously, I do appreciate you agreeing to help out."

"Mollie, considering all you do for me, it's the least I could do in return," Charlotte said. "Besides, I've had a blast, and I think Stanley, by the end, even managed to enjoy himself as well," she added, looking over her shoulder in the direction of the loo. "You know what, he's been in there an awfully long time by now, hasn't he?" she thought out loud. "Stanley!" she called out. "Stanley, is everything okay in there?"

"No!" came the immediate response, after which the door gradually opened. "Mum, I can't get the rest of this paint off my face," a now-changed Stanley remarked, presenting himself before them for examination. "I've been scrubbing for ten minutes and got some of it off, but not all of it. And now I just look like I've been swimming in Ribena."

Mollie was first to react, extending a few fingers to gently prod Stanley's face. It was, after all, her overzealous application of paint that'd resulted in him looking like he had dangerously high blood pressure. His face was now dry, and no makeup residue came off on her fingertips as she felt his skin, but a stubborn stain somehow remained there.

"I'm sure the rest of it'll come off eventually," Mollie suggested, although she didn't sound entirely convinced. "It'll come off, won't it, Lotti?" she asked, turning to her friend for support.

"Hang on," Charlotte said, scurrying off for a moment to retrieve the bottle of Strawberry Red from where they'd placed it. "Okay, let me see..." she advised, bottle procured and in hand as she returned. "Just a moment here," she went on, reading the label to herself as she ran her other hand through her headpiece of frilly greens, which she'd yet to remove. "Oh," she said suddenly, looking up and flicking her eyes over to Mollie and Stanley. "Oh," she said again.

"Oh, what?" Mollie asked, looking like she didn't really want to hear the answer.

"Mum?"

Charlotte's eyes fell down towards the plastic makeup bottle again. "Uhm, well, the thing is..." she offered, looking as if she'd just read through an extortionate electricity bill.

"Mum!"

Charlotte offered an exaggerated gulp before answering. "It states on the instructions that the paint should be applied, well, like Marmite," she told them.

"On toast?" asked a confused Stanley.

"No, I meant spread thinly," Charlotte clarified. "*Sparingly*, as it says here."

"Sparingly? Auntie Mollie spread it on with a trowel!" Stanley wailed.

Mollie didn't take offence because the boy was on point with his assessment. "All right, so maybe I was a wee bit heavy-handed with my application. What do the instructions say about that? Anything?"

"Hmm," said Charlotte, scanning the label once more.

"Well?" asked Stanley.

Charlotte looked back up. "I'm afraid it says the effects may be permanent," she advised gravely.

"*Permanent?* Mum, I can't stay like this forever! I've got the school disco to go to only next week!" Stanley moaned, pressing a hand against his discoloured cheek.

"We could probably make you a little balaclava," Charlotte offered, sounding like she was trying her best to cheer him up. "Then nobody would see your face, yeah?"

"Yeah, you'd look like a ninja, Stan. And you always said that ninjas were *well cool*," Mollie entered in.

But before Stanley's lower lip started quivering, Charlotte put the poor tyke out of his misery. "Relax," she said. "We're just teasing."

Stanley looked annoyed and relieved in equal measure. "So this will eventually wash off?" he said.

"I'm sure it will, kiddo," Mollie assured him. "Nothing a bit of your mum's cold cream won't sort out once you get home."

"Clotted cream?" Stanley asked, misunderstanding. But before he could chastise the annoying grown-ups or say anything else, his mum's mobile rang, distracting them.

"Stan, be a dear and grab my phone?" Charlotte asked. "It's in my bag beneath the counter, and I really don't fancy attempting to bend over in this tight-fitting costume."

Stanley did as requested, grumbling to himself as he trudged towards the counter area. "I'll get you both back," he said, already plotting his revenge. He followed his ears until he'd retrieved the phone, as directed. "Mum, it's someone called Darren Shipley," he advised, relaying what he could see on the phone's display.

"Is that not the fellow from the BBC?" Mollie remarked.

"Are you winding me up?" Charlotte asked, suspecting her son had already started to implement Operation Revenge.

"Nope," Stan said, handing over the phone. "See for yourself."

"Oh, so it is," Charlotte said, flashing Stan an apologetic smile for ever doubting him.

Charlotte took the phone from her son's hand and adopted her most professional, work-sounding voice reserved for occasions such as this. "Hi, Darren, it's good to hear from you," she said, once she'd removed the head portion of her carrot costume as Mollie had earlier. "No, this isn't a bad time at all," she replied, in response to the polite question posed. "I'm just in the garden tending to my vegetable patch," she explained, offering Stan and Mollie a playful wink.

Mollie placed her hand on Stan's shoulder. "Come on, boyo. Let's leave your mum to take her call, and perhaps we can have another go at cleaning your face while we wait, yeah?"

"With some clotted cream?" Stanley asked.

"Well, let's try some simple soap and water first, okay?"

And shortly, at the kitchen sink in the rear of the shop, poor Stanley's cheeks were being scrubbed more furiously than the ice at a curling tournament. And while Mollie wasn't going to suggest his initial effort might have been substandard in any way, it wasn't too terribly long before his skin tone was returned to a more natural shade. "Ah. Success. That's looking much more like it," Mollie informed him, handing Stanley a cloth. "You dry yourself off while I go and make sure no customers are waiting to be served, all right?"

"You do know you're still wearing your carrot costume, Auntie Mollie?"

"Oh, I hardly noticed because it's so comfortable," she joked, shuffling awkwardly towards the door. "Anyway, I just might adopt this as my new work uniform, as the few customers we've had seemed to like it."

Fortunately for Mollie — but not for the till — the shop remained relatively quiet, what with it being late afternoon and a typically slow time. She looked around for Charlotte to see how her friend's phone call with Darren had turned out, and found Charlotte staring at a display of leeks, scallions, shallots, and a few assorted onions. "Everything okay there, Lotti?" Mollie asked. "Lotti? You look like you've seen a ghost," she said to her currently glassy-eyed friend.

"What?" Charlotte replied, snapping back to the present. "Oh, yeah, I'm fine. It's just something Darren has said that's rather caught me off guard."

"He does know you've got a boyfriend?"

"No, no, it's nothing like that, Moll. I must have mentioned that we were going away to Center Parcs with some of the gang next week, and Darren suggested we meet up in person while I was over there in the UK."

"And you're *sure* he knows you've got a boyfriend, Lotti? Because from what you're saying, it sounds like—"

Charlotte shook her head in the negative. "No, it's not that, Mollie," she assured her. "It's... well, you know how he did that feature about me and the Crafternooners, right? Well, because of that, I guess, and the interest he's shown in crafting, he's apparently been approached to host some sort of crafting show on the television."

Mollie raised her orange-hued eyebrows in response. "What sort of show, exactly?"

"He couldn't tell me, as it's all a bit hush-hush at the moment. That's why he wanted to meet up in person to discuss what he wanted to say."

Mollie's jaw fell slowly open. "Hold on," she said after a moment. "What if Darren wants you to appear on this new TV show of his?" she suggested.

"I know," Charlotte said, daring to dream. "Apparently, from what he did reveal, there's going to be a major craft and home design exhibition going on not too far away from where we're staying. It's during this that the BBC is going to announce the new show, and Darren asked if I could meet him there."

"This is completely unbelievable, and quite frankly shocking if you ask me," Mollie answered, sounding almost cross.

"What, that I could be on TV?" Charlotte asked, a little taken aback by the sudden stern tone of her friend's voice.

"No, Lotti. The fact there's going to be a major crafting show near to where we're staying, and you knew nothing about it!"

Chapter Six

Charlotte and the others were only leaving their fair isle for three short days. But with a list of logistical considerations as long as your arm to sort out before her departure, the preparations felt to her like she was leaving for a year-long, around-the-world cruise.

Fortunately, following a herculean effort, Charlotte had managed to clear all outstanding items on her considerable 'to-do' spreadsheet, delivering an assortment of adorable keepsakes to their respective forever homes. In addition, she'd rescheduled all her existing weekly crafting-related commitments, taking time to ensure those affected by her absence had sufficient projects to keep themselves occupied until their next meeting (as Charlotte for one knew precisely how stressful life could be without sufficient crafting projects to keep oneself occupied).

And while she was delighted to be heading off-island for a well-deserved break with a superb group of friends and family, Darren's phone call from earlier in the week was still in the back of her mind. Intrigued as she was, Charlotte couldn't help but feel a pang of guilt for agreeing to meet with him at the crafting event. She was acutely aware that the lovely, thoughtful man in her life, Calum, had arranged and paid for a bit of wonderful time off for herself and her friends, and now she was thinking about wandering away for a good chunk of one of the days, leaving him and the others abandoned.

As such, with Stan at his father's for the evening, Charlotte hoped to soften the blow by cooking Calum's absolute favourite meal, toad-in-the-hole, followed by a generous helping of sticky toffee pudding smothered in ice cream for afters.

But Calum's head didn't button up the back, and when Charlotte presented him with a bottle of his favourite expensive red wine that evening as well, he knew he was being buttered up for something. Though what, precisely, he wasn't sure. And that's when she came clean about the slight amendment to their holiday schedule. Presented with this information, Calum put in an Oscar-winning performance of playing the wounded soldier. But it didn't last too long, just enough for him to head off and retrieve a brown envelope that he'd stashed in the other room for safekeeping until such time as he could properly present it to her.

Unbeknownst to Charlotte, Calum had, fortuitously enough, already stumbled upon the details of the exhibition whilst researching the area of their holiday destination. Suspecting that such an event may hold a certain appeal to a group of crafting-mad dafties, Calum had taken it upon himself to purchase tickets for the ladies. He'd hoped it would be a nice surprise, and indeed it was. Needless to say, Charlotte was beyond delighted with the selfless gesture. And her gratitude for having such a caring, wonderful boyfriend didn't end once the bottle of wine was polished off, and Calum certainly wasn't complaining.

And the next morning, with what Charlotte hoped might turn into an annual excursion, the Crafternooners were off on their eagerly anticipated adventure in the minibus Calum had rented as their gleaming chariot for the next few days.

"Oof, bloody Nora," Joyce remarked, fanning her face with her fingertips. "Have you been eating poached eggs?" she asked, shooting her good friend Beryl a sideways glance. "You know how they make you flatulent, dear."

"Cheeky thing!" Beryl replied, giving Joyce a playful jab with her elbow. "First of all, that's just rubbish. Eggs don't give you gas. And secondly, that smell is nothing to do with me, it's—"

"We're driving past a farm," Charlotte interjected, looking over her shoulder after overhearing their conversation from her position up in front. "So it's not Beryl," she advised. *This* time, at least," she added, though muttering this last bit under her breath to herself. But she needn't have worried about being overheard, because ever since picking everyone up from the pre-agreed meeting and collection point at Union Mills Methodist Church, there'd been a constant stream of boisterous banter from the rear of the minibus, plenty loud enough to help drown out her mumbled observation anyway.

It was only a relatively short drive to the nearby Isle of Man Sea Terminal, where the trusty workhorse *Ben-my-Chree* awaited to ferry them across the Irish Sea to the town of Heysham, over in Lancashire.

"Everything okay, Lotti?" Calum asked from the driver's seat, spotting his co-pilot fidgeting through the corner of his eye.

"What? Oh, yes," Charlotte replied, although without much conviction. "You know that scene in *Home Alone* when they all go on holiday...?" she asked a moment or two later, sounding a bit uncertain with herself.

"Do you think you've forgotten something?" Calum ventured. "That's impossible, Lotti," he assured her. "I personally watched you tick off every item on your list. And then you checked it and double-checked it."

"Did I leave the rubbish bin out?"

"No, Lotti, you didn't," Calum calmly advised, turning off the main road to join the queue of vehicles lined up in the sea terminal carpark, all waiting their turn to drive aboard the ferry. "But that's only because I placed it out last night myself, remember? Relax, Lotti. You're on holiday and you've got everything under control."

Charlotte leaned across to give Calum's left knee a gentle squeeze. "You're right," she said. "I'm sure I'm worrying about nothing. I'm sure there isn't anything we..."

"Charlotte?" Calum asked, concerned when she'd frozen mid-speech, appearing as though she was having some sort of funny turn.

With the minibus now at a halt, Charlotte unfastened her seatbelt, quickly spinning around for a view of the rear. "One... two... three..." she said, tapping a finger in the air as she counted heads. "Oh for the love of...!" Charlotte shouted abruptly. "Larry! We've bloody forgotten Larry!" she said, in response to the conspicuously empty seat she'd just spotted in the back row.

Calum laughed, initially assuming this to be simply a joke on Charlotte's part. "Wait, you're serious? But that's impossible," he told her. "I know he was with us. I was just talking to him before we left the church, when everyone was popping inside for a last-minute trip to the loo. We've not locked him inside the building, have we?"

Mollie, who was sat near to the front, leaned forward. "No, I closed the church myself," she advised, shaking her head. "And I first checked there was nobody left inside. I made sure of it."

"Then where on earth...?" Charlotte replied, running her eyes around the interior of the minibus to confirm she'd not missed poor Larry the first time of asking. "Larry, my love!" she called out, as if the modest minibus were some sort of Tardis where he could have gone unnoticed during the previous roll call.

"Uhm," said Stanley's friend Eric, raising a tentative finger in the air, hoping the adults wouldn't mind too terribly if he spoke up. "Is Larry the man with hairy ears?" he offered, although not in an unkind way, this being an innocent observation on Eric's part, as Larry really did have quite hairy ears.

"Yes! Yes, that's him!" Charlotte answered. "Why, do you know where he is, Eric?" she said, her excitement nearly sounding like anger.

Young Eric shuffled nervously in his seat, conscious that all eyes were now upon him.

"It's okay, Eric," red-haired Bonnie assured him, the pale skin and lovely freckles on her smiling face serving to soothe the boy. "We just need to know where he is. Do you have any idea?"

Eric fidgeted with the collar of his shirt. "When we were outside the church..." he began, pointing over his shoulder towards the church now several miles behind them. "He said something about forgetting his hat inside one of the vehicles, and then he wandered off in search of it. I'm sorry, I never realised he didn't come back. Not until just now."

"His captain's hat!" Beryl entered in.

"Eh? What captain's hat?" Charlotte asked.

"He thought it would be fun to wear one of them fancy caps like the captain on the boat wears," Joyce explained. "He must've left it in the back of the car when you turned up in the minibus."

"He's had us searching charity shops all week looking for that special hat," Beryl remarked. "And then he goes and forgets the flippin' thing!"

"Oh no, Larry," Charlotte moaned, slumping back in her seat. "Calum, we need to—"

But Calum had already pressed down on the turn indicator. "On it," he said, skilfully manoeuvring the minibus from out of the queue of vehicles. "Hold tight, guys," he announced, "I may need to put my foot down if we're going to make it back here in time for our ferry."

※ ※ ※

The *Ben-my-Chree* eased off her berth on schedule, her departure confirmed by a deafening toot on the ship's horn signalling she was leaving for another day at sea. A crowd of passengers lined up on the outside deck, waving away to those still on dry land who'd come to offer them a fond farewell.

Many of those on board would be departing holidaymakers, returning home after enjoying a visit to this lovely little jewel in the middle of the Irish Sea. And it wasn't too difficult to spot them, for they would be the folks taking in one last appreciative look at the rolling Manx hills as the ship chugged steadily away from Douglas, leaving them with a batch of fond memories and perhaps a yearning to return the following year.

Also standing on deck (thanks to Calum's quick detour back to the church) was Larry, wiping away a salty, wind-induced tear from his cheek with his crisp white handkerchief. Or, it could've been a tear in response to his friends nearly leaving him behind. Either way, he looked resplendent in his smart navy-blue blazer and recently purchased captain's hat, with Larry receiving several puzzled glances from passengers who likely wondered why he was stood there enjoying the view when he ought to be busy at the helm.

"Everything okay, Larry?" Stanley asked, appearing alongside him. "I said to Mum that I should come and check on you."

Larry wiped away another tear before glancing down at his young travelling companion. "Roger that, good buddy," Larry asserted. "A little bit of sea spray in the old peepers, is all," he offered as an explanation for his watery eyes.

"It looked like you were sad we were going?"

Larry placed an arm around Stanley's shoulder pulling him in closer. "Ah, well I'm always sad to say goodbye to our fair isle, Stanley," he said, pointing his free hand in the direction they'd come. "But you know what puts a smile back on my face?"

"The circus jugglers who ride those funny miniature bicycles?" Stanley suggested, drawing from his own experience.

"Oh, of course," Larry replied, in immediate agreement. "But I was going to say the thought of a few days away with my pals," he offered as an alternative option. "Although, at my advanced age, I didn't think there'd be any more trips off-island if I'm being honest."

"You're not that old," a buoyant Stanley offered, eager to perk his mate up.

"Well, there's not much room for many more candles on my birthday cake, Stanley," Larry said gently, after which they stood together for a bit, saying nothing.

Stan enjoyed the moment a while longer, although watching two seagulls battle for aerial superiority rather than the diminishing vista behind them. "Wellsir, I reckon I'd better get back downstairs and rescue my friend Eric," Stanley said eventually. "Beryl and Joyce had him hemmed in on both sides when I left, threatening to teach him how to crochet. You coming?"

Larry shook his head, releasing Stanley from his grip. "Not just yet, Stan," he advised, returning his attention to the island getting smaller in the distance. "I think I'll take in the view a while longer. Besides, If I head down now, Joyce and Beryl might get their crafting hooks into me."

"So long as you're okay, Larry. I'll see you in a while, yeah?"

"In a while, Stan. That you will. And thanks."

"For what?" Stanley asked over his shoulder.

"For looking out for me."

"That's what mates do," Stanley said, offering a raised thumb.

After a short hop and skip back to the passenger lounge on the lower deck, Stanley was greeted by Eric throwing him a panicked, *what-the-heck-have-you-got-me-into* sort of glance.

Stanley returned this with a prompt *welcome-to-my-world* type of glance, as he noticed his friend bookended by both Joyce and Beryl. Like a juicy fly landing onto their web, the pair of them probably sensed they could pull another crafter into the fold.

"Did you find Larry, then?" Charlotte asked, sliding over on the bench seat and patting the available space.

Stanley parked himself beside her as directed, giving the appearance of a young man with the weight of the world on his shoulders. "Yeah," he offered glumly, casting an eye over to the card game that Sam, Mollie, Bonnie, and Abigail were currently engaged in. "Hey, are they playing for money?" he asked, briefly perking up and sensing the opportunity to perhaps bolster the paltry contents of his wallet. "Oh, it's just for buttons," he added a moment later, answering his own question.

"Stan?" Charlotte pressed.

"What?" Stanley asked. And then, "Ah. About Larry," he said, upon realising what his mum was after. Stan tilted his head to one side, staring through one of the porthole windows. "He was reading a note when I found him," he disclosed.

"Oh?"

"Yeah, but I saw him shove it into his pocket when I turned up," Stanley revealed. And then, leaning closer to his mum, "And he looked like he'd been crying," he added softly.

"Crying?" Charlotte said, her protective instinct kicking in.

"Larry said it was the salty sea air in his eyes, but I dunno," Stanley offered, along with a shrug. "He just didn't appear to be his usual happy, crazy self."

Charlotte could see the concern written all over her son's face. "Well how about we keep an extra special eye on him?"

Stanley considered this idea for a moment. "Sounds good," he replied. "But don't tell him I thought he was crying, okay? I think it'd make him embarrassed and even more sad."

"I promise," Charlotte promised, reflecting on how she'd raised such a thoughtful, caring boy. "Now, do you think you should go and save Eric?"

Stanley looked across at his mate but realised Eric was going nowhere fast. Indeed, Eric appeared much like a prisoner sitting between two guards on his way to the nick. "Nah," Stanley said, rubbing his hands together. "This is actually payback for when he told Selina Bostock I wanted to take her to the school disco."

"Oh? What's this?" Charlotte asked, but before Stanley could elaborate, Calum suddenly returned with a tray crammed with various refreshments.

"I've got drinks!" Calum announced. "Now, who here wanted java...?"

"Over here," Joyce and Beryl offered in unison.

"Get that hip flask of yours out, Beryl," Joyce instructed, while taking possession of their coffees.

"Uhm, you do know it's only just gone nine in the morning?" Calum asked, passing them a couple of plastic stirrers.

Beryl dipped her hand into her bag, rummaging around for what she was looking for. "It's okay, as we're on holiday," she declared, without looking up.

"Besides," Joyce chipped in. "It's five o'clock somewhere!"

Chapter Seven

Calum stared intently at the display screen, drumming his fingers atop the steering wheel. "Why's she not working?" he asked, with a rarely heard hint of frustration in his voice. "Why are you not working?" he demanded of the satnav directly, his new purchase still featuring the Isle of Man's sea terminal as their current destination. "Oh, come on, you!" he barked, as if this would in some way encourage the uncooperative device to catch up with their current location.

"Have you tried turning it off and then back on again?" Sam, Mollie's obliging beau, helpfully suggested, leaning forward in his seat in the minibus.

"Oh, yes," Beryl chimed in, sounding like quite the authority on such matters. "Yes, you need to turn it off and on," she confidently declared. "Oh, and slap it a couple of times to wake it up, too. I find that always helps."

Joyce screwed up her face, throwing her best mate a funny look. "And what do you know about satellite thingamawhatsits?" she scoffed. "It took you two whole months to figure out how to get your solar-powered calculator working, for heaven's sake."

"Well how the heck was I to know I was meant to remove the label from the solar strip?" Beryl shot back, offended by the insinuation. "They should've made it clear, if you ask me."

"So the *'remove before use'* written on the label didn't somehow tip you off?" Joyce pressed.

But Calum, up front, had tuned their conversation out by this point, more concerned that the ship's watertight doors securing the vehicle deck were slowly opening, meaning they'd soon be on their way. "I don't know where I'm going," Calum whispered to Charlotte, not wishing to alert his other passengers. "Once we exit this ferry, I've no idea which way to drive."

"Uhm," Eric chimed in, a bit bolder in speaking up now, and breaking his attention from the crafting project he'd been assigned earlier. Although he couldn't hear what Calum was saying, he could see the expression on Calum's face and must have worked out what the panicked whispering to Stanley's mum was all about. "This usually happens to my father's car when we sail here," Eric said, struggling to be heard over the still-bickering Beryl and Joyce. "The getting annoyed with the sat-nav, I mean."

"Ladies!" Charlotte admonished both Joyce and Beryl, like a schoolmarm bringing order to the class. "Eric?" Charlotte then said calmly, turning in her seat so she was facing the boy. "You were saying, dear...?"

Eric released his crochet hook, casually extending a finger towards the offending technological device. "Once we're clear of the boat it should start working," he advised. "Well, I assume it does, because that's usually when my dad stops swearing at it."

"Ah, it must be because we've been trapped inside the ship," Charlotte suggested, swirling her hand in the air to indicate the interior dimensions of the ferry. "It must block out the signal or something."

Eric was proving to be a valuable member of the team, and fortunately for Calum, the boy's assessment from a moment ago was accurate, because immediately upon driving away from the ship Cindy the sat-nav burst into life, offering her overly anxious driver an assured tone and concise directions as to where they should be travelling.

The journey northward up the M6 motorway to Center Parcs Whinfell Forest, just outside the Lake District in Cumbria, went by without incident. Well, apart from an impromptu singalong session, slaughtering the soundtrack to the movie *Grease* to pass the time. Indeed, Eric's parents would likely be surprised to discover that their son had already grasped the basics of crochet, as well as now being able to recite the lyrics to "Hopelessly Devoted to You," amongst other selections from the 1978 film.

And although appearing happy enough on the surface, the only person not exactly entering into the frivolities was Larry. Sure, he made a token effort, joining in when he knew some of the words to a particular song, but he was not his usually chirpy self, it seemed to Charlotte. Following on from Stanley's observations from up on deck, Charlotte had made several attempts to engage with Larry back on the ferry, but each time they were disturbed by one thing or another. Now, every time she turned to offer him a friendly, reassuring smile, he'd simply smile back and doff his captain's hat in response, giving the impression that everything was rosy even if Charlotte could sense that it was not.

※ ※ ※

The check-in process at Center Parcs was efficient enough, considering that about two hundred thousand cars arrived all at roughly the same time. Well, Stanley's estimate as to the number of vehicles may have been something of an exaggeration, but there was certainly the mother of queues to collect the keys to one's accommodation. Unfortunately, Calum then made the common rookie mistake, out of politeness, of nodding to the reception staff when asked if he understood the directions to their lodge, when really he didn't.

"At least we're getting the scenic tour," Mollie offered brightly, putting a positive spin on things as they circumnavigated the vast lodge area for the third time.

"Right-ho, campers!" Calum eventually declared, finally pulling up the minibus outside a charmingly inviting rustic wooden structure, their home for the next three nights.

"Well done," Charlotte said, leaning across to plant a kiss on Calum's left cheek. "And good work, navigator. You're my hero," she added.

"Aw, shucks," Calum said, waving away the compliment. "It comes naturally when—"

"No, I was talking to the sat-nav that time," Charlotte clarified. "Good work, Cindy," she said playfully, patting the top of the magic box that had successfully guided them there to the park, if not to the specific lodge.

Calum turned his nose up in response. "Yeah, but I'll bet the sat-nav won't be able to toast us all marshmallows on the campfire later, like I can," he pointed out, just before climbing out of the minibus and whistling a happy tune.

Vehicles were only permitted to be parked up at the lodges for a short period of time, for unloading purposes, before then being directed towards the nearby carpark for the duration of one's stay. As such, Calum cajoled the gang to help transfer the copious amounts of luggage inside their lodge. Beryl and Joyce were, of course, excused from such duties. Not only because of their advanced years, but also due to them being a bit lethargic after the long journey and one too many slugs from their hip flask along the way. They were assigned the crucial task, then, of heading inside to fire up the kettle for a much-needed cuppa.

Calum hadn't paid too much attention to the bright blue Range Rover next to them in their shared gravel parking bay, not at first, other than a mutual nod to its driver upon arrival, as they'd both been preoccupied with emptying the contents of their respective vehicles. But eventually he observed the chap giving him the most curious of looks as the fellow stared down at the pile of bags lying at Calum's feet along with several more hanging out of his vehicle's boot area. "Ah. You'd think we were staying for a fortnight, wouldn't you?" Calum remarked, along with a friendly chuckle.

"I hear that," the weary driver said with a laugh, stretching out a crick in his neck. "But at least there's only three of us in my crew," he commented, offering Calum's mountain of luggage a sympathetic smile.

"And it's remarkable how my young assistants have vanished into thin air when there's some heavy lifting to be done," Calum observed, offering a friendly, outstretched arm to his pleasant-looking fellow traveller. "Calum," he said by way of introduction. "I'll be your neighbour, at least for the next few days."

"My name's Richard. Richard Townend," Richard answered, accepting the handshake. "I suspect your helpers are exploring their new, temporary abode, like my wife is doing, and perhaps laying claim to the largest room available," he suggested. "Oh, and this is our new arrival, by the way," Richard added, gesturing vaguely.

Calum looked down at the bags by Richard's feet, assuming this to be what Richard was referencing, and wondering why on earth the friendly chap had felt the need to extend to Calum a formal introduction to his luggage, as fine a set as the bags were. "Okay?" Calum answered, not wanting to be impolite, unsure what else he could say on the matter and not wishing to offend someone he'd only just met. "Ehm... they're lovely?"

Richard shook his head, offering a jolly smile. "I'm not talking about my luggage," he explained, nodding towards the narrow strip of grass lawn between their holiday lodges, a child's car seat plunked down there in the nice, shaded area. "That's the new arrival I was talking about, enjoying the gentle breeze after the stuffy car journey. This is Trinity Fae Townend."

"Oh," Calum said with a *what-am-I-like* laugh, now looking at what he was supposed to be looking at, which was the populated car seat. What he saw sitting inside was a beautiful, fair-haired child, dressed in a cosy floral-patterned baby onesie. Calum felt certain that Charlotte was going to love both the flowery fabric and the child it protected.

"She's adorable," Calum offered, and he was being absolutely sincere. "Is she always so happy?" he wondered aloud. "It's just that she's smiling, even now, as she's asleep."

Richard laughed. "Oh, she can be a terror on rare occasions, as I suppose anyone's child can," he admitted. "But the vast majority of the time, she's hardly any trouble at all. In fact I think she was put on this earth to provide us with an overabundance of joy, which she does, and I don't believe I'm saying that simply because I'm her father."

Calum smiled. "I'm sure that's true," he agreed, as who was he to disagree with a doting dad.

As pleasant as this was, fussing over babies had never been one of Calum's strongest talents. It just didn't come naturally to him, and when he attempted to slide into that role there was the danger of things becoming awkward, as they were right now. Hearing footsteps on the gravel path, Calum looked over, hoping Charlotte might be coming to his rescue. After all, she was a grand master at cooing over wee ones. But unfortunately it was only Stanley and Eric, both of them trudging slowly along like they were heading to put in a shift digging down a mine.

"Mum's filling the fridge. And she told us to, uhm..." Stanley started to say. But it was clear he'd already forgotten whatever information he'd been instructed to convey only seconds earlier.

"Do you two strapping lads want to grab some of those bags?" Calum suggested, suspecting this to be the reason the boys had been sent outside. Then, turning his attention back to Richard, Calum became aware that he was being eyed somewhat suspiciously. "Ehm, everything okay?" Calum asked, concerned he'd somehow upset his new neighbour.

Richard tilted his head like a butcher considering which cut of beef he'd start with, looking Calum up and down with great interest.

"Richard...?" Calum said, shifting his weight uneasily from one foot to the other. There was plenty of meat on his bones, yes, but Calum felt confident — or at least hopefully optimistic — that Richard was no cannibal.

"Oh, forgive me, Calum. This might sound silly, but I'm sure we've met somewhere before. Your face is very familiar."

"We're not from around here," Calum advised, although considering they were both at a holiday park this revelation probably didn't come as a surprise. "We've just sailed over from the Isle of Man."

Richard snapped his fingers like a genie granting a wish. "I knew it!" he said. "So have we," he added. "And that'll be why I recognised your face."

"Yes, we met at the Hospice Gala Ball, didn't we?" Calum said, slapping his thigh as the drawer in his memory banks opened. "We ended up bidding against each other in the auction?"

Richard nodded in fond recollection of the evening. "A glass of vino or seven and a charity auction is always a recipe for a dinted chequebook," he commented. "Still, it's all for a good cause, am I right?"

"I hear that, Richard."

Then, spotting his partner standing in the lodge doorway, Richard said, "Lucinda, you're not going to believe where our neighbours are from." And right after this, he said, "Oh, forgive my manners. Lucinda, this is our neighbour Calum. Calum, this is my wonderful wife Lucinda."

Calum gave a friendly wave to Lucinda, a striking woman with a long dark mane of hair and an impish smile.

"And you can see where Trinity Fae gets her good looks from," Richard said self-effacingly, in the way that loving husbands often do. "Anyway, what do you reckon, dear?"

"About where Calum is from? Hmm," Lucinda answered, appearing to give the question some consideration. "What about... maybe, the Isle of Man...?" she offered, only a moment later.

"What? How...?" Richard answered, perplexed.

Lucinda wiggled her fingers mysteriously, as if she'd just been in contact with some helpful, unseen spirits regarding the matter.

"Can I guess that you've spotted our Manx registration plate?" Calum entered in, suspecting he'd solved this little mystery.

But before Lucinda could reveal the source of her insight, her expression hardened. "Richard," she said, approaching their car with her eyes trained on the remainder of their luggage still lying in the boot, untouched.

Richard held his hands out in submission. "I know. Sorry, I got sidetracked, but I'm bringing them in now."

But Lucinda's pace quickened, her attention now drawn to the passenger compartment of their vehicle. "Richard?" she said, pressing her nose to one of the rear windows. "Richard, where's

Trinity?" she asked, panic evident in her voice as she threw open the car door.

"It's fine," Richard assured her. "She's enjoying the afternoon breeze over by..." he began to say. "Oh, stone the crows," he added, whispering this bit to himself so as not to upset his wife any further than she already was. Richard looked over to Calum for answers. After all, they'd both been peering at Trinity's car seat mere seconds before his wife's arrival. "Calum...?"

But Calum shrugged in response, being clueless himself as to how a baby could have just disappeared into thin air like that. That is, until the possible source of this little mystery presented itself in the form of two distracted chatting-nonsense-about-YouTube-videos lads reappearing from the lodge, ready to load themselves up for another trip inside.

"Stanley...?" Calum said, interrupting the boys' conversation. "Stanley, have you just, ehm... well, have you just perhaps taken a baby into our lodge by mistake, by any chance?" he asked.

"A *baby*?" Stanley replied with a laugh, unsure if this was a joke he wasn't getting. "Calum, we're not completely useless, you know," he added with an audible tut-tut. "I mean, we can tell the difference from luggage, as we *do* know what babies look like."

"Don't forget we both used to be one," Eric chipped in, eager to join the joke he didn't really understand himself.

"So, just to be clear. You've not taken, by mistake, a baby in a car seat, picked up from just there, over in the—" Calum started to say, but stopped himself short as he witnessed Charlotte appear from their lodge, car seat in hand.

"Calum?" Charlotte enquired. "Any idea why there's a baby in our lodge?"

"I think these two storks delivered her in error," Calum advised, pointing out the two guilty parties. "Charlotte, meet one Trinity Fae. Trinity, this is Charlotte."

"Oh, my word," Charlotte gushed. "She's absolutely *adorable*," she said, glancing over to who she assumed to be the proud parents. "I'm going to get my travelling craft bag and start knitting you a little bonnet," she told Trinity, who was currently gurgling happily away, pleased to be the centre of attention. "Yes I am, Trinity," Charlotte went on. "Yes I *am*..."

※ ※ ※

"Listen to that lot," Charlotte said, directing her ear towards the laughter flowing from the outside decking area. "They're having an absolute blast," she remarked fondly, reaching across the table for Calum's hand. "Aww, thank you so much for arranging all of this," she told him, giving his fingers a gentle squeeze.

Calum looked through the glass doors towards Joyce, Beryl, Bonnie, and Abigail, who were partially obscured by the steam rising from the warm water. "Joyce and Beryl were particularly eager to get their new swimming costumes on and jump in the hot tub," he recalled with a smile. "Ah, good times with good people," he declared, as a general observation.

"Good times, indeed," Charlotte agreed. "And poor Stanley and Eric didn't know where to look when Beryl and Joyce, our resident oldsters, strutted through the lodge modelling their new outfits."

"Yeah, but the boys weren't too sheepish, I couldn't help but notice, when teenaged Bonnie and Abigail stepped out in their swimwear," Calum commented with a chuckle.

"Oh, don't," Charlotte said, releasing her grip on Calum and then holding her head in her hands, as if she were in pain. "He's still my little boy and I want him to stay that way forever," she insisted, though it was obvious she was saying this playfully. "Hmm, and speaking of little boys..." she said, looking up and glancing about.

"They've gone for a quick kickabout outside," Calum advised, figuring that's what Charlotte was about to ask. "I saw them take their ball with them," he explained. "Perhaps I should—?"

"You just want to go for a bit of footy with the lads, don't you?"

"Absolutely. And I'll give Sam a shout and see if he wants to join us as well?"

"He's gone out with Mollie," Charlotte informed Calum. "A romantic stroll through the grounds, as Mollie put it. Although Sam described it as simply a wander to the shops."

Calum pushed back his chair, taking to his feet. "Well, I shan't let that stop me," he said. "You coming to see my silky skills?" he asked with a grin, doing keepy-ups with an imaginary football.

"Tempting, but no," Charlotte teased. "While it's quiet, I think I'll try and have a chat with Larry, actually. He's not been himself, ever since the ferry ride over here, I think, so I want to make sure that everything's okay."

With David Beckham on his way to football practice and the girls happily boiling in the hot tub, Charlotte climbed the creaky wooden staircase to the lodge's upper level, unsure what she was going to say, exactly. All she had to go on was Stanley's account of him possibly appearing upset, plus the fact Larry'd been a bit reserved and uncommunicative since they'd left the island. It wasn't concrete evidence that something terrible was afoot, but she'd sleep easier knowing she'd at least checked in on their very dear friend.

"Permission to come aboard, Captain?" Charlotte asked, after giving a gentle rap of the knuckles against his bedroom door.

"Permission granted," came the prompt response.

Charlotte eased open Larry's door, finding the skipper lying on his bed, a newspaper resting on his chest. "I'm not disturbing you, am I?" she asked.

"Oh, not at all. You'd never disturb me, Lotti. I'm just catching up on the day's events."

Larry swung his legs around until he was sitting upright, placing the newspaper down on the bedside table next to his captain's hat. "If you're here to tempt me into the hot tub then I must decline as I wouldn't inflict my nobbly knees on anybody," he joked. "Beryl and Joyce have already tried without success to lure me in, and they're rather persuasive."

"I just, ehm..." Charlotte started to say, tripping over her own words. "That is... what I mean is... Larry, I wanted to—"

"Out with it, Lotti," Larry gently chided her. "No need to stand on ceremony with me. Even with my fine headwear," he said, placing his hat back on his head with a grin.

Charlotte composed herself for a moment. "Larry, I can't tell you how happy we all are that you've joined us."

"But?" a concerned Larry replied, leaning forward. "I feel like a *but* is coming."

"No, there's no but, Larry," Charlotte assured him. "Did I tell you how excited Stanley has been about you coming on our little holiday?"

Larry lowered his head, reflecting on this point. "He's a credit to you, Charlotte," he offered a moment later. "A real good 'un."

"I don't mean to pry..." Charlotte said, trying her best to sound like she wasn't doing precisely that.

"Is this about Stanley seeing me up on deck?" Larry enquired. "He doesn't miss a trick, that boy," he offered. "Sharp as a tack," he added fondly.

Charlotte stepped in closer to Larry, lowering herself down so she was at eye level. "Well, yes. It is about that, actually," Charlotte confessed. "And also because you've just appeared a little gloomy lately, ever since Union Mills. Which isn't like you, Larry. You're usually the life and soul of the party."

Charlotte placed a hand on Larry's shoulder.

"Larry, I just wanted to check in and make sure you're okay. You know you can always talk to me, right? Is it– is it that we left you behind and had to come back for you? Because, Larry, I can promise you that we were horrified when we—"

Larry started chuckling to himself. "No, it's not that. It's nothing. Really," he assured her between laughs.

Larry liked to make light of any situation, even when any of those situations might concern a potentially serious topic. But when he could see that Charlotte wasn't buying it this time and was continuing to stare at him intently, his extra cheery disposition lessened.

"Ah, you know me too well, Lotti," he said.

But Charlotte didn't reply, offering him a warm smile of encouragement instead, allowing Larry to answer in his own time. With his jovial facade removed, Larry now looked rather vulnerable in Charlotte's eyes.

He released a long, slow sigh, staring down at his feet. "I was reading a message I'd received," Larry admitted. "I read it earlier in the day," he explained. "But I don't think all the details had properly registered for me the first time around. So I was reading it again, and that's when Stanley came out to see me."

Charlotte didn't want to assume the worst, but when your friendship group consists of elderly folk, it's often a sad reality that any upsetting news might well be medically related. "You've not had bad news, Larry...?"

Larry nodded in response, choking up as he tried to speak. "Not the best," he confided eventually.

"You know I'm here for you, Larry, dear," Charlotte said gently. "And not just me. All of us."

"I know."

Charlotte didn't want to delve too deeply into what was obviously a tender subject, unsure if she should press Larry for details or simply leave him to his thoughts. "Whatever you need, Larry," she offered. "If you need a chauffeur to take you to medical appointments once we get back to the island?" she told him, attempting to sound bright and breezy. "Then I'm your woman, yeah? I'll even get myself a chauffeur's hat, and you can still wear your captain's one."

Larry smiled, appreciative of the gesture. "Wait," he said a short moment later, pointing at himself. "You mean me? Oh no, I'm fine, Miss Lotti. No, it's not me that's doing poorly."

"You're fine?" a relieved, yet confused, Charlotte replied. "But I thought..."

"I'm bright as a button," Larry insisted. "No, it's my pen pal who's really having a difficult time. Honestly, you just wouldn't believe what that poor woman's been through this year."

Larry lowered his head, visually emotional at the thought of his friend's troubles.

"You have a pen pal?" Charlotte enquired, this revelation taking her by surprise. "You never mentioned anything about a lady friend."

"It's not like that, Lotti. Veronica and I are just friends."

"Veronica? Ah. That's a lovely name," Charlotte remarked. "So what's happened to get you so upset, Larry?"

Larry recalled the details of the correspondence, the pain of the news evidenced by his mournful expression. "That poor, poor woman, Lotti. First, she had to undergo a kidney operation that nearly killed her. Then, just as she was starting to see blue skies again, just as things were starting to look up for her, her young son needed urgent medical attention as well. That was the news that tipped me over the edge, Lotti. As if she hasn't been through enough already, yeah? And then there's her precious lad, about the same age as your Stanley, going through his own desperate troubles. I couldn't help but think of him when I read through Veronica's message."

Charlotte listened a while longer, conscious that this was clearly important to her beloved friend. And it soon became obvious to her that the emotional turmoil he experienced was having a most detrimental impact on his general well-being. But a problem shared is a problem halved, a point she made to Larry before leaving him alone for a much-needed power nap.

Charlotte headed down the stairs to the lounge area of the lodge, finding Calum slumped on the sofa, nursing a sore ankle.

"Remind me that I'm older than I think," Calum joked, rotating his foot and offering the occasional grimace. "Stan and his mate have just run me ragged," he advised. "Everything okay...?" he asked, as Charlotte cuddled up next to him, a look of concern splashed across her face. "Did you speak with Larry?"

"Yes," Charlotte answered, resting her head against Calum's shoulder. "I'm pleased to report that Larry's fit as a fiddle, at least physically."

"Oh, that's excellent news."

"Yes it is. But I suspect the same can't be said for poor Larry's bank balance."

"Eh? His bank balance?"

"Yeah," Charlotte replied. "Unfortunately, from what he's just told me, I think our dear friend is being taken for a ride by some scam artist calling themselves Veronica. He's yet to be convinced of that fact, and I haven't put it to him just yet, but I do believe this person may have already lightened the contents of his bank account, and is now asking for more."

Chapter Eight

Sleep eluded Charlotte for much of the night. Perhaps it was the creaks and groans of the lodge, the settling building sounding like an old sailing vessel out at sea. Or perhaps it was the unfamiliar bed she was sleeping in. But the primary cause of her intermittent sleep was most definitely anxiety over Larry after learning of this new so-called friend of his.

For someone ordinarily so very chatty, Larry was worryingly guarded on the subject, clamming right up whenever Charlotte pressed for additional details. From the limited information she had been able to glean, however, she learned that Veronica had initially made contact with Larry by way of an unsolicited email, which only further confirmed Charlotte's worst fear that the poor fellow was being 'played'. Charlotte couldn't help but think Larry had also been brainwashed by this Veronica person to some extent, owing to the fact he wouldn't reveal the true nature of their friendship to those closest to him.

Unsure how to handle the sensitive situation, Charlotte had discussed the matter with Mollie's boyfriend Sam, who was an experienced nursing home director. On his suggestion, Charlotte had reached out to phone Emma, the manager of the living facility Larry called home. Fortunately — or unfortunately, as it should happen — this was a problem Emma was apparently all too familiar with, having encountered the same sort of scenario with other various residents throughout her career. Ever the professional, Emma had put Charlotte's mind at rest, assuring her that she'd speak to Larry's bank first thing in the morning and put them on standby, seeking their advice on what to do next.

For now, however, all Charlotte could do was to be there for Larry when he was ready to open up, and also be hopeful that he would eventually get into the holiday spirit for the few days they were at the lodge.

The next morning, following several mugs of coffee and a light breakfast, Charlotte and the female contingent of the travelling party were chauffeured to the exhibition hall, the venue of the craft & home design extravaganza.

"You're sure you don't mind us abandoning you for the day?" Charlotte asked of Calum, staring lovingly into her man's eyes.

Calum's shoulders slumped, as if heavily burdened by the mere thought of it. But then he smiled. "Well, it's going to be a real struggle without you, what with a full day of action sorted with the lads including archery, rock climbing, go-karting, and so forth, and I think a nice swim in the early afternoon as well, if we don't over-indulge at lunch, that is, in which case we'd just lay around like beached whales for a bit until we recover," he playfully advised, putting Charlotte immediately at ease.

"So I don't need to feel guilty?" Charlotte asked, planting a wet kiss on his cheek.

"No, I promise," Calum assured her. "Now go and enjoy your crafty day and I'll come back and pick you all up later. Oh, and let me know what the BBC chap says, yeah?"

"Of course, and thanks," Charlotte said, clapping her hands in delight. She was now completely energised for the day, the previous night's sleep deprivation offering no hindrance. "Are we excited, ladies?" she asked of her crafting entourage.

"Excited?" Beryl replied, reaching for her handbag. "The last time I was this excited I'd just opened up that *Magic Mike* DVD Joyce had given me for Christmas. Ooh, that hunk of beefcake, Channing Tatum..."

Charlotte, Mollie, Joyce, Beryl, Bonnie, and Abigail all eagerly handed their tickets to the check-in team in the foyer, each of them receiving a decorative floral wristband in return. "These are nice," Charlotte remarked, appreciating the attention to detail as she secured the hand-crafted item around her wrist. "And it's lovely they get us a complimentary cuppa as well," she added, leading the way towards the main exhibition hall. "Which I'm certainly not complaining about."

"Holy crap," Joyce remarked, rather succinctly, as their group approached the entrance and clapped eyes on the scale of the event.

"It's flippin' massive," Abigail commented, struggling to even see the far wall in the distance. "It's a good job I'm wearing my trainers," she added, looking over to the rest of their gobsmacked gang.

In every direction, stallholders plied their wares, with everything on offer from small independent retailers selling homemade lampshades to the major wholesale manufacturers showcasing products that'd soon appear in shops across the country. If you were even remotely interested in anything crafty, then you'd truly reached Mecca. The only two concerns you probably had were if you'd brought along enough money to spend and if the day was long enough to navigate your way around this vast utopia.

The original intention, discussed on the drive there, was that the girls would stay together, hunting in a pack, as it were. But that plan soon went straight out the window, with Bonnie and Abigail first to veer off, unable to resist the allure of a stall selling sparkly things that, according to Bonnie, were going to look absolutely fabulous on their new dresses. Shortly after, Joyce and Beryl were snared in by a spirited chap peddling his homemade slippers which he confidently declared were the comfiest that would ever grace one's tootsies. It was a bold claim, but with his polished sales patter and the pull of his lilting Irish brogue, the spider had soon snagged himself two flies only too ready and willing to reach for their purses.

"I've got a sneaking feeling we might all be getting slippers for Christmas from those two," Mollie joked, with her and Charlotte continuing on, as a pair, with their own exploration. "I'll bet this place is like Disneyland for you, isn't it, Lotti?" Mollie ventured, a little further on.

Charlotte nodded, linking her friend's arm. "Oh, it really is, Moll," she confirmed, inhaling deeply and taking the place in. "You can just smell fabric and wool in the air!" she exclaimed, entirely satisfied.

Mollie took a tentative sniff herself, but alas, did not possess the same ultra-heightened, extra-discerning senses of the crafting bloodhound next to her. "I'll have to take your word for that one, Lotti," she said with a gentle grin. "Anyway, so where are you supposed to be meeting this Darren fellow?"

"Stall One-Twenty B," Charlotte immediately answered, that detail engrained in the memory.

"Which is where, exactly?"

Charlotte shrugged. "I haven't the faintest clue. But there's plenty to have a gander at while we find our way," she declared, smelling the air again like a child near a candy floss stall, letting the glorious aroma fill her lungs.

With her modest cottage back home in Laxey already bursting at the seams with crafting-related miscellanea stuffed into every nook and cranny, Charlotte was determined to show restraint as she perused the vast array of items on display. And her determination was not just impressive, Mollie observed, but surprisingly so. Well, it was impressive for the first seven minutes, that is— at which point Charlotte's resolve collapsed like milk-drenched Weetabix.

"I simply can't help myself," Charlotte offered weakly, as she handed her well-hammered bank card to yet another grateful retailer. "Do you think I have a problem?" she asked of Mollie.

"Yes, you do," Mollie was quick to agree. "And that problem is that you're soon going to run out of hands to carry all of the stuff you *weren't* even originally going to buy," she added with a smirk.

"You've not done too badly yourself," Charlotte said, pointing out the bags resting by her friend's feet while Mollie considered which scarf to add to her already healthy inventory.

"Ah, but there's such lovely stuff here," Mollie answered, running her hand over one particular Angora wool scarf that especially tickled her fancy.

But before too much more time had passed and either of them could drain their bank accounts entirely, Mollie suggested a strategic respite, phoning the other ladies to arrange a much-needed rendezvous in the refreshments area. Unfortunately, if the throbbing crowds were anything to go by when Mollie and Charlotte arrived, they weren't the only ones to come up with this same brilliant idea.

Mollie stood up on her tippy-toes, attempting to peer over the sea of heads. There were loads of people milling about who were, same as them, all hopeful of snagging the next available table. "Oh, we're never going to find them in all this," Mollie declared, once her heels had returned to solid ground. "It's absolutely jam-packed, and—"

"Wait, I see them," Charlotte cut in, extending a pointed finger towards Bonnie's mop of gorgeous flame-red hair, which stood out like a Belisha beacon amidst the crowd to guide them through the masses.

With Mollie in tow, Charlotte was soon able to cleave a path through the throng, delighted to find their mates already seated upon arrival, along with a freshly poured cup of tea and a thick slice of sponge cake waiting for them both. "Oh, I could kiss you!" Charlotte said, taking a seat and looking around the table for whichever one of their friends was the generous benefactor.

"We all chipped in," Abigail explained, happily tucking into her own piece of cake. "We were grateful for Mollie's suggestion, and if your feet are half as sore as ours by now, then we knew you'd appreciate having something already here waiting for you, something to recharge those batteries," she advised.

"And I see you've all been busy!" Mollie cheerfully remarked, having spotted, as she'd pulled up to the table, the collection of well-stuffed shopping bags resting beside everyone's respective chairs. And there was one other thing she'd spotted before sitting down. "Ehm... Joyce?" she said, looking across the table, and taking great pains to sound as respectful as possible. "Joyce, dear, you do realise you're wearing one shoe and one slipper...?"

Joyce nodded in the affirmative, as if this sort of thing was perfectly normal, and no cause for alarm. "Yes, of course," she said. "I was showing Bonnie and Abigail my new slippers..." she continued, pausing only briefly to brush away a few cake crumbs that'd spilt onto her jumper. "But afterwards, when I went to put my shoes back on, I realised my feet must have swollen from all the walking, because I could only manage to get one shoe back on."

"Ah, okay," Mollie answered, now starting to get the picture. "So your plan, I take it, is to put the missing shoe back on once the swelling subsides...?" she surmised.

"Nah," Joyce offered. "I think I'm done with shoes for the day, to be honest. The slippers are so bloody comfortable, I think I'll just wear them instead for the rest of the afternoon. I simply haven't got round to changing the other foot yet, because that's when the cake arrived, and that was more important right at the moment."

"When you get to a certain age you can get away with wearing slippers in public," Beryl explained with a wink, sounding quite the authority on the subject. "Dressing gowns too."

Bonnie offered the two elder stateswomen an affectionate grin. "I guess we've got that relaxed dress code to look forward to in a few years, then," she entered in, before turning her head towards Charlotte. "I was just wondering, Lotti, when you were meeting that chap from the BBC? Has that happened yet?"

"No, not yet," Charlotte answered. "We meet in about thirty minutes," she said, after taking a quick glance at her watch. "At least I know where it is now," she added, pointing a finger in the general direction of where she needed to go. "And it was all very mysterious when we walked by there. We were staking the BBC stand out at first, from a safe distance, but then we swooped in for a closer look. Didn't we, Moll?"

"Oh, yeah. Very mysterious," Mollie agreed. "Everything was hidden by tarpaulins, and there were even a couple of security guards making sure the nosey parkers didn't get too close."

"Nosey parkers like us," Charlotte confessed. "We were politely asked to move on."

"It's all very cloak and dagger," Bonnie enthused, wiggling her fingers in the air as if she were tickling an invisible hedgehog. "And Darren the reporter hasn't given you any clue as to what's going on?"

"Nope. Well, nothing except for what he mentioned over the phone about him hosting some sort of crafting TV show. Other than that, he's not said a dicky-bird. Hence the big reveal to the press today, at which point I'll find out what's going on just like everybody else."

Abigail placed her elbows on the table, leaning in close so as not to be heard by the neighbouring tables. "Oh, Lotti," she said, wide-eyed. "Imagine if they did want you to be a contestant?"

However, Charlotte didn't appear to be too convinced by that potential outcome. "I know, it *would* be a hoot," she said, drifting away to imagine that possibility for a brief moment, and then snapping herself from her reverie. "But honestly, when Darren was visiting the island, he asked if I would help him with some sewing lessons. So, really, I expect him wanting to meet with me is more to do with that, actually. More likely, you know, getting himself upskilled and such before filming starts, so he can impress the powers that be."

"Ah, well. Whatever happens today," Beryl offered, "know that we're in pleasant company, drinking tea and eating cake, with crafting goodness in every direction. It doesn't get better than that, in my book."

"Oh, it does," Joyce ventured, bending over and fidgeting under the table. Then, once entirely upright again, she offered a sigh of contentment and relief. "All of what you just said is even better when you're wearing both your new comfy slippers," she insisted, giving a little squirm of delight as she repositioned herself in her chair. "Ah. Now where was I?" she said, directly before getting back to the important business of eating cake.

※ ※ ※

With an empty plate and her teacup fully drained, Charlotte trotted off for her pre-arranged meeting with Darren. She didn't anticipate it taking too long, assuming he likely just wanted a quick word before the BBC presentation thingy would start. As such, she'd been happy to take up the generous offer to leave her multitude of shopping bags with Mollie and the girls to babysit while she was gone.

Making her way through aisles that seemed to stretch out in every direction, Charlotte contemplated whether such an event would work back home on the Isle of Man. It would have to be on a slightly smaller scale, of course, but would still be a chance for local crafters and homeware enterprises to exhibit their goods to a captive Manx audience. It was an idea worth sticking a pin into, Charlotte reckoned, something for future consideration once she returned home.

After successfully navigating back to stall 120b, Charlotte was flabbergasted to see the transformation from only an hour or so earlier. Gone were the drab tarpaulins, revealing the uber-cool space they'd been concealing, now illuminated by a collection of snazzy, strategically placed lighting displays. Indeed, Charlotte was initially put in mind of the modern staging behind which you'd find Huw Edwards presenting the evening news on BBC1.

Other than a sign promoting the impending announcement of a new television show, there were still no clues, as far as Charlotte could see, which would offer an insight into the nature of this as-yet-unnamed programme. This, however, didn't stop a steady stream of visitors rubbernecking for a good gander as they walked by.

Charlotte stood by the perimeter of the raised stage, hopeful of locating Darren as arranged. However, she was starting to feel rather uncomfortable, conscious that she likely appeared as a right snooping so-and-so, someone loitering about in hopes of some kind of sneak preview, not content to wait patiently for the big reveal like everybody else. And her heightened anxiety levels were not eased when she could find no sign of Darren, or even anyone to ask. For a moment she wondered if she'd got perhaps confused about the meeting time, until suddenly she noticed a pair of Timberland work boots poking out from beneath the large, shiny desk being set up for the presenters. Whoever it was, they looked to be on their hands and knees, perhaps running some wiring through the desk, though Charlotte could see little of them at the present moment except for their booted feet.

"Excuse me?" Charlotte said, a bit timidly, hoping to attract the person's attention. "Hello?" Charlotte said, a little louder this time when no response had been received. But again, there was nothing, and with the scheduled meeting time rapidly advancing, Charlotte bravely ventured onto the platform and across the stage, towards the pair of protruding boots. "Yes, hi there," she offered, hoping there was an entire body under there attached to the boots, and hopeful it would appear. The boots wiggled a little, but beyond this there was still no answer.

With no other option, Charlotte walked fully around to the rear of the desk, and from this improved position, she could now clearly see a workman in a high-viz vest making adjustments. Unfortunately, at least from Charlotte's present perspective, the industrious chap offered a bird's-eye view of a builder's bum you could quite easily park your bicycle in.

"Excuse me," Charlotte said, doing her level best to keep her eyes averted. "I just wondered…" she started to explain. That is, until she heard a rhythmical beat originating from the area of his head. Suspecting the breezy-bottomed fellow was distracted by his earphones rather than simply ignoring her, Charlotte gently tapped her foot against the sole of one of his boots, hoping to politely interrupt him.

But gently interrupting him was the very last thing she did as the poor chap received the fright of his life. Reacting in shock, he promptly smacked his head on the underside of the desk, after which he collapsed to the floor, groaning in pain as he rolled over onto his back, free now from the confines of the desk.

It was only then that he finally came face to face with a horrified Charlotte. "My bloody *head*," the man complained, furiously rubbing his scalp.

"Oh, I'm ever so sorry!" Charlotte offered, although her apology still had to compete, at least partially, with the music blaring through the wounded workman's earphones. With one earbud having just fallen out, Charlotte could now easily make out the song the fellow had been listening to— "Dancing Queen" by ABBA.

"Let me have a look," Charlotte suggested, happy to offer her keen medical advice and apply whatever first aid might be necessary, although her expertise in such matters largely consisted, to date, of attending to scraped knees and applying Vicks VapoRub. "I called out to you several times," she said, trying to explain herself, stepping in closer to commence her assessment of the patient. But she didn't advance very far at all before the sole of her shoe landed somewhat unceremoniously on a screwdriver, it rolling under her foot and sending her pitching forward. She came to earth with an abrupt halt, finding herself in a rather intimate position, her legs straddling the builder's waist and her face an inch away from his.

It was just then that Darren ultimately appeared into view, adjusting the knot on his tie. "Charlotte, I thought I recognised your voice. So sorry I'm late," he said, walking and talking. And then, after looking up, "Ah. I see you've met Jack, our set designer," he added casually, his delivery impressively deadpan, as if the scene before him were in no way unusual.

Watching on from the sidelines, a bespectacled lady nudged her mate. "The lengths some people will go to get on the telly is really quite shocking," she could be heard to say, in reference to Charlotte's current predicament.

"Maybe I should audition, myself," her friend replied with a mischievous cackle. "It looks like fun."

Unable to resist a wry smile at Charlotte's expense, Darren helped her up so that Jack might complete what he'd been working on before being rudely accosted. "It's really good to see you again," Darren said, escorting her from prying eyes to a curtained-off area at the rear. "We're just getting the final preparations ready, as you can see," he advised, regarding the hive of activity now within view to Charlotte, with some people fixing their hair and others tweaking the appearance of their stage props.

"Hmm, for some reason I thought you'd be wearing a knitted jumper, rather than a formal suit," Charlotte remarked, making conversation and now entirely put at ease by Darren's friendly manner.

"Well, with your help, Charlotte, I'll be knitting like an old pro in no time. And that topic brings me along nicely to what I'd hoped to talk to you about."

"Ah, I must confess I was intrigued after your phone call."

Darren offered an apologetic smile. "I'm genuinely sorry for the whole hush-hush approach," he said. "But when the BBC commissions any new project, it's a case of mum's the word until further notice."

"But you can tell me now?" Charlotte assumed, as otherwise why else was she there, she wondered.

"Well," Darren said, glancing over his shoulder to build the suspense. "The official reveal is still an hour away, but I'm sure you can keep it a secret?"

Charlotte fastened an invisible zip over her lips, turning an imaginary key as well and then throwing it over her shoulder.

Darren raised his hands, holding up his palms like he was preparing to set the scene. "Imagine, if you will..." he said, moving his hands in small circular motions. "A new weekday, afternoon show based around crafting..."

"I'm sold," Charlotte said, immediately sold.

Darren was getting into his stride, buoyed by the positive response. "It's two teams of two, each given fifty pounds apiece, and they'll need to buy items from a charity shop, make them into something else, and then sell them for a profit. The team making the most profit wins."

"Oh, I like. So, you mean I'd buy a really naff jumper, turn it into a showstopper, and then sell it for as much as I can?"

"Exactly, Charlotte. And the name of the show?" said Darren. *"The Crafternoon Showdown,"* he was delighted to reveal.

Charlotte couldn't help but notice Darren may have taken inspiration from her own organisation's name, The Crafternoon Sewcial Club. But as she quickly appreciated, Charlotte had, at one time, likely borrowed that inspiration herself. Regardless, she still wasn't able to work out what Darren's angle was here, the reason for her being present and privy to the exclusive details being revealed, as wonderful as they were.

"Ah. Brilliant," Charlotte offered, not wanting to dampen his enthusiasm. "So... you're wanting those crafting lessons you mentioned, are you? Trying to show the bosses how good you are at crafting?"

"Absolutely, Charlotte. But that's not why I wanted to speak to you today."

It was at this point in the conversation that Charlotte's eyes lit up, daring to dream that he might actually wish to have her appear on his new programme. "So, if it's not a lesson you're after...?" she said, teeing Darren up to put her out of her misery.

"I want you on the show," Darren said, clapping his hands in delight. "I've told the producers all about you and shown them the videotape from our interview. And like me, they think you've got a personality that our viewers will simply love."

Charlotte shifted her weight excitedly between her feet, placing her hands against her cheeks. "Oh my!" she said, fit to burst. "I can't believe this, Darren!" she yelled, before recalling the entire sworn-to-secrecy thing. Then, lowering her voice to an enthused whisper, "I'm going to be a contestant on a new crafting show," she said, scarcely able to believe the words that were coming out of her mouth. "How amazing is that."

Darren had listened as Charlotte spoke, narrowing one eye, his forced smile making his face ache. "A contestant on the new show?" Darren eventually repeated back to her, making sure he'd heard her correctly. "Charlotte, no, I'm sorry, I didn't mean you were going to be a contestant on the show," he told her.

Charlotte immediately blushed. "Is that not what you...?" she said, realising she must have just made a colossal mistake, completely misunderstanding what he had been saying. "Oh, I must have, you know..." she waffled on, laughing out loud to hide her inner pain. "What am I like," she added, lowering her head to conceal her cheeks, which she reckoned must be scarlet by now. "So when would you like your first crafting lesson?" she asked, staring down at her shoes.

Darren hooked a finger under Charlotte's chin, gently raising her head until they made eye contact. "Charlotte," he said, clearly amused by her anguish. "Charlotte, I don't want you to be a contestant on the new show—"

"Yeah, you might have mentioned that."

"Charlotte. The reason you're not going to be a contestant is that we want you to be the *co-host*. Hosting the show, Charlotte. Hosting the show, with me."

Chapter Nine

"Turn it back on," Larry instructed to any of his loyal subjects who might be listening, relaxing back with a glass of fizz pressed to his lips, like Lord Muck, just as Beryl had described him previously. "Oh, I'm glad you talked me into this, Lotti," he said over the rush of the hot tub jets as they suddenly burst back into life, as requested.

"Oh, this is the life," Beryl suggested, holding her empty glass up for one of their diligent attendants to notice. "Waiter?" she joked, swirling her glass around to make clear that it was empty and in desperate need of being refilled. "Waiter? *S'il vous plaît?*"

"On it," Stanley replied, happy to oblige. He didn't understand the magic of how it worked just yet, not at his age. But he was amazed at how even a modicum of fizz, provided at regular intervals, could always keep adults in such high spirits.

For the second evening of their holiday, Stanley, along with his business partner, Eric, had assumed the role of entertainment directors for the evening's festivities and were having a whale of a time, refreshing drinks, choosing the music, and, because they had direct access to the snacks, secretly eating more snacks than you could shake a stick at.

In the hot tub, boiling like lobsters, Larry held court with a bevy of beauties — namely Beryl, Joyce, and Mollie — who were hanging on his every word. Or at least that's what he probably believed after a glass of champagne or three.

On the other side of the outdoor paved decking, safely out of reach of the splashing water, Charlotte sat with Calum and Sam around a lovely outdoor firepit. As Calum stood to give the fire some needed attention, Charlotte leaned over to speak to Sam.

"Thank you, Sam. I can't tell you how happy I am to see Larry smiling like that again," she whispered, nodding towards the water babies, her affection for Larry and the others evident in her sparkling eyes. "He didn't mind opening up to you about the whole Veronica situation?"

Sam waved as Joyce — whose ears may have been mistakenly burning, thinking they were talking about her — blew a kiss in their direction. "No, no," he said, returning his attention back to Charlotte, after taking a quick sip from his glass. "We had a good call with Emma at his nursing home. He trusts Emma, and between the two of us, we explained to Larry how we were both convinced he might be the victim of some callous fraudster."

Sam paused for a moment, taking care, out of due respect for Larry's privacy, that young ears weren't overhearing their conversation. But the two boys were only interested right now in loading marshmallows onto a stick, in preparation for toasting.

"Anyway," Sam continued. "Poor Larry couldn't comprehend how anybody could be so cruel, making up such heart-rending stories in order to trick people into giving up their money. But of course it happens all the time, especially with good-natured yet slightly gullible people like Larry. And no offence meant to him when I say that, but it's that sort of kind-hearted naiveté that makes people like him the perfect marks to these unscrupulous scammers out there. Fortunately, working with vulnerable folk as we do, nursing home management on the island have an excellent relationship with the police and the banks."

"So you spoke to them about Larry?" Calum asked, plopping back into his seat after successfully placing another log onto the fire, and signalling to the nearest maître d' that his glass was requiring a top-up.

"Yes, we followed up with both of them, and they were amazing," Sam advised. "The police explained to Larry how this wasn't his fault, for instance, but how the letters he'd received were full of red flags, and how they were certain nothing being described in them was true. They'd seen it all before, they told us, and they could practically guarantee this person called Veronica didn't even actually exist. It was all a fiction. And once he knew that nobody was ever in any pain, danger, or anything like that, it appeared to put Larry at ease."

"I could bloody swing for those scuzzballs," Charlotte insisted, teeth clenched, in a rarely seen show of aggression. "Preying on someone as sweet and kind as Larry? Just unbelievable."

Sam nodded, appearing to be in complete agreement. "It's an awful situation, but it could even have been so much worse," he offered. "Apparently, the fraudster had so far convinced Larry to send a little over two thousand pounds. We learned this from the bank, after alerting them of the situation. And as terrible as that is, the bank mentioned they've seen victims relieved of five-figure sums in these types of scams. So, again, at least we nipped this one in the bud when we did."

"Did they mention if they can recover Larry's funds?" Calum asked.

Sam shrugged, as sadly he didn't have all the answers. "They're going to investigate, but the likelihood is that the money will already have been moved on, making the trail even more challenging to follow," he explained. "But there is one positive out of this whole sorry affair."

"There is?" Calum said, gratefully accepting the refill from an obliging Eric. "Thank you, young sir," he offered to their under-aged bartender.

"There is," Sam told Calum, glancing over in Larry's direction again. "The Crafternoon Sewcial Club, as well as the island's various Make It Sew groups, now proudly boast their very own Fraud and Risk Training officer."

"Oh, what a man Larry is for volunteering his time," Charlotte remarked, like a proud parent. "And it really is a superb idea, because a large number of our members are getting on in years, and are all susceptible to those... those..."

"Scuzzballs?" Stanley chipped in, repeating his mum's earlier terminology, suggesting that young ears were indeed listening into the conversation. "Anyway," he continued, taking a nibble of his now-toasted marshmallow. "Anyway, me and Eric were helping Larry design his new business cards, and we think he might need to change his job title."

"Oh? Why is that?" Charlotte innocently asked.

Stanley couldn't stifle a giggle, recalling their earlier strategy session with Larry. "You see, Larry wanted it to be something snappy on the card, right? Something people would remember," Stanley explained. "So we condensed his job title down into one of them... 'action man' thingies, I think Larry called it...?"

"Acronyms?" Charlotte guessed.

"Yeah, that's it," Stanley answered. "Anyway, so that meant that Fraud And Risk Training got shrunk down to... got shrunk down to..." he attempted to say, but he was unable to continue, a fit of giggles overtaking him.

"FART!" Eric shouted, taking over for his friend. "It means Larry's a *FART* officer!" he howled. "Larry even said he now had a *'nose'* for fraud and he'd help his friends *'sniff'* out a scam!" he related, laughing at Larry's comical words.

"Are you two carrying on about earlier?" Larry asked, walking over with wet feet and a towel wrapped around his dripping torso. "What's going on? Are you boys having a laugh at my expense?" he asked, smiling at the two boys who were still sniggering happily away to themselves. "Because if you two little rapscallions are making fun of me, I'll know it," he playfully admonished. "And you know how I'll know?" he asked. "Because I can *sniff* it out in an instant!" he told the pair, answering his own question. "And that's because Larry Beasdale is the Isle of Man's first and topmost FART officer!"

"Does– does that mean..." Stanley tried to ask, through tears of laughter. "Does that mean we can be trainee FARTers...?" he was eventually able to say.

Larry considered the promotion request for a moment. "I dunno," he pondered, caressing his chin like he was giving this idea some serious consideration. "Yeah, go on then," he allowed. "Trainee FARTers, it is, then. Welcome to the team, lads."

✼ ✼ ✼

Charlotte often struggled to sleep if she'd been drinking too much champagne, the acid reflux playing havoc with her insides and churning around like a washing machine. But even knowing this was a likely outcome, it hadn't stopped her from enjoying several refills. After all, they were on holiday, and her friends were desperate as well to toast the amazing opportunity she'd been given that afternoon of becoming a crafting star on the television box.

Lying there in the darkness, staring up at the ceiling with the sound of Calum's nostrils vibrating beside her and keeping her company, Charlotte was still trying to make sense of the good fortune thrown her way. She knew absolutely nothing about the world of TV, other than the fact that she liked watching it. A lot. Too much, in fact.

Although it wasn't a done deal with contracts signed on the dotted line, the clear message from Darren was that this thing was hers if she wanted it. According to him, the producers were anxious to sign up a relatable, person-living-next-door kind of personality to co-host the show, someone with an interest in all things crafting. All boxes that, in Darren's opinion, Charlotte more than adequately ticked. And this was an opinion which, after having watched his news interview with her, the production team were apparently in complete agreement.

There was still the small matter of a face-to-face meeting with the production team and the formal signing of the offer — both of which could happen in the near future. But, for now, Charlotte needed to reconcile the potential change of career in her own mind.

From the time Darren first mentioned it, there was a sense of disbelief on Charlotte's part. Indeed, the rest of the afternoon at the craft fair, along with her subsequent journey back to the lodge, had passed by in something of a blur. She still scarcely believed it. This can't be real, she told herself over and over, with a case of imposter syndrome now present in her mind.

But it was real, all right. She'd just had a once-in-a-lifetime deal land squarely in her lap, which was likely to come with a not-insignificant boost to her bank balance as well. What's the worst that could happen? she pondered, giving Calum a gentle nudge in the ribs to bring her a temporary reprieve from the snoring. *I can do this*, she added optimistically, imagining herself up on the small screen, wandering around the set peering over the contestants' shoulders, offering up pearls of wisdom as she flashed the camera a cheeky smile. Although, granted, while it all sounded like jolly good fun right now — lying there in the safety of a comfortable bed without the studio lights, the weight of expectation, and a couple of million people watching, wanting to be entertained — the reality, she suspected, would be rather more nerve-jangling.

There was the idea of being away from Stanley to consider. The proposed filming schedule would require her to be off the island for three days each week, from what she understood. Fortunately, with a favourable air link, she'd be able to leave first thing each morning and return on an evening flight, apart from the occasional time she'd need to stay overnight. And as for those times, well, Stanley would often spend a couple of nights staying with his dad each week anyway, so any overnights here and there could hopefully be worked out and wouldn't create too much of a problem, she reckoned. As far as taking Stanley to and from school, both Calum and Stanley's dad were more than happy to pitch in when required. And Stanley, for his part, appeared completely unbothered by any potential disruptions in their normal routine, thrilled as he was with the bragging rights that came along with having a mum appear on the telly. As he'd been quick to point out, his classmate Nigel was still dining out from his dad appearing in a set of poxy adverts for some rubbish dishwasher tablets or other. By comparison, his mum's new gig would bring untold fame, fortune, and glory Stanley's way, he was quite sure. For that reason alone, if nothing else, he was all for this grand new adventure of hers.

There were other things to consider. But even with the increased workload that this new endeavour entailed, Charlotte had just about managed to organise her hectic schedule so that there'd be no disruption to the rollout of her other crafting initiative, Make It Sew, which continued to gain in popularity in nursing homes and beyond. Sure, she'd be stretched thin for a time, but she was confident she could make things work. For a crafting aficionado, Charlotte Newman was living the dream, and all things considered, the television show was an opportunity she simply couldn't refuse.

Having thought through and considered every concern, every eventuality — several times over, in fact — her mind eventually purged of all doubt, Charlotte's eyelids felt heavy. It was only natural to have reservations, she told herself, but felt reassured that everything was under control, everything accounted for, in her decision-making process. As such, she snuggled her head into her soft pillow, willing herself to relax.

Then, just as sleep's cosy embrace started to take hold, she sat bolt upright, nearly giving herself whiplash in the process. "Oh, no!" she said, a thought having suddenly occurred to her, shattering the relative calm inside her head.

"Was I snoring...?" Calum mumbled, half-asleep, as he rolled over onto his side. "Sorry, Lotti," he snuffled, before returning to the land of nod.

But it wasn't Calum, at least not this time, that'd snatched her away from slumber. In all of her methodical planning, she couldn't believe she'd completely omitted from her revised and now-completely-packed schedule one of the things nearest and dearest to her heart. "How have I missed that?" she moaned in the darkness. "How have I forgotten about my beloved Crafternoon Sewcial Club?"

Chapter Ten

By the third day of their holiday, poor Joyce and Beryl were "absolutely goosed," as Joyce had so eloquently put it. Despite their combined ages totalling a very impressive Mensa score, the two of them hadn't shied away from many of the activities that Center Parcs had to offer, even those considered slightly more adventurous. Indeed, for a time, even Stanley and Eric were struggling to keep pace with the two most energetic pensioners in Whinfell Forest.

So far, the pair of ladies had enjoyed a pony ride, been down every waterslide at the swimming pool, and even braved the aerial tree trekking course, amongst other things, which included whizzing down a seventy-foot-tall zipline at the end of it, to top things off. But when the idea of hiring bicycles for an adventure tour was bandied about by the group at large, they decided to sit that particular excursion out, instead opting for a leisurely afternoon indulging in a relaxing and rejuvenating spa treatment — an idea that was rapidly seized upon by the other weary females in their group as well, and also by an inquisitive Larry, whose interest was piqued by the option of an anti-ageing facial.

And so, stretched out on the loungers surrounding the spa pool, Larry, plus Charlotte and the other girls, all waited in turn to be called in for their own selected treatment.

"You know," Bonnie said, peering into her half-drunk kale smoothie, "this whole business of relaxing really is hard work."

Abigail nodded her head in agreement, draining the contents of her own colourful beverage. "I'm going to need another holiday to recover from this," she joked, removing her terry-towelling bathrobe to put in another arduous shift in the heated pool.

"Beryl and Joyce?" the bubbly spa technician said, presenting herself before the group. "If you'd be kind enough to follow me, where the team are ready for your hot-stone massages," she politely informed them.

"Lead on, young lady," Beryl instructed, fastening the belt on her robe. "Oh, and did you get our memo?" she asked, shooting a grin over to Joyce.

"Memo?" the technician asked, running her eyes over the clipboard in hand, concerned she might have missed some crucial detail on the booking.

"Yeah," Joyce chipped in, following her friend's lead. "We requested the hunky rugby-type masseur," she advised.

"Two of them, in fact," Beryl clarified. "One each, if you don't mind."

"Oh, I see," the friendly technician replied. "In that case, I'll ask reception to send out for two of them immediately," she said with a playful wink.

Witnessing all of this, Larry pushed himself forward so he was sat partially upright in his lounger. "You can't take those two anywhere," he remarked to the others, shaking his head in a *what-are-they-like* manner. "Honestly, if I came out with merely half of what they do, security would be called to escort me from the building."

"I'm sure the girls wouldn't mind sharing one of their hunky rugby-style masseurs for your anti-ageing facial," Mollie offered. "Would you like me to make some enquiries?" she gently teased.

Larry ran a hand over his cheek, attempting to iron out some of the wrinkles. "So long as they can make me look five years younger, I don't mind who they send," he commented.

And Larry didn't need to wait too long to find out, as a moment later he was whisked away to commence his restorative treatment. "Remember what I've got on, ladies," Larry suggested. "Because you might not recognise me when I return!"

Mollie couldn't help but smile as Larry set off with a spring in his step. Then, running her eyes over the magnificent interior of the spa, its ornate mosaic tiles putting her in mind of an ancient Roman bathhouse, she offered a contented sigh, happy as a cat lazing before a roaring fireplace. "Can I make a suggestion?" she said in general, not speaking to any particular one of her remaining friends specifically. "I've had such a lovely time and I definitely think we should make this an annual tradition. Whaddya think?"

"I'm in," Abigail offered, bobbing gently on the water.

"Oh, flip, yeah," Bonnie immediately added. "I've loved every minute of it."

Expecting some further input from Charlotte that didn't arrive, Mollie prompted her friend for a response. "Has that soothing music lulled you to sleep over there, Lotti?" she asked.

"What's that?" Charlotte answered, removing her cooling ice-gel eye mask intended to relieve tired eyes.

"We were saying about making this an annual event," Bonnie explained. "The Crafternoon Sewcial Club on tour."

Charlotte stared blankly, appearing at first like perhaps the lights were on but nobody was home. "Oh. Yes, of course," she offered after a moment or two, although sounding relatively unconvinced by her own words.

Knowing her friend as well as she did, Mollie didn't need to be Miss Marple to recognise when something was wrong. "Everything okay over there, Lotti?"

"I'm fine!" Charlotte replied, even though her forced smile suggested a different story. "Oh, who am I kidding," she added, quickly thereafter. "To be honest, there's something I've overlooked, something important I should have remembered but then forgot about completely."

Mollie adopted a sympathetic tilt of the head, happy to be the shoulder her friend apparently needed. "Is this about the legs?" she asked.

"The legs? Mollie, what are you on about?"

Mollie pointed a discreet finger at the portion of Charlotte's legs visible below the bottom of her dressing gown. "The hairy legs," Mollie suggested flatly.

Charlotte pulled her knees into her chest, placing a protective arm around her stubbly shins. "No, it's not about my limbs being in need of a shave," she shot back. "Although," she conceded, "they are overdue some attention, I admit."

"The honeymoon period with Calum must be over," Bonnie teased, a remark which managed to raise a grin from Charlotte. "So if it's not about bristly pins, Lotti, then what's up?" Bonnie put forth.

"It's this TV show," Charlotte admitted.

"You're having second thoughts?" Mollie asked.

"No. At least I don't think I am," Charlotte answered. "But I spent most of yesterday thinking about my schedule, working out how to fit everything in with Stanley, Make It Sew, and all my other commitments, yeah? But with one thing and another, I'd completely forgotten about factoring Crafternoon into the equation. And now I don't see how I can possibly squeeze it in. I just don't have enough hours in the day!"

Abigail climbed out of the pool, reaching for the towel lying on the edge of her lounger. "We could run it for you when you're off-island," she suggested, darting a finger between herself and Bonnie. "If you wanted us to, that is?"

"Yes!" Bonnie readily agreed, happy to have been volunteered. "We could open up the church, dish out the crafting supplies. Ooh, ooh... and when you're off-island we could have a team conference call to discuss what projects we should be working on. It'd be fun!"

"You know what, girls?" Charlotte said, her cheery demeanour nearly restored, "I couldn't think of two people I'd want to look after the Crafternoon Sewcial Club more."

"But...?" Mollie pressed, sensing there might be a *but* on the tip of Charlotte's tongue.

"Oh, it's selfish on my part," Charlotte confided, struggling to say what was on her mind.

"Out with it, Lotti. We're all friends, and I tell you *everything*, remember?" Mollie pointed out.

"Sometimes a bit too much, in fact," Charlotte answered with a laugh. "Anyway, having the girls look after the club is a massive relief, no doubt about it," she said. "But attending is one of the high points of my week, a time I set aside to spend with some of my favourite people in the whole world," she explained, turning somewhat serious again. "And not having that to look forward to is something I'm going to struggle with, you know? Is that silly of me?"

"Not at all, Lotti," Mollie answered. Sensing a hug was likely required, Mollie moved over to Charlotte's lounger. "And it's not like it's forever," she said, pulling her friend in close for a cuddle. "You'll still see your pals periodically, and Crafternoon is still going to be there once filming is finished, yeah?"

Charlotte knew what she was hearing was correct, but it still didn't alleviate her concerns. Not completely, at least. "It's not just that," she confided. "The thing is..." she started to say, glancing around to make sure Joyce and the others hadn't returned just yet. "Oh, I feel awful for even thinking about this. But the thing is, some of the Crafternooners are getting on in years," she said. "I'm just worried that what time we do have together, as a group, is already so precious. And now I'm off gallivanting when I should be with them. Do you know what I'm saying? Is that completely irrational?"

"It's not irrational at all," Mollie assured her. "It's perfectly natural."

"Wait! I've got it!" Abigail declared, taking a sudden break from towelling herself down. "FaceTime!"

"Yes, perfect," Bonnie agreed, apparently on the same wavelength as her friend. "If you're off-island, Lotti, we'll patch you in so you can join the Crafternoon Sewcial Club remotely," she explained. "Easy-peasy," she insisted.

"Lemon squeezy," Abigail added promptly. "And that way you can offer us a sneak peek, as well, into what's going on behind the camera, right?" she suggested. "So it's a win-win situation all around, I should think, yeah?"

"You guys!" Charlotte gushed. "You'd do that for me?"

Bonnie and Abigail both nodded firmly in the affirmative. "Of course we would," Bonnie further assured her. "And, besides, you'd be helping us."

"I would?" Charlotte asked, unsure what Bonnie was referring to.

"Sure," Bonnie told her. "Don't forget, you're the only one who can keep Joyce and Beryl under control!"

Just then, the spa technician returned, casting an eye down at her clipboard. "Charlotte Newman?" she said, looking around the pool.

"That's me," Charlotte declared.

"Wonderful," said the attendant, drawing a tick next to the name. "If you'll follow me? Ellen, one of our best, is all ready for your full-body massage."

"Oh, that'll be heaven," Charlotte said, rubbing her hands in delight. "And thanks, guys," she offered the gang before rising to her feet. "I really don't know what I'd do without you lot."

"Oh, miss!" Mollie called over, attracting the attention of the technician, before she and Charlotte could disappear from view. "You might want to warn Ellen not to be too heavy-handed with Charlotte," Mollie helpfully advised.

"Oh?" the woman replied, reaching for her pen. "Is there an injury I need to make her aware of?" she asked of Charlotte.

"Nah, it's not that," Mollie answered on her friend's behalf. "I'm concerned that if Ellen rubs Charlotte's legs too hard then she's in danger of starting a fire, what with those Sasquatch-like limbs of hers!"

※ ※ ※

Later that same evening, fully relaxed, revitalised, and now with smooth legs to boot, Charlotte enjoyed a nice gin & tonic as she applied the finishing touches to her makeup. With it being the final evening of their holiday, the gang decided a nice meal at one of the onsite restaurants was preferable to slogging away in their lodge kitchen.

"How's the pain?" Charlotte asked, wincing as she spotted the constellation of small lacerations dotted around Calum's back, along with some associated bruising. "Do you want me to apply more Savlon cream?"

"Thanks, but I'm all right," Calum replied, gingerly slipping a polo shirt over his head. "I already smell like a hospital after the first application," he advised. Then, even though he had his back currently to his beloved and couldn't possibly see what she was doing, "I can hear you smiling, you know," he added.

"Oh? How can you *hear* me smiling?" Charlotte protested, even though smiling was precisely what she was doing.

"And," Calum went on, "if I'm not mistaken, you're resisting the urge to tell me I should be old enough to know better?" he asked, turning to face Charlotte. "Tell me I'm wrong?"

Charlotte made out like she was about to proclaim her innocence, but she didn't like telling fibs. "Well, if you'd listened to my words of caution earlier this morning, before you'd left, you wouldn't have ended up travelling so fast, gone over the handlebars of your bike, and landed in a thorn bush as a result, would you?" she lectured, with no attempt to conceal her smile, though of course entirely sympathetic to the pain he was in.

"But reputations were at stake, Lotti!" Calum insisted.

"You knew the boys were always going to clean you and Sam's clocks, Calum. They're boys. Tearing around on their bicycles is what they do best."

Calum went quiet for a moment, lowering his head like a dog just caught snaffling sausages from the kitchen worktop. "Uhm, yes, well about that..."

With her gin now polished off, Charlotte applied a coat of lip gloss. "Wait," she said, looking over at the naughty pooch. "You weren't actually racing the boys, were you?"

"Nope."

"You and Sam got carried away, thinking you were kids again, didn't you," she surmised, offering a disapproving shake of the head.

"Yeah, but Sam also fell off and he's got a graze on his knee," Calum reported, the tattletale that he was. "Plus, I was winning the race until I hit that tree stump and took a swan dive into the gorse bush."

"I'm very proud of you," Charlotte offered up, though any further plaudits were interrupted by a tentative knock.

Calum walked over to answer the door, as he'd been closest. "Hello, boys," he said, upon finding Stanley and Eric on the bedroom doorstep.

"If you've come to challenge Calum to a race, then I'm afraid the thorn bushes have already won!" Charlotte called over, happily chuckling away to herself, satisfied with her own impeccable wit.

Stanley spoke up first, skipping over his mum's comment. "Uhm, Calum...?" he mumbled, appearing sheepish as he shifted his weight from one foot to the other.

"Ask him," Eric cut in, giving his pal an elbow in the ribs.

"Ask me what?" Calum said, unsure where this conversation was headed.

"We were just wondering..." Stanley continued, rubbing his side. "That is, Eric, wondered—"

"Oi, it's not my idea, Stan!" Eric jumped in, threatening another jab with his elbow. Then, likely sensing that Stanley's waffling might continue on for some time, Eric bravely took the lead. "Calum, you know how we're going out for a meal tonight?" he said. "Well, Stan and I were just wondering if you had... you know?" he asked, offering a knowing wink.

Calum stared down at his young visitors and wondered what the heck the pair of them were up to. "Erm, you two don't think I'm going to give you alcohol, do you?" Calum whispered out of Charlotte's earshot, wondering if this was what they wanted to say, but perhaps didn't know how.

"What? No. Of course not," Stanley offered. "Well, unless you wanted to...?" he joked, gauging Calum's reaction.

Calum didn't need to verbally respond to that, his narrowed eyes doing the talking for him. "Spit it out, boys."

"Well, we just wondered if maybe we could borrow your aftershave?" Stanley eventually managed to say.

"And hair gel, if you've got any?" Eric added to the shopping list.

Calum nodded in agreement, as this was an easy enough request to fulfil. "I'll be just a tick," he told them, heading towards the bathroom to retrieve the asked-for items. "Now go easy with that," he advised a moment later, first handing over the aftershave. "It's good stuff, so you don't need much."

"Thanks, Calum," the boys said in unison.

"We'll come and see you about the beer in a year or two!" Eric added, raising a giggle from the pair of them.

With the door soon closed, Charlotte couldn't hide her surprise. "What on earth was all that about?"

"Dunno. I suppose they wanted to make an effort on our last night?"

"Hmm, I'm not so sure about that," Charlotte offered, somewhat sceptical of Calum's assessment. "I mean, make an effort? Stanley? *My* Stanley, who could quite happily go an entire week wearing the same pair of underpants if I'd let him?"

Then, Calum had a moment of clarity. "Ah. Got it."

"Got what?"

"The reason the boys want to smell nice and gel their hair."

"Bonnie and Abigail...?" Charlotte ventured, jumping onto Calum's train of thought.

"Exactly. Brad Pitt and George Clooney are putting the effort in to impress the girls."

"Ohhh," Charlotte groaned. "My little baby's growing up. Do you think we should caution the girls?"

"No point," Calum warned.

"No?" Charlotte asked.

"If the boys are wearing my aftershave, then the ladies won't be able to resist them, I'm afraid."

Unfortunately, at least for Stanley and Eric's sake, Calum's prediction was soon found to be considerably wide of the mark. It wasn't that his fragrance wasn't pleasing on the nose, necessarily, because it was. Rather, it was more that the generous quantities in which the boys had apparently doused themselves — despite Calum's earlier warning — wasn't proving to be such a hit with the girls (or, for that matter, anybody else within a three-table radius).

Aside from that small issue, everyone in the group enjoyed themselves just fine around the dinner table, and feeling replete after finishing a delectable serving of haddock, Charlotte took Calum's hand in hers, giving it an affectionate squeeze. "Thank you for organising this trip, and for putting up with all of us," she said.

"The pleasure's all mine, Lotti," Calum assured her. "If you'd told me two years ago I'd be going on holiday with a bunch of mad-as-a-hatter crafters, and that I'd adore every minute..."

"You're lovely, do you know that?"

"You're not so bad yourself, Lotti," Calum said with a grimace, closing his eyes in pain.

Confused, Charlotte released his hand. "What, I'm not squeezing your hand that tightly, am I?"

Calum leaned abruptly to one side, shifting his weight in his chair, and for an awful moment Charlotte thought he was about to break wind.

"No, you're fine. It's not that," Calum answered. "When I said earlier that we'd managed to remove all the remnants of the gorse bush, I may have been a little bit premature in my conclusion," he confided.

"Ah, is there some way I can help?" Charlotte kindly offered, although uncertain as to what aid she might be able to render there at the dinner table.

"No, but thanks," Calum whispered, wincing in pain as he tried to find a comfortable position in which to sit. "Due to its location, I think I'll probably need to take care of it myself..."

But before Calum could excuse himself to the loo to remove his uninvited lodger, Larry pushed his chair back, holding his drink aloft. "Ladies and gentlemen," he said, tapping his spoon against the glass to attract the attention of those sitting around the table. "If everybody has a drink, I'd like to propose a toast, if I could be so bold. On the last night of our terrific trip..." he said, running his eyes slowly around the table, "I'd like to toast to good friends and good company."

"To good friends and good company," came the collective response, accompanied by the noise of chinking glasses.

Once dinner was finished (and Calum's uninvited hanger-on was successfully dislodged), the gang returned to their cabin for an early nightcap, conscious they needed to be up and out at the crack of dawn for the return leg of their trip.

"Oh, can we stay just one more night?" Mollie asked, nursing a small glass of Scotch whisky that Sam had poured her.

"If you want to stay another night, then it's a sure sign you've enjoyed yourself," Charlotte offered, after which she located the welcome pack they'd received upon arrival, rummaging through it again, as she remembered something she'd spotted in there.

Mollie relaxed on the sofa with her feet resting up against the coffee table. "I've had the best time, Lotti," she answered. "I just need to buy a winning lottery ticket so we can do all this again. It wouldn't be fair to make Calum pay for it every time."

"A-ha!" Charlotte said, holding up an envelope-sized piece of paper decorated with a gilded edge. "I knew I'd seen this."

Mollie peered over. "Oh? Is that my winning lottery ticket?"

Charlotte shook her head, managing her friend's expectations. "Nope, but it's the next best thing, I reckon."

Calum leaned across the sofa for a nosey. "A voucher for fifteen percent off our next stay," he read aloud, for the benefit of the others.

"It must be fate," Joyce suggested sleepily, half-dozing in her chair after having enjoyed one too many drinks for the evening.

Charlotte wiggled the voucher in the air, waving it around as she cast her eyes around the group. "Should we book it before we leave in the morning?" she asked. But before she received an answer from anyone, her phone began to vibrate on the table beside her. "Ah. Sorry about that," she offered, reaching over for her mobile. "Let me just turn this off, and then I'll..." she started to say, but then she noticed the caller's details displayed on the screen. "Oh, that's strange. What does Darren want, calling me at this hour? Sorry, guys, I better take this..."

Charlotte retreated to the kitchen area, leaving the others to discuss the assorted virtues of rebooking for the following year. Center Parcs weren't daft, of course. They knew most folk would be disappointed having to head home at the conclusion of their stay, back to the drudgery of school, housework, day jobs, traffic jams, et cetera. As such, offering a wee bit of a discount to help live the dream again was a relative no-brainer. And their marketing incentive appeared to be a winning gambit, if the positive chatter from the lodge's living room was anything to measure by.

When Charlotte reappeared a short while later, she stood in the kitchen doorway with her phone clutched to her chest, not immediately saying anything.

"Charlotte?" Calum said. "Everything okay?"

"It's not bad news, Lotti?" Mollie asked, clocking Charlotte's faraway expression.

"Not bad news, no," Charlotte replied, with a hint of a smile emerging. "Darren was just sharing a quick progress update," she explained. "They've been inundated with applications from people wishing to appear as participants on the show. Which is good."

"Well? Out with it, Lotti," Mollie prompted, fully confident that there must be more to her friend's phone call than just that.

Charlotte remained tight-lipped, at least until she parked herself back down on the sofa. "Well..." she teased, permitting herself a huge, cheese-eating grin. "So aside from accepting specific applications for contestants, the production team are always just generally on the lookout, constantly keeping their eyes peeled for the ideal candidates. You know, those people whose natural charisma and charm will shine through onscreen and help them drive up the ratings."

THE CRAFTERNOON SEWCIAL CLUB: SHOWDOWN

Mollie waved her hand in a tight circle, like a policeman directing traffic, in hopes of drawing out further detail. "And...?" she asked.

"And it turns out it wasn't only *my* effervescent personality the producers were appreciating on Darren's Crafternoon news piece," Charlotte replied. And then, shifting her attention to the sofa opposite to hers, she asked, "What are you two doing several weeks from now, on a Tuesday?"

"Who, us?" Beryl asked, pointing first to herself, and then to Joyce. "You're talking about us?"

"Yep!" Charlotte confirmed. "If you'd both like to?"

Joyce, who was now suddenly wide awake, leaned forward in her seat. "Bloody right we do!" she insisted, taking the liberty of answering for them both. "You get right back on the phone and tell that darling man from the BBC that we're in!"

"No need for all that," a grinning Charlotte offered. "Because that's what I've already told him!"

Chapter Eleven

Returning to work after a delightful break away from the island wasn't a chore for Charlotte like it would be if she were, say, working in some kind of soul-destroying, monotonous office job as she'd once done in the past. As the old saying goes, *Choose a job you love, and you'll never have to work a day in your life*. And with this currently being the case for Charlotte, she thus couldn't wait to get back into the thick of it.

Waiting for her in an already-congested email inbox were several enquiries about Crafternoon membership from around the UK, a couple of schools hoping to become involved with the Make It Sew initiative, and a small handful of requests for special crafting commissions. Of course, what with everything going on with her current workload, Charlotte simply had no capacity to accept any new crafting commissions such as memory bears and the like... which is why she replied straight away, confirming that she'd *absolutely* be delighted to help.

"Oh, I simply can't say no," Charlotte told an amused Calum as she hit the 'Send' button on her computer screen, right after composing a response to the first of her email commission requests. "They're the adorable school uniform bears with the itsy-bitsy shorts that are just so darned *cute*," she explained, sounding like she was trying to convince herself as much as she was Calum.

Included amongst her busy schedule, there was a crucial face-to-face meeting with the TV production people to attend to. As such, Charlotte was invited to meet the team in their offices in MediaCityUK, Salford, in the Greater Manchester area. She'd only travelled to the UK all by herself on one previous occasion, when she was due to attend a work conference in Birmingham. Unfortunately, that visit hadn't gone without incident when she fell asleep in transit, waking up as her train pulled into London's Euston terminus, over one hundred miles from her intended destination.

So, with the memory of that previous incident still raw, even after all this time, Charlotte was understandably a bit apprehensive about travelling to the 'Big Smoke' unaccompanied. And despite both Calum and Mollie offering their chaperone services, Charlotte felt like she had to ride this particular horse on her own, brave little sausage that she was. And so before long, no sooner had she returned home to the Isle of Man than she was off to the UK once again, although this time travelling solo.

Fortunately, this little sojourn required only one quick flight and a short train journey to get there. And thanks to several coffees on the morning of travel, she remained alert and conscious throughout. *Un*fortunately, with a cocktail of nerves mixed with caffeine overload, Charlotte was considerably wired once she arrived safely at her destination, with her being much more excitable than usual. In fact, Charlotte chattered away like a monkey throughout her tour of the studio, at one point bizarrely taking hold of three balls of wool laid out as props, apparently deciding it to be an ideal time to showcase her impressive juggling skills, leaving poor Darren likely wondering who on earth he'd put his name and reputation to.

But rather than being dissuaded by her unorthodox manner, the production team were suitably impressed by Charlotte's natural charisma and unpretentious personality. So much so that contracts were soon signed and the proposed filming confirmed by all parties, leaving Charlotte to return to her home isle once more, scarcely able to believe people she didn't even know were willing to pay her so much money just to do what she already adored.

Oh, and there was one unexpected extra that was the icing on what was already a deliciously oversized cake, which Charlotte was soon to put to exceptionally good use. And so, safely back to the Isle of Man *yet again*, Charlotte and Mollie thus set about in perusing the fine apparel in the ladieswear section of the local Tynwald Mills Shopping Centre...

"Honestly, with your luck, Lotti, you need to put some money down on the ponies at the racetrack," an incredulous Mollie suggested, running an admiring eye over the seriously posh dress Charlotte was considering. "Is it harsh of me to call you a jammy cow?" she asked. And then, not waiting for an answer, "In fact, that's exactly what you are. A jammy cow."

Charlotte couldn't deny Mollie's way of thinking, accepting the affectionate slur with a nod of the head. "I know, it's bonkers," she said, pressing the dress in her hands against her torso, checking herself out in the nearby full-length mirror. "What do you think?" she asked of her fashion consultant.

"Ooh, that's bloody lovely, Lotti," Mollie offered, before leaning in for a closer inspection. "Wait, is that Ralph Lauren?"

Charlotte reached inside the dress, pulling out the tactfully concealed price tag and label. "Yup," she said, shielding the price from Mollie.

But it was too late, as judging by the look of shock, Mollie had already caught a glimpse of the item's cost. "Buy it, Lotti. You'll look stunning in that, and you bloody deserve it."

Charlotte carefully placed the designer dress in her shopping basket next to the other garments she'd already selected. "I feel just like Julia Roberts in *Pretty Woman*," she suggested, giving the contents of her basket an appreciative glance. "Well, minus the part about being a call girl, of course," she clarified.

For someone who considered herself generally frugal, taking articles of clothing costing hundreds of pounds apiece from the rack didn't come naturally to Charlotte at all. Indeed, most of what she wore on a daily basis were items she'd created herself. So, to now find herself in possession of a pre-paid credit card, provided by her new employers, with instructions to go out and splurge, supplementing her wardrobe ahead of filming, was the stuff of dreams.

"So you don't need to pay any of this back?" Mollie asked. "And the clothes are yours? You get to keep them?"

"I think I get to keep them, yeah," Charlotte advised, although not appearing overly confident on that particular detail. "Although I was kind of in shock when the production assistant told me they were giving me a clothing allowance of three thousand pounds to get myself camera-ready, so…" Charlotte added, wondering if she did indeed get to keep them after filming was over. "Oh, hang on," she said a moment later. "I wonder if that means they didn't like what I turned up wearing?" she asked, pondering aloud, wondering if she should be offended.

"I'd turn up wearing an empty coal sack with armholes cut out if it meant getting a three-grand clothing allowance," Mollie put forth. *"Jammy cow,"* she exclaimed again, for added emphasis, though it was delivered with the best of humour and not any ill intent. "Anyway, I need to head over to the little girls' room. How about I grab us a table in the café area afterwards, and I'll meet you there?"

"It's a date," Charlotte said, returning the Ralph Lauren to the sales rack, deciding it was a touch too decadent for her tastes, even if the Beeb was footing the bill.

Once at the checkout, the sales assistant was more than happy to serve Charlotte, likely meeting her weekly sales target in one fell swoop. But as the items were being scanned and the tally on the till display steadily increased, Charlotte couldn't help feeling an overwhelming sense of guilt. For longer than she could perhaps remember, money had always been tight, especially after separating from Stanley's father. Any spare cash she did find herself with never went on extravagances, such as fancy new clothes, it was willingly spent on Stanley so he didn't go without. Not that she minded, though, as it was just the way things were.

With her purchases bagged up and the final amount more than the price she paid for her first car, Charlotte handed over the credit card with intense trepidation. She still struggled to comprehend that she'd been given the clothing allowance and, somewhat irrationally, worried whether this might be some sort of practical joke initiation ceremony implemented by her newfound colleagues. Indeed, she'd already figured out the quickest and therefore least-embarrassing exit from the store should the credit card be declined.

"It won't be too long," the cheerful shop assistant announced, one hand resting on the payment terminal. "It often takes a moment or two to connect."

Outwardly, Charlotte appeared unconcerned by the delay, but her stomach was churning like an agitating washing machine as she willed the 'Approved' display to come up on the screen.

"Are these purchases for a nice trip away?" the shop assistant asked by way of conversation, tapping the machine with her finger as if this would speed things along.

With her eyes fixed squarely on the payment terminal, Charlotte shook her head. "Oh no, it's nothing like that," she said. "I'm starting a new job, you see. Well, that is, I've still got my old job. But this is a new one, in addition to the existing one."

"How exciting," said the salesperson, continuing to make a bit of friendly small talk as the two of them waited. "And what's the new job? Oh, listen to me being so nosey."

"It's fine," Charlotte assured her. "Believe it or not, I'm going to be on the television!" she revealed. And then, "My goodness, it sounds so strange when I say it out loud."

Fortunately, the card terminal erupted into life, spitting out a receipt, and confirming that Charlotte's line of credit was perfectly legitimate and that she wasn't, as she had feared, a victim of hazing by her new colleagues. But that didn't mean their chat was over. The shop assistant was keen to know more, it not being every day a potential celebrity popped into the shop. For Charlotte, this was the first person she'd told outside her circle of friends and family, and it felt surreal, as if she was talking about somebody else. Still, she was happy enough to toot her own horn a bit, and toot it she did. And it was a good job there wasn't a queue forming behind her, because the lovely and curious saleswoman was currently getting an earful, with Charlotte not sparing any of the details.

Indeed, it was only a hungry Mollie appearing from the adjacent café, wondering why she wasn't presently eating cake, that prompted the conclusion of Charlotte's conversation

"Well, I think I've just secured a new viewer," Charlotte was delighted to report, as they started off in the direction of the promised food.

"Nice. So the credit card payment went through without any issue?" Mollie remarked, noting the overstuffed carrier bags in Charlotte's possession.

"Yeah, but I'm still waiting for a tap on the shoulder from one of the store security guards," Charlotte joked, glancing around just in case.

Once in the café area, the two of them took a seat by the window, casting their eyes over the menu. It was a pointless exercise, really, as they were regulars and ordered the same thing on each and every visit.

"It's my round, so I'll go put our order in at the counter," Mollie suggested. "The usual?" she asked.

Charlotte closed over her menu. "Yeah, why not?" she agreed. "Carrot cake and coffee it is, then." But before Mollie could get up, Charlotte reached down for one of the shopping bags at her feet. "Here, before you go," she said, handing the particular bag she'd selected across the table. "This is for you."

Confused, Mollie accepted the bag, taking a peek inside. "It's that jumper I was looking at while we were over there," she remarked, information Charlotte was already aware of. "I'm impressed we share the same good taste," Mollie commented, assuming Charlotte had been inspired by her fashion sense.

"It's not mine, silly. I bought it for you," Charlotte answered. "And just in case the BBC is somehow listening, that was on my credit card and not theirs."

Mollie removed and unfolded the cashmere sweater, flicking her eye over to Charlotte and back. "Not that I'm complaining, mind you, but..."

THE CRAFTERNOON SEWCIAL CLUB: SHOWDOWN

Charlotte pre-empted the upcoming question, gently cutting Mollie off. "Because you're the best friend I've ever had and I love you to the moon and back," she said.

"Ah, fair enough."

"And not only that, Moll, you're the most selfless person I've ever met, do you know that?"

"You're going to get me tearing up in a moment."

"I'm serious, Moll. You're always there for me, without question, no matter what. You're seriously the best mate ever, okay? So I just wanted to buy you a little something as a token of my gratitude, for being, well... for just being you."

"Aww, shucks," Mollie answered, a little embarrassed, but gracious enough to accept the compliment without any complaint. "You're very welcome," she said, tucking the jumper safely back into the bag. "And you didn't need to do that, but thanks," she added, rising to her feet. "Oh, and if there's any room left on that credit card, I hear Paris is lovely this time of the year, and I'm sure I could wangle a few days off work?" she cheekily suggested, speaking over her shoulder as she set off to place their order.

Chapter Twelve

One of the many joys of living on a relatively small island was that nowhere was particularly too far away. In practical terms, this enabled Charlotte to complete a whistlestop tour of most of the Make It Sew venues in short order.

By now, word of Charlotte's involvement on the new TV show had filtered through to most of the club members and, indeed, most of the Isle of Man at large by this time. But she was still determined to put in a personal appearance to assure those involved that there would be no dilution in the offering provided. This was important to Charlotte because she knew from personal experience the club wasn't just about developing crafting skills, but was also a way of encouraging valuable social interaction.

And ever since Calum's company, Microcoding, had stepped forward with a charitable grant, Make It Sew had evolved from a part-time crafting project in one nursing home, operated by the goodwill of those involved, to an island-wide initiative welcoming hundreds of participants collectively each week, and expanding not just to other nursing homes but to schools as well, and even a prison! Additionally, the trustees of the grant, quite rightly, would also expect to see limited disruption considering the funding they'd so generously provided.

But with nearly two dozen Make It Sew clubs in operation and impressive growth aspirations, Charlotte always knew that flying solo wasn't sustainable in the long term. It wasn't practical for Charlotte to attend each and every meeting at each and every location (although she often tried), but she did ensure that each individual club was fairly self-sufficient once they were up and running. She still needed to develop and roll out an evolving crafting curriculum relevant to the differing skillset of the varying memberships, though. For example, what might be manageable for a group of experienced crafters in a nursing home, for instance, might be too challenging for a selection of primary school children who'd never picked up a crochet hook before. So considerations such as this certainly kept Charlotte on her toes.

Indeed, enlisting additional help had long been on her mind even before the opportunity with the BBC had presented itself. So, after discussion with and approval from the charity trustees, Charlotte was presently on watch for a bit more formal arrangement rather than relying on the support from big-hearted volunteers she'd previously managed to rope in on an ad hoc basis.

Unfortunately, finding a single crafting-mad assistant willing to commit to a few hours a week was proving impossible. So that's just why Charlotte had to settle for *two* of them.

"So what do you think, then?" Charlotte asked, sitting at her kitchen table, her palms pressed together like she was saying a little prayer. "Can I welcome the two of you as the newest additions to Team Make It Sew?" she asked, sliding a plate of chocolate digestives across the table as if this would in some way serve to sweeten the deal.

"I didn't know you were inviting us here for a job interview, Lotti," Bonnie commented, extending a tentative hand towards the biscuits. "I'm sure you mentioned pizza and a movie?"

"Oh, that's coming," a hopeful-sounding Charlotte teased.

Looking perplexed, Abigail, sitting on Bonnie's left, felt the need to get something clarified that she'd just heard in the sales pitch. "Lotti, can I ask you a question?"

"You can ask me two if you like. Or three, if it helps," Charlotte offered, with something of an awkward laugh.

"If I've heard you correctly, you want to *pay* Bonnie and me to help you run the Make It Sew crafting initiative?"

"That's correct," Charlotte was happy to confirm. "And please, these biscuits aren't going to eat themselves."

Abigail declined the kind offer, saving up her appetite for the promised pizza. "But we'd happily help you for *free*," she noted. "And we'd do it because we *enjoy* it," she pointed out, looking over to Bonnie for support. Something Bonnie was happy to provide.

"Lotti, you don't need to pay us for doing something we love," Bonnie agreed.

Charlotte understood the sentiment, which is one of the reasons she already knew the girls would be ideal candidates for the newly created official positions. "Ah, this I know, girls," she told them. "And I really appreciate it, as do the members. But with me potentially spending more time away from the island, I was hoping to expand the remit of the role to include curriculum development as well as hands-on assistance. All of which will require much more of your time. Time I wouldn't feel comfortable asking for without you being paid in return."

Bonnie appeared conflicted, like she wanted to leap at the chance and bite Charlotte's hand off for the opportunity, but yet still harboured certain reservations. "But wouldn't we be taking money from a charity?" she asked. "Money that could go towards buying crafting materials?"

"Oh no, not at all," Charlotte assured her. "Part of the grant we received includes a budget to employ staff if we expand the programme, and the programme has already expanded. Currently, I've just been spinning plates, relying on the kindness of volunteers to plug the occasional gap. But I'm now at the stage where I need to think of a more regular, long-term solution."

Bonnie nibbled her way around the outer edge of her biscuit, mulling over what she'd just been told. "I dunno, Lotti," she said, giving the matter serious consideration, but not appearing entirely convinced. "It's a tough sell, if I'm being honest."

"It is?" Abigail entered in, likely wondering if she'd been listening to a different conversation.

"Getting paid to do something we adore doing?" Bonnie advised gravely, as if this was something wholly terrible, though with a grin slowly emerging. "Why, yes. Yes, of *course* we'll do it,

Lotti," Bonnie added, her grin now turning into a full-fledged smile. "And we've got so many great ideas bubbling around!"

"So many, Lotti!" Abigail was quick to agree, gazing out the kitchen window, imagining the possibilities.

"So you're both on board?" Charlotte asked, happy as a clam.

"Aye, Captain, the two of us are on board," Bonnie confirmed, accompanying this with a sharp salute, an action immediately replicated by Abigail.

Charlotte clapped her hands together in delight. "Excellent! Now how about we celebrate with that pizza I mentioned?"

"Pizza?" a young voice called out from the upstairs landing. "I could eat pizza, Mum!"

"When I ask him to bring his dirty washing down, he's deaf as a doorknob," Charlotte dryly remarked. "And yet that boy has the hearing of an owl when food is mentioned..."

✽ ✽ ✽

Up until this point, the reality and magnitude of appearing on a national television programme hadn't quite sunk in for Charlotte just yet. It was similar to nature's gift of becoming a parent for the first time, in that for many, things don't start to become real until the newborn actually pops out to say hello, accompanied by an ear-splitting wail that announced their arrival to the world. And receiving a call later that evening from Phillipa, one of the production assistants from *The Crafternoon Showdown*, was the moment Charlotte felt as if a screaming baby had just been placed onto her chest.

"Yes, it was lovely to meet both you and the team," Charlotte offered at the outset of the call, exchanging pleasantries. "Oh, me too, I'm definitely looking forward to getting stuck in," she said, punching the air in excitement as she said this. She then listened for a moment, pacing across her kitchen floor as Phillipa spoke. "What's that? Do I remember you mentioning about the press junket?" Charlotte asked, making certain she'd heard Phillipa correctly. "Oh, yes. Yes of course I do," Charlotte confidently declared, absolutely lying through her teeth.

THE CRAFTERNOON SEWCIAL CLUB: SHOWDOWN

It wasn't that Charlotte hadn't been listening when she met with the production team, but more that there'd been an awful lot of information to digest. As such, some of her recall in certain areas was perhaps a bit sketchier than others. Although now that Phillipa mentioned it, Charlotte did have a flicker of recollection, but only because the words she thought she'd heard previously were "press *drumkit*." Words which hadn't made a lick of sense to her at the time, and something she had just chalked up as being some kind of strange television backstage terminology she wasn't familiar with.

Of course, not wanting to reveal that she may have zoned out during certain sections of their introductory meeting at the Media City studio, Charlotte was happy to agree to anything right now, up to and including participation in a press junket, whatever precisely that might be.

"Yep, sign me up, Phillipa," Charlotte said brightly, eager and enthusiastic colleague that she was. "A pen? Sure, wait there just a tick," she added, pulling open drawers on the sideboard hoping to locate one amongst the discarded batteries, picture hooks, and other miscellanea that'd been dumped in there. "Right. Got one," she said, now armed with a writing implement, though with no paper to go along with it. Ever resourceful, Charlotte was prepared to write down what she was about to hear onto the back of her hand. "Ready when you are, Phillipa."

With her mobile phone now set down and placed on speaker, Charlotte set to work, writing as furiously as she could on the back of one's hand. Pretty soon, the available skin was filling up with scribble, and if Phillipa didn't stop talking, Charlotte was worried she'd need to swap hands to continue taking notes.

Unfortunately, once again the words she was hearing weren't fully registering. And it wasn't that she wasn't listening this time, because she absolutely was. Rather, it was more a case of being so determined to quickly transcribe the information being relayed to her that it simply didn't have a chance to sink in as it travelled from her brain straight to her pen.

"Yes, got it," Charlotte was pleased to report, utilising the last available free space on her thumb for the final detail. "Wait..." she said a second or two later, checking her notes to confirm that what she thought she'd heard was in fact what she'd heard. "You're being serious?" she asked, pausing for a moment to hear the response. "What's that? A problem? Oh no, not at all, Phillipa. I'll look forward to it."

With the call ended, Charlotte collapsed down onto her sofa, staring intently at the back of her hand, trying to make sense of the agenda transcribed there. She laughed. But it wasn't the sort of laugh you might offer a funny joke. No, it was more of a *what-the-bloody-hell-have-I-just-signed-myself-up-to* sort of laugh.

Charlotte sat in silence for a while, her peace occasionally interrupted by Stanley shouting at something upstairs in his bedroom, probably a result of him defending himself against an assault by aliens or whatever such enemy was assailing him in the current video game he was playing. Deliberating as to whether she ought to crack open the drinks cabinet, Charlotte eventually settled on calling the one person who was always very adept at assuring her everything would be okay.

"Mollie, it's me," Charlotte said into her phone. "The girls? Oh, yes, Bonnie and Abigail are signed up and onboard," she advised, after which she exchanged a bit more casual chitchat. "Mollie," Charlotte pressed, shifting the conversation in a more relevant direction. "Mollie, if I said the words *press junket*, would you have absolutely any idea what I was talking about?" she asked, pausing to await her friend's reply. "Ah, yes, that's correct. Some sort of media roadshow," she said, surprised her friend was as knowledgeable on the subject as she was. "So I guess it's just me that's never heard of it, then," she added, mildly despondent. "How's that? Is it a big deal?" she continued, in response to what Mollie was saying. "Well, I guess you could say that, Moll, yeah. Because it would appear that I've just enthusiastically agreed to join one for the new TV show."

Charlotte got up and resumed pacing back and forth, a sense of falling flat on her backside, figuratively speaking of course, washing over her. "Mollie," she said, "I'm not sure if I've perhaps bitten off a bit more than I can chew. I'm starting to feel like I've got imposter syndrome, like all of this *ought* to be happening to somebody else, not me. Mollie, I don't know what to do."

Charlotte headed towards the drinks cabinet, thinking that maybe it hadn't been such a bad idea after all. "I don't know if it will be fun, Moll," Charlotte said, sounding distinctly uncertain on that particular idea. She reached for a bottle of red, before immediately returning it, deciding she was too rattled to drink.

"Oh, no, Moll," Charlotte said, along with a vigorous shake of her head. "This press junket isn't just a simple newspaper interview or something. If it was as minimal as that, I wouldn't have the type of heart rate set to give me an aneurysm. No, this is significantly higher profile. Moll, they expect me to go on BBC National Television to talk about the new programme. For starters, I'm meant to be appearing on *The One Show* next week, and it's going to be a bloody live interview!"

Chapter Thirteen

Charlotte squinted, the bright lights being trained on her face uncomfortable, but fortunately also distracting in a way, helping to take her mind away from the nerves consuming her. Or at least for a moment, they did.

"You're sure I'm not wearing too much makeup?" she asked, inwardly suspecting she looked much like a circus clown, what with all the excess colouring slapped onto her cheeks. "I could always go and..." she suggested, pointing in the general direction of where she'd just arrived from, back to the dressing room area and makeup chair.

"You're fine," an authoritative voice insisted, assuring her that she was perfectly camera-ready. "Just hold steady, as we're due to go live at any moment."

"Yeah, but..." Charlotte said, squirming on the solid, disagreeable bar stool that was currently irritating her coccyx. She raised a hand, hoping to shield her eyes from the piercing lights, but it was hopeless. And with her vision impaired the interviewers remained silhouetted, appearing like ghostly apparitions staring facelessly back at her.

"I'm not sure about this, if I'm being honest," Charlotte said, the evident stress levels in her voice increasing. "Maybe we should re-think the—"

"Five seconds!" a voice in the shadows called out, putting paid to any thoughts of Charlotte making a sharp exit.

Despite drinking several glasses of water beforehand, Charlotte's mouth felt drier than a camel's two-toed hooves, and the pre-rehearsed script she thought she had consigned to memory was dripping away from her brain like hot candle wax. She just wanted to up sticks and go, but her legs didn't appear to be receiving the memorandum.

"Three, two, one, and... Action!"

Given her cue, it was Charlotte's time to shine. Her moment in the sun, as it were. "I-I-I..." she stuttered before pausing, inhaling deeply and on the verge of hyperventilating. "That is..." she eventually managed to say, before drawing another blank. "Oh, this is useless," Charlotte declared, jumping down from the uncomfortable stool. "I knew when the time came, I'd just completely fudge things up," she moaned. "And will you turn those bloody lights out? They're giving me a headache."

"We're on live TV," the voice from the shadows reminded her.

Frustrated, Charlotte grabbed hold of the lights — which, in actual fact, were simply two large torches strapped together onto a coatstand using duct tape — twisting them down with some effort so that the dual beams were redirected towards the floor.

"Folks, I must apologise for this disruption, and we'll be right back after a quick word from our sponsor," said the announcer, having to swiftly improvise based on Charlotte's sudden refusal to cooperate.

"Oh, forget about it, Larry," Charlotte said, presenting herself before the table where Joyce and Beryl were sitting in their capacity as TV interviewers for the day, with Larry, nearby, wearing several hats as cameraman, director, and announcer.

Joyce raised a finger above her head. "You don't want to give it another go?" she asked, though fairly certain she already knew the answer.

"No, I don't," Charlotte replied, looking like a child who'd just let go of their favourite balloon. "I'm going to dry my armpits and try and take this bloomin' makeup off. In that order."

The exercise had been a good idea in principle, Larry felt certain, and why he'd convinced Charlotte to participate in the first place. Aware of her live-TV anxiety, he'd suggested a few of them meeting up for their scheduled Crafternoon session early, using the church hall to put their nervous friend through her paces in what could be considered a safe environment. For the afternoon,

Larry had secured beforehand two large torches from the nursing home janitor, fashioning them into studio lights once at the church in the hope of making the interview experience as authentic as possible. Hair and makeup services were provided by Beryl and Joyce, but owing to them both chatting incessantly as they worked and carrying on for far too long, Charlotte's makeup application may have ended up slightly overcooked.

Unfortunately, while anticipated to give Charlotte a much-needed confidence boost, Larry couldn't help but feel his well-intended suggestion had gone decidedly pear-shaped, with her now possibly in a worse state than she was before.

With the rest of the Crafternooner crew slated to arrive soon, Larry, Joyce, and Beryl placed out the usual table and chairs to welcome them. "Right," Joyce said in Larry's direction, after that chore had been accomplished. "How about we see if that tea urn of yours is up to temperature, and then we'll all have a nice brew before the gaggle arrives."

But before any of them could venture forth from the main hall to the kitchen, Charlotte emerged from the washroom with several thick applications of makeup now successfully unspackled from her face.

Poor Larry felt awful, as it was apparent Charlotte had been upset by the reddening of her eyes. "Lotti..." he began. But before he could continue, Charlotte walked over to the three of them, scooping them up in her arms.

"Uhm, everything okay?" Larry asked, unsure if he was being cuddled or throttled at this point. "You're not annoyed with us?"

"No," Charlotte said softly. "No, I'm annoyed with myself," she explained. "You've gone to all of this effort for my benefit, and then I have a temper tantrum when things get a little difficult. How am I so lucky to have such kind and thoughtful friends?"

"We've still got time to try another rehearsal," Beryl offered, from somewhere amidst the scrum. "If you'd like, that is?"

"Mm-hmm," Charlotte agreed. "I'd really appreciate it."

"Do you want me to fetch my makeup brush?" Joyce enquired.

"Ehm... no. But thanks."

✳ ✳ ✳

Ordinarily, Thursday afternoons filled Charlotte with a giddy sense of excitement. The Crafternoon Sewcial Club was something she looked forward to all week, a chance to find out who'd been up to what and how their crafting projects were progressing, all while keeping one eye on the church door hoping to see and welcome any new recruits arriving in addition to the steady stalwarts.

But today felt different. Knowing her filming schedule would likely clash with their weekly meeting for the foreseeable future left Charlotte with a heavy sense of melancholy. For a brief period, she'd considered if moving the club to a different day was a viable option. But with over thirty regular attendees, she knew it was selfish to expect so many people to disrupt their own diaries to accommodate hers. However, she took immense comfort knowing the club would flourish under the stewardship of Bonnie, Abigail, Larry, et al. Besides, she'd make every effort to put in an appearance as and when her commitments permitted. For now, however, Charlotte made a conscious effort to enjoy the moment, soaking in each and every moment while she could.

As Charlotte circled the church hall, offering words of wisdom, or perhaps some much-needed encouragement for when the crafting gods happened to conspire against you, as occasionally they did, each and every person in attendance had their own intriguing backstory. And finding out what those stories were was just one of the many charms of the club.

For example there was Lois, one of their newest members, who now regularly attended with Cassie, Lois's eight-year-old granddaughter. Running a highly respected accountancy firm, spare time for Lois was virtually unheard of. So when she'd recently asked Cassie what she wanted for her birthday, she was caught off-guard when the reply was for two hours of exclusive Gran time without the distractions of a mobile phone. But that's precisely what young Cassie had received in the form of weekly visits to Crafternoon, even if the present had proven challenging to gift wrap. And it was, in Cassie's own words, "the bestest" present she'd ever received. Indeed, it was also a time that Lois had come to cherish, two hours of quality time learning how to knit with her granddaughter, and socialising with some lovely new people as well. And to ensure Lois remained undisturbed and 'unplugged' from business, Cassie took great delight in securing Gran's mobile in the car glove compartment before each meeting. It was the human stories, such as these, that Charlotte so enjoyed. And knowing she wouldn't get to play a direct part in them for the next few months was a bit less than desirable.

And then there were the characters whose company could forever bring a ray of sunshine to her life even on the dullest of days. And one of those characters was undoubtedly Larry, who was presently holding court, teapot in hand, delivering what appeared to be the punchline to a particularly lively joke.

"Any tea left, Larry?" Charlotte asked, once he'd finished his conversation.

"For you, Lotti? Always," Larry offered, liberating a cup and saucer from his refreshments trolley.

"Isn't it wonderful we've now got two television celebrities at Crafternoon?" a seated Carole asked, glancing up from the partially knitted jumper she was diligently working on.

Charlotte smiled in response, unsure if this had something to do with the joke Larry had just dispensed. She knew she was going to be on the telly, of course, as were Joyce and Beryl. But she wasn't sure who Carole was referencing here.

"So you've not heard about Larry?" Joyce offered, when it soon became apparent that Charlotte didn't have any clue as to what Carole was on about.

Charlotte gratefully accepted the cup of tea Larry had graciously poured for her. "What've you been up to?" she asked, eyeing him with friendly suspicion.

"He's going to be on a series of adverts and they're going to be paying him," Beryl chipped in on Larry's behalf. "He's just been giving us an impromptu performance."

"He's like a young Laurence Olivier," Joyce suggested, fluttering her eyelashes like a starstruck groupie.

Charlotte looked quizzically at their Laurence Olivier. "Larry? What's going on?"

"I was going to tell you earlier, Lotti, but I didn't want to distract you from your rehearsal whilst you were in the zone," Larry replied, sounding like quite the authority on the subject (and this despite the fact that Charlotte had most certainly *not* been "in the zone"). "It's important that creatives such as me and yourself immerse ourselves completely when the moment calls for it, as I'm sure you'll agree," he added with a confident sniff.

Larry filled the other empty teacups nudged in his direction, recounting his fortunate news for Charlotte's benefit. He was delighted to report that his bank had eventually agreed to refund every penny that his so-called friend Veronica had swindled out of him. And while his initial misfortune had been immensely distressing at first, the timing of it was, as it should happen, rather fortuitous, Larry went on to explain. In an effort to combat rising levels of fraud against their clientele, the bank was rolling out a national advertising campaign to highlight just how easily it was for people to fall victim to scams, as Larry himself had recently experienced. And rather than using an actor in the campaign, the advertising agency for the bank was hopeful of securing a person whose real-life experience would shine through, having a real impact on the viewing public.

"And that's why they wanted yours truly as their poster boy," Larry proudly announced. "They emailed the first of the proposed scripts through earlier this morning, so I was just giving this lot a virtuoso performance of my role in it."

Knowing Larry as the practical joker he was, Charlotte remained unsure if he was having a laugh at her expense. She ran her eyes over his face, searching for any indication that he was somehow teasing her. "You're serious?" she asked, when she was fairly certain he wasn't teasing. "Larry, that's brilliant news and I'm sure you'll be an absolute star."

Larry's expression was an absolute picture, with him beaming happily from ear to ear. "Filming starts early next week, and the bank is hosting a glitzy shindig in Liverpool further on next month to launch their national campaign, and..."

"And?" Charlotte asked, looking to see if the ladies were privy to whatever it was Larry was about to say.

Larry held out for a moment, building up to his big reveal. "And they're inviting me and a few friends to attend the launch party," he disclosed, after the pause. "In fact my cheerleaders are already signed up," Larry advised, pointing over to Joyce, Beryl, and Carole. "And there's an invite with your name on it as well, Lotti, if you'd like to come?"

"Oh of course I would, Larry," Charlotte confirmed. "It's just..." she started to say, before stopping herself short. "Yes, I'd love to come, Larry."

Just then a raised hand indicated Larry's invaluable services were required elsewhere. "Marvellous, Lotti," he said, pushing his trolley towards where it was needed next.

Still smiling, Charlotte took a sidestep to where Bonnie was busy cutting out fabric pieces for a cushion she was working on. "Bonnie," Charlotte said, once Larry had moved onward, crouching down and talking to her through the corner of her mouth. "Bonnie, you don't think—"

Bonnie leaned in close, so as not to be overheard by the others. "That it sounds a bit too good to be true? Yeah, I was thinking exactly the same thing, Lotti," Bonnie answered, suspecting she knew what Charlotte was thinking. "In fact, if you hadn't come over when you did, I was going to talk to you next."

"So you think?"

"Yeah," Bonnie said gravely. "I don't know what anyone might possibly have to gain by it, or what their game is exactly. But I do believe our dear friend Larry could very well be the victim of yet another scam, for the second time this month."

Chapter Fourteen

Stanley ran his index finger down the menu, making little murmuring noises to himself while he considered which particular variety of pizza might hit the spot.

"Hmm, what about..." he offered eventually, sounding as if he'd reached a crucial decision. "No, maybe not," he said a second later, returning his attention to the menu for another gander, with his finger at the top of the page, ready for another pass.

Calum and Charlotte, who'd already given the waiter their own individual orders, watched on with anxious, hungry anticipation. "How about pepperoni with jalapeño peppers?" Charlotte proposed, a winning combination the last time they'd visited La Mona Lisa for one of their sumptuous pizzas.

Stanley shook his head, immediately discounting his mum's suggestion, moving his nose closer to the menu for further consideration as the waiter stood poised, pencil at the ready, like a journalist on the verge of an exclusive scoop. "I could come back in five minutes if you'd—"

"Pepperoni with jalapeño peppers, please!" Stanley declared, coming to his own decision with firm confidence, as if his mum hadn't just suggested this exact same selection only a moment or two before.

"Excellent choice, sir," the attentive waiter offered, dutifully scribbling the order down on his notepad. "One small pepperoni and jalapeño pizza, coming right up."

For Stanley, Friday night was rapidly becoming his favourite night of the week. With their recently instituted tradition, not only did Friday mark the end of an arduous, brain-sapping week of school, but it also meant pizza, followed by a lazy evening with a good film and plenty of snacks within reach. An arrangement Charlotte and Calum were happy to provide, especially when you threw a nice bottle of red into the mix for themselves. And with no gaming consoles or iPads in sight, a most welcome consequence for Charlotte was in having her son's undivided attention and scintillating company for the evening.

There were many parents, Charlotte noticed, who would tear their hair out listening to yet another chapter and verse conversation about who was doing what on Minecraft or what crazy antics their child's favourite YouTuber was up to. But this was what kids of Stanley's generation were into. And even if Charlotte didn't have a clue what a lot of it actually meant, she was happy to listen to Stanley nattering away for hours on end. Because she knew, one day, he'd fly the nest and she'd miss these random discussions.

With their meals soon delivered and thus Stanley's gob subsequently full of pizza, it did however present Calum an opportunity to get a word in edgewise, and so he seized his chance. "So, Lotti. It's good news that everything's in order with Larry, yes?" he remarked, making conversation as he reached for their bowl of shared chips.

Charlotte discreetly shook her head, hoping to bring this line of conversation to an abrupt conclusion.

"Wait, hang on," Stanley interjected, taking a sudden break from chewing. "What's that about Larry? He wasn't ill, was he?"

Charlotte rolled her eyes, but not in an unkind manner. "He's fine, I promise," she quickly assured him. And knowing Stanley as she did, she knew he wouldn't be satisfied leaving it at just that. "I didn't want to worry you by saying anything, Stan, but we thought, for a short time, that Larry might have fallen victim to another scam."

"But he hasn't?" Stanley asked, drawing his fingers into a fist, just to be sure, protective friend that he was.

"No, definitely not. Larry showed me the correspondence from his bank, and everything appears totally legitimate."

"*What* appears totally legitimate?" Stanley pressed, hungry for both pizza and further details.

Charlotte gave Calum a friendly scowl, in a playful, *look-what-you've-started-now* sort of way. "Well, you're just going to have to wait," Charlotte informed Stanley, not wishing to reveal Larry's exciting news. "Larry knows you're coming with me for Make It Sew tomorrow, and he wanted to tell you himself."

"But, Mum..."

Charlotte fastened an imaginary zipper across her mouth. "I'm sworn to secrecy, Stan. He can tell you himself tomorrow."

"Muumm..." Stanley pleaded.

Charlotte, however, stuck to her guns and stayed tight-lipped throughout the remainder of their meal. Which was impressive considering she'd enjoyed a large glass of merlot which would, ordinarily, have loosened her tongue considerably.

Soon, completely stuffed, the three of them resisted the desserts menu, opting to save what little space remained in their bellies for their movie-time snacks back at Charlotte's cottage.

Once outside the restaurant, Charlotte enjoyed a lungful of the salty breeze blowing in from the Irish Sea. "How about a short walk down to the shore before we head home?" she suggested.

"I could go for a walk," Calum replied. "Stan?"

"Can we skim some stones while at the beach?" Stanley asked.

"Of course," Calum readily agreed. "In fact it's illegal to visit the beach without skimming stones," he insisted. "Well, or at least it should be."

Charlotte treasured living in the lovely, picturesque village of Laxey, known historically for its industrious mining and fishing trade. Cosy stone cottages lined the narrow, winding streets. Popular with both tourists and locals alike, you were never too far from a friendly face. Though it was rarely too crowded, with peace and tranquillity also available in spades. Or a bucket and a spade, rather, if heading to the beach was your thing. And, for Charlotte, heading to the beach was absolutely her thing.

And, for Charlotte, the changing seasons didn't spoil her enjoyment either. In the brighter months, such as at present, long summer evenings meant leisurely strolls, with perhaps a glass of something cold in one of the available outdoor beer gardens. Wild winter days, on the other hand, meant bundling up in your thickest coat, maybe watching the waves crash against the shore, before heading home and huddling up next to the log burner with a steaming mug of hot chocolate to warm your bones.

Down by the beach today, other than an adventurous couple packing up their paddle boards, they had the entire stretch all to themselves. Charlotte parked herself down on the pebbly section of the coast, fondly watching on as Calum led Stanley in their search for the optimum skimming stones. "It's all about smooth surface," she heard him say to his young Padawan. "And throwing at a twenty-degree angle," he continued, extending his right hand before mimicking the perfect arm action, what with him being a self-proclaimed Master of Skimming.

Charlotte felt a brief inclination to join the boys and show them how it was really done. But they were both so engrossed in their friendly one-upmanship that she felt it best to leave them to it. Besides, it was a delight to see the pair of them bonding over a common interest, even if that interest was just hurling lumps of rock into the waves. So for now, Charlotte was perfectly content to just watch from a distance as the gentle sea breeze caressed her cheeks.

With the failing light, and her soft derrière losing its battle with the knobbly rocks, Charlotte eventually called time on their beach activities. If she hadn't, there was every likelihood the boys would still be going strong the following morning.

"Thirteen bounces across the sea!" Stanley announced with enormous satisfaction, on the walk back up to the street. "I did, didn't I, Calum? Thirteen bounces."

With a shrug, Calum had no choice but to hand over his laurel crown. "That you did, Stan," he humbly submitted. "And I'm sure Barnes Wallis himself would have been impressed by the display."

THE CRAFTERNOON SEWCIAL CLUB: SHOWDOWN

Stan didn't really understand the compliment, as he had no idea who this Barnes Wallis fellow was or what the chap was famous for, but he was more than happy to receive the plaudits nonetheless. "And the highest number wins a fiver, right?" he was keen to remind his conquered companion, as per the details of their previously negotiated bet, a bet that Calum appeared to have absolutely no recollection of, curiously enough.

Calum reached for his wallet, however. "You're sure I agreed to that?" he asked, pulling a note out from the crease.

Stanley thrust out his hand. "Yep. And that's what overconfidence gets you, Calum!" he joked, seizing the crisp five-pound note, the spoils of his impressive victory.

Charlotte wandered unhurriedly up the cottage-lined street, hand in hand with the boys on either side of her. It wasn't that she was worn out by the steep incline of the road. Rather, she just liked to have a discreet look inside the cute cottages they passed, nosey little so-and-so that she was. Stan, on the other hand, was less discreet, all but pressing his nose up to the glass.

"You know, I was just thinking..." Charlotte offered, a little bit further along.

"Oh, dear. That usually means I need to fetch my drill, tape measure, or ladders," Calum observed.

"Nope, no DIY on this particular occasion," Charlotte clarified, along with a laugh. "No, it's just, you know these press interviews I've agreed to?"

"Yeah," Calum and Stanley both answered in unison.

"Well, they're supposed to be happening next week, and I've not heard anything about travel arrangements, hotel bookings, or anything like that. I was wondering if I should maybe give somebody a wee reminder. You know, a little nudge, perhaps? But I didn't want to sound like I was being cheeky or anything."

Stanley waited a moment to see if his mum had anything else to say on the matter, any explanation as to what she meant, because... "Mum?" he asked, looking up at her. "Mum, did you not say they were Zoom meetings?"

Charlotte was impressed her son had been listening to her. "That's right. Zoom. In and out, quick, one after another," she said, chuckling happily away to herself. "Zoomy-zoom-zoom!"

"Mum. Do you know what a Zoom meeting is?"

The fact that she was being asked this by Stanley somewhat dinted Charlotte's confidence, making her less sure that she actually knew the answer. Still, she pressed on. "Yes, of course," she said, as she gazed inside yet another of the quaint stone cottages, comparing it to her own. "Zoom. As in to move quickly. Fast and energetic. Power meetings, concise and to the point?"

Calum felt the need to jump in at this stage. "Lotti, if they're Zoom meetings, what that means is that they're going to be via video conference interviews rather than face-to-face meetings. And if you've not heard any travel agenda, that would be why?"

"Oh," Charlotte replied, unsure what else to say just now, as she was a little too embarrassed to say much else.

"So you probably didn't need to spend all that time rehearsing with Larry and the others, right, Mum?" Stan helpfully pointed out. "Mum? I was saying that you probably didn't need to—"

"Stanley," Calum cut in, hoping to spare Charlotte's blushes. "Stan, if you've never used Zoom it's an easy mistake to make."

"Ah," replied Stanley, receiving the message, especially after noting the look on his mum's face. "Yeah, absolutely," he agreed. Then, tugging on her hand, he said, "Right. Come on, Mum, the first one in the house gets to choose tonight's film."

❈ ❈ ❈

Charlotte's confusion regarding the meeting terminology was, as it turned out, a blessing in disguise, in that she was now significantly over-prepared following the several gruelling prep sessions that had been conducted previously by Larry and his improvised production team. And the idea of an interview via the miracle of modern technology — rather than in person, live in the studio — came as a huge relief and was a much less nerve-wracking proposition to Charlotte. As such, she now found herself fairly looking forward to the sessions.

THE CRAFTERNOON SEWCIAL CLUB: SHOWDOWN

There were six ten-minute interviews scheduled with various media outlets. And to make things easier for all concerned, they were due to take place on the same morning, one after another. With Calum's assistance, she'd worked out where to place her laptop with a favourable camera angle, and thus, what the viewing public would eventually see on their screens. In preparation, Charlotte had dressed her kitchen-cum-office for the morning so it resembled a crafting workshop, replete with a sewing machine positioned strategically beside her on the tabletop, surrounded by balls of wool and rolls of colourful fabric. And all favourably basked in complementary natural light courtesy of the broad kitchen window.

Of course, she wouldn't be alone, with her co-host Darren also dialling in to join her. The media interviews were a crucial opportunity to pitch their new show, selling the idea to the public who would determine the show's success and, vitally, if it would ultimately be commissioned for a second season. As such, nothing was left to chance, with Charlotte and Darren having several calls in advance to discuss the running order and the key points they wanted to address. And with Darren's extensive career in broadcasting, Charlotte was delighted to have somebody so experienced to hold her hand, so to speak.

Fortunately, with the interviews happening on a school day, there was no chance of a young person wandering in the kitchen half-dressed while looking for something to eat. And with her mobile phone turned off and a prominent sign hanging on her front door politely advising any potential visitors that she was not to be disturbed, Charlotte was all set for her very first press junket.

For the first of the press interviews, conducted by a strait-laced reporter from the *Daily Telegraph* newspaper, Charlotte initially struggled. With a slight delay in the Zoom connection and butterflies in her stomach, she ended up talking over herself to the point that she was virtually stuttering. Fortunately, Darren, the consummate professional that he was, stepped in to rescue his floundering colleague.

But it didn't take too long to get into her stride and by the third interview of the morning, Charlotte's natural charm and passion for crafting shone through unhindered. Indeed, by this stage, even Darren was struggling to get a word in, although he didn't appear to mind too much because her unscripted, spontaneous approach definitely seemed to strike a chord with those asking the questions.

Later, with her voice getting hoarse from all the back-and-forth conversation, Charlotte was relieved to get safely through to the last interview without too much incident. And, surprisingly, she found herself rather enjoying her debut press junket, which required her to talk about crafting, something she was rather accomplished at. Although she did experience a flutter of nerves ahead of the final interview with *The One Show*. After all, this was a TV programme she watched each evening religiously. So, to see her favourite presenter on her laptop screen smiling back at her was, putting it mildly, a surreal experience for Charlotte. And knowing she would be appearing on the show herself was absolutely bonkers, Charlotte couldn't help but think.

Asked about the inspiration behind the Crafternoon Sewcial Club, Charlotte paused to consider her response. Right at that moment, though, a skulking figure outside the kitchen window caught her attention, distracting her away from the question at hand. She stumbled over her answer, much to her chagrin, holding one eye on the computer screen and the other on the window. Even though she knew the Zoom interviews weren't going out live, and would also most certainly be edited before broadcast, she still wanted to come across as professional as possible and avoid any potential slip-ups.

It didn't take Charlotte too long to figure out that her visitor was Postman Harry. Suspecting beforehand that Harry would likely appear on his postal rounds at some point, he was actually the principal reason she'd left an explanatory and polite 'Do Not Disturb' notice on her front door. Being a busy fellow, she suspected he'd likely forget their conversation about the timing of her interview commitment, so she'd hoped the sign would serve as a friendly reminder. Sadly, this didn't seem to be the case, as judging by Harry's current position and behaviour, her cunning idea didn't appear to have quite gone to plan.

With the sun beating down on the window, Harry strained his eyes, struggling to see beyond the glare into the kitchen beyond. "Charlotte!" he called out as he squidged his prodigious beak against the glass, using a hand to shield his eyes from the sun's rays in hopes of improving his view. Then, after catching a glimpse of Charlotte sitting rigid at the kitchen table, her attention focused squarely on her computer screen, he tapped his finger on the glass. "Lotti!" he called out, certain she must be able to see him there. "Lotti!" he said again, wondering why she wasn't answering him.

But in the kitchen, Charlotte was consumed with trying to conclude her interview, having just been asked what her aspirations were for the new show. As such, she was currently speaking from her soul about how she hoped to bring the wonderful world of crafting to an even wider audience, showcasing the various benefits of such a rewarding hobby. Being a subject close to her heart, she spoke eloquently and with passion, all while attempting to shoo Postman Harry away with a series of discreet, out-of-camera-view gesticulations. However, this wasn't having the desired effect, with Harry seeming to take this signalling as some kind of secret request for assistance.

Seeing his dear friend Lotti sitting there, without any type of acknowledgement — when she clearly knew he was stood there — told him something was amiss. He could witness her chatting away, but just couldn't see with whom. This was strange behaviour indeed, even from Lotti, he reckoned. As such, Harry could only assume she was in trouble. What sort of trouble exactly, he couldn't be sure. But trouble was definitely afoot, in Harry's considered opinion, of that he was certain.

"Lotti, is everything okay?" he asked, rapping his knuckles on the glass. But again, Charlotte remained talking, appearing to ignore his presence, and yet continued to make the most peculiar hand gestures. "Right," said Harry, having seen enough to know something was not right. "I'm coming in, Lotti!" he announced, loud enough to be heard. Harry removed his satchel in short order, dropping it down on the garden path and rushing over to the front entrance. He tried the latch, but the door was strangely locked. Being a seasoned postman, Harry had seen a fair few doors in his time, and based on his vast knowledge, he reckoned this one would offer little resistance to the application of a firm shoulder.

Unsure what to expect and concerned about any potential peril that might await, Harry armed himself with a small, three-pronged hand rake that he found in the outdoor flower garden. Without overthinking his approach, Harry positioned himself accordingly, took a deep breath, and then launched his shoulder towards the wooden door. As he thought, the lock mechanism yielded without much opposition. But Harry's forward momentum sent him staggering through the hallway, with the living room door eventually bringing him to an abrupt halt.

Slightly out of puff, Harry wielded his tiny little rake, raising it over his head. "Lotti, it's me!" he bravely announced, bustling through the living room and jumping into the kitchen like a brave knight rescuing his damsel from a menacing dragon.

"Lotti? Lotti, it's me!" Harry said again, when curiously Charlotte's attention remained fixed to the screen of her laptop computer. "Lotti, are you all right?" he asked, darting his eyes around the kitchen, trying to make sense of her odd behaviour.

"I'm sorry about the noise," Charlotte offered, followed by an awkward laugh. "What's all the commotion?" she said, repeating the question she'd just been asked. "Oh, that's just my friend Harry the postman breaking into my house," she explained. "He probably needs a signature for a parcel, and he's awfully committed to his job," she joked, just as Postman Harry appeared over her shoulder and was thus captured by her laptop's camera. "And I'm fine, Harry, thanks for asking. But as you're here, you may as well say hello to *The One Show*, which you'll most likely be appearing on shortly. Oh, and you can go ahead and put your weapon down, if you like."

Chapter Fifteen

George ran a weathered hand across the equally weatherbeaten splintered wood, assessing the damage inflicted. "Old Harry did this?" he asked, appearing surprised but also somewhat impressed.

Charlotte had just arrived from the kitchen, a tray of tea and biscuits in hand, when George asked her this. "Indeed he did," she confirmed, taking up a position inside her front doorway. "Bless him," she added fondly. "He thought I was being held hostage or, bizarrely, that I was somehow being hypnotised. Possibly both, I'm not sure. But in any case, it's comforting to know he's keeping an eye out for me, I suppose."

"Well, if he ever gets bored being postman, a career as a rugby player awaits," George remarked, reaching for his toolbox.

"So you can fix it?" Charlotte asked, jiggling the packet of biscuits she'd brought along hoping to keep George happy. The biscuits were Tunnock's Caramel Wafers, his favourite, and she'd had a devil of a time securing a place to hide them from Stanley, as Stanley would surely gobble them up in an instant if he'd been lucky enough to have found them.

"Yeah, no problem. But let Postman Harry know I'm reinforcing the area around this lock, so he might dislocate something if he tries the same manoeuvre again."

"Right. Will do," Charlotte answered. "Although I'm hopeful he won't be making a habit of breaking in," she said, surveying once again the damage from Harry's last effort. "Oh, and you're sure you don't mind, George? You know, about me having to go away earlier than expected for the TV show?"

George shook his head as he set to work with the claw end of a small prybar, carefully separating one section of wood from another. "Of course not, Lotti. I love having Stanley stay over," he replied. "Hang on," he said, a thought occurring to him. "Did you not say it was your boyfriend's birthday tomorrow? I thought we'd already swapped my night with Stan anyway, as you were taking Calum out for a slap-up meal?"

The reminder brought Charlotte a pained expression. "I've not mentioned it to him yet. I only found out about the revised schedule this morning. It's not ideal, of course, but I didn't think I could really say no to them. I'd hoped to catch the last flight back tomorrow, so that I could meet up with Calum in the evening. But so far everything's already fully booked."

Unfortunately, it was a slightly tricky situation she found herself in. Originally, she'd not been due to leave the island just yet. But due to some unplanned last-minute rescheduling, the producers were starting to film much earlier than anyone expected. And as well as being away for Calum's birthday, it also meant that she would now have to miss several Make It Sew classes pencilled into this week's diary. Mollie, Bonnie, and Abigail, bless their hearts, were all kind enough to volunteer to help where their work and school timetables permitted. But not putting in appearances at the various Make It Sew sessions as she had promised, and thus letting those people down, put a slight dampener on her enjoyment of an otherwise very exciting development in Charlotte's career, as filming of the TV show was now about to commence.

"Right, that's me finished!" George called out, an hour or so later, after having successfully remedied the damage caused by a determined Postman Harry.

Charlotte arrived to inspect George's handiwork with a crochet hook secured in her mouth and her purse in hand. "What do I owe you?" she asked through occupied lips.

George packed up his toolbox. "*Pfft,*" he said. "You honestly think I'm going to charge the talented mother of my son to fix her door? Please."

"Wait, you think I'm talented?" Charlotte asked, removing the crotchet hook so she could speak more clearly. Charlotte had that look you get when you meet a friend's new Labrador puppy for the first time. "You know, George, you're a right decent bloke when you want to be," she suggested, giving his shoulder a playful punch.

"Oi, not so loud! Don't be telling everybody that," George said, glancing about the neighbourhood. "I don't know how many other doors Harry's put through, and I could very well be here all day," he joked. "But seriously, about the TV thing, Lotti? Go and smash it," he advised.

"Smash my TV...?" Charlotte asked, misunderstanding for a moment what George was saying.

"No, not that. I meant give 'em hell!" George explained with a laugh. "Show those boys what you're made of, yeah? Honestly, we're all damned proud of you for this."

"Oh, stop it, you," Charlotte protested, though only mildly. "You're going to get me going in a minute."

Fortunately, the fancy restaurant Charlotte had booked for the next day was understanding and able to cancel her reservation. And while Calum was disappointed that she'd be away for his birthday, he understood the situation was out of her control.

So later that day, after having kissed both Calum and Stanley to within an inch of their lives, Charlotte drove herself towards Ronaldsway Airport for the start of the first chapter in her new, grand adventure. Calum had hoped to escort her there and see her off, he'd informed her, but a pressing business engagement sadly took precedence, apparently.

It was funny, Charlotte observed as she drove along, how her perspective of the island had changed since the formation of her various crafting clubs. Rather than being merely geographical areas dotted around, the villages she drove through were now the homes of her club members. She knew where many of them lived, what crafting projects they were working on, and even in some cases the personal business of many of their neighbours (as her members did like to gossip!).

And again, missing out on playing a regular part in the lives of these friends, not maintaining a steady presence, made her a bit sad. For a fleeting moment passing through Ballasalla, in fact, only a short distance away from the airport now, she had an overwhelming urge to turn a hundred and eighty degrees and head straight back in the direction she'd just come.

"Oh, Charlotte," she said to herself, willing away the gloom. "It's just nerves, you silly thing." Then, thinking about how excited Joyce and Beryl had been about appearing on the show alongside her, this managed to raise a much-needed smile from her as well. "Right. This is an absolutely fantastic opportunity," she reminded herself aloud, as she pulled into the airport carpark. "No going back now, Charlotte."

Charlotte collected her things, wheeling her modest suitcase towards the terminal, when a strange realisation hit. Previously, Charlotte was unknown to the majority of people, just another pleasant face in the crowd. But soon, once the show started to air, what impact would it have on her life? Sure, Charlotte loved talking to new people, but how would appearing on the show change things, she wondered, a fresh wave of nerves washing over her. Would she be recognised each time she left the house, with people coming up to say hello? And what if people didn't like her? What if people said mean things about her online?

All of these possibilities darted through her mind, all the way until the vast automatic doors at the terminal entrance. A blast of warm air from the overhead heaters buffeted her hair as she went through, snapping her from her thoughts, just in time for her to come to such an abrupt halt that her suitcase bumped right into her heels. "What on earth are you doing?" she asked, scarcely able to believe what she was seeing.

"Surprise!" came the throaty response from the group of people assembled in the terminal building, all looking like a football team waiting for their photograph to be taken.

"Aww, you guys. What am I going to do with you?" Charlotte said, stepping forward, with passersby likely wondering what the commotion was all about.

Standing there, holding a banner that stretched out wider than a bus, were Calum, Stanley, and Mollie, accompanied by a dozen or so of the usual suspects from her loyal Crafternoon family as well. Charlotte read the words on the group's banner:

Good luck Lotti. You'll SEW smash it!!!

"You lot are the absolute best," she said, extending her arms to embrace whichever one of them was closest. "I can't believe you've done this," she said, her voice temporarily muffled against someone's shoulder. "And you. I thought you had a meeting?" Charlotte offered a moment later, lifting her head and looking over at Calum.

"I lied," Calum answered with a shrug, while smiling like a fool.

"Make sure to get that hunk of yours from the BBC warmed up for our imminent arrival!" Joyce instructed, followed by one of her trademark cackles.

"Hunk?" said Calum. "What's all this about a hunk...?"

"Oh, don't you worry, you're the only fellow in my life," Charlotte promised, shifting her position so she could wrap her arms around him. "Oh, and you too, mister," she quickly added, along with a wink, for Stanley's benefit. "And thank you for this, guys," she told the entire group. "Honestly, I love you all, and you're the best group of friends a girl could ever hope for."

❋ ❋ ❋

Long after her plane had soared up and away from the Isle of Man, Charlotte was grinning from ear to ear, still chuffed to bits about the unexpected departure committee. And even though she wasn't leaving for a six-month world tour or anything like that, it was the pick-me-up tonic she desperately needed at just the right time.

"Excuse me," a friendly lady said, leaning over from across the aisle and gently tapping Charlotte's arm. "I'm sorry to bother you, but you wouldn't happen to be Charlotte Newman, would you?"

"Oh," Charlotte replied, surprised she was being recognised like this already, even before she'd appeared on the upcoming TV programme, but figuring it best to just go with the flow. "Yes. Yes, I am," she proudly declared, wondering if the lady may have seen the recent news interview she'd done with Darren Shipley. "If you'd like to take a selfie with me, you'd be my first," Charlotte advised, strangely relaxed and slipping into the role of minor celebrity with aplomb. Perhaps being accosted by members of the adoring public wouldn't be such a horrible or intrusive thing after all, Charlotte mused.

"A selfie?" the lady replied, puzzled, over the sound of the engines. "Uhm... no," she said, holding out an item in her hand for Charlotte's consideration, although Charlotte couldn't identify what it was just yet.

Charlotte rolled her eyes in a *what-am-I-like* manner. "Oh, you just want my autograph?" she asked, assuming the item to be a piece of paper or some such thing.

"What? Why would I...?" the woman started to say. "No. No, I've just found this debit card on the floor, and I was only trying to find its owner," she explained, handing over the bank card with Charlotte's name printed on it. "Maybe it fell out of your purse somehow, while you were settling in?"

Charlotte took quick possession of her property, offering her sincere thanks before burying her head in the partially completed jumper she'd brought along with her to work on during the flight. Not once had Charlotte anything that could be considered to even remotely resemble an ego. And if fame and modest fortune were ever in danger of changing that personality trait of hers in the future, all she need do was remember this incident on the plane. It was funny, Charlotte thought to herself, that the most grounded she'd felt in a long time was when she was currently twenty thousand feet in the air.

After a short hop, consisting of no more than forty minutes or thereabouts, Charlotte was soon back on terra firma, in Old Blighty. Walking through the luggage reclaim area, she couldn't help but blush as the debit card lady from the plane offered her a cordial wave to send her on her way.

Charlotte scanned the arrivals hall, hoping to see Phillipa, the production assistant she'd met on her previous visit, who had kindly offered to pick her up. Staring back was an ocean of people likely waiting to greet their returning friends or loved ones. But as far as Charlotte could see, Phillipa was not there among them.

Standing near the vast revolving doors that led outside were what she assumed to be taxi drivers, with all of them holding small placards noting the surname of the passengers they were there to collect. Wondering if there might have been some sort of change of plan, Charlotte moved closer to read each of the signs in turn, offering an apologetic smile for not being the person the drivers had written on their plastic boards. With no more drivers to smile at, Charlotte started to fear she'd arrived at the wrong time or, irrationally, even at the wrong airport.

"Hmm," she said, switching her phone off aeroplane mode to see if she'd received any messages. She walked towards the exit with her nose pressed into her phone, considering if she should just jump into one of the long line of taxis she'd seen snaking around the terminal building.

"Oh my days!" a startled Charlotte exclaimed, looking up as somebody jumped directly in front of her, blocking any further progress rather suddenly.

"Taxi for Ms Newman?" a familiar voice said, accompanied as well by its owner's familiar face.

"Darren, what are you doing here?" Charlotte said, delighted to see her soon-to-be co-host. "You're not here for me, are you? I was expecting Phillipa."

"May I?" Darren asked, reaching for the handle on Charlotte's suitcase. "Phillipa double booked, so I offered to come and pick you up," he explained, directing her through the exit. "M'lady?" he said, once outside. "If you'd like to follow me to where your carriage awaits."

Once on their way, Charlotte gazed out the passenger-side window, taking in all the sights of a bustling city centre. The concrete jungle that was Manchester was a world apart from her bucolic existence back on the sleepy Isle of Man. And now, the realisation that this vibrant new world would play a significant part in her working life was daunting, yet exhilarating.

"You okay, Lotti?" Darren asked as he checked his sat-nav for directions to Charlotte's hotel, noticing Charlotte was awfully quiet over there in her seat along their drive.

"Oh, yes. Wonderful, in fact. I was just taking it all in, Darren."

"Ah, I think this is you," Darren advised a short while later, turning into the hotel carpark. "Nice. Good choice, this," he remarked, noting the five-star rating boldly displayed on the hotel name's signage.

"Phillipa was kind enough to book it for me," Charlotte replied, appearing rather delighted with Phillipa's selection. "I must offer her my sincere thanks," she added, just as a well-presented concierge wearing a tall hat hurried over to greet them.

"Now, about dinner tonight, Lotti."

"Dinner tonight?" Charlotte said, smiling as the concierge opened the car door for her.

Darren climbed out of the car to fetch Charlotte's luggage from the boot. "Of course, Lotti. You don't think I'm going to let you arrive in town and not show you our famous Manchester hospitality, do you?" he told her. "Honestly, what sort of host would that make me?"

Charlotte tried her best to appear grateful when, in truth, she really just wanted a quiet night in the hotel room with her travelling knitting project for company and some room service. "Oh, well in that case, I'd feel awful for offending such a gracious host," she answered.

"Pick you up at seven-thirty? My friend owns a superb Italian nearby."

"I'll look forward to it," Charlotte said cheerily, stretching the truth just a little. "Although..."

"You don't like Italian? It's no problem, we can—"

"No, no, I do love Italian food," Charlotte advised, placing her hand against her belly. "It's just that I didn't want to be out too late tonight. You know, to stay bright-eyed and bushy-tailed for the first day of filming tomorrow?"

The concierge took possession of Charlotte's suitcase, waiting patiently to escort her safely inside.

"Ah, no need to worry about an early start, Lotti," Darren said confidently, clearly having not seen Charlotte the morning after a late night. "Tomorrow's a free day, so I was thinking you might perhaps like a tour of the area? I hear Tatton Park is lovely this time of year, and I'm fairly certain they've got a tearoom for refreshments. And then the hard work only starts the day after."

Charlotte felt her left eye starting to twitch at this point. "A free day?" she asked of Darren, whilst offering the patient concierge a polite smile. "Sorry, but I was under the impression that *filming* was going to start tomorrow, as after all, that's why I'm here a week early?" she said, trying not to sound too cheesed off.

"Ah, my mistake," Darren confessed, as if this seeming mix-up were only a minor gaffe. "I think there might originally have been a production meeting scheduled. So I may have given Phillipa the wrong dates. Sorry about that. But at least you're here now, eager and raring for action, yeah?"

But all Charlotte could think about was how she was going to miss Calum's birthday thanks to a scheduling oversight. For a fleeting moment, she thought about jumping into a taxi and heading straight back to the airport. "It's just that..." Charlotte started to say, but decided that getting off on the wrong foot wasn't an ideal start to their working relationship. "You know what, Tatton Park sounds lovely," she acquiesced, determined to be cordial and trying her best to hide her bitter disappointment.

"Marvellous, Lotti. I'll see you later this evening, then, and make sure to bring your appetite."

Chapter Sixteen

Charlotte had tossed and turned for much of the night. It might have had something to do with the fantastically generous serving of gnocchi followed by the equally generous helping of tiramisu, both of which had been happily gurgling away in her stomach. Or, more likely it was the fact she'd be missing her boyfriend's birthday to spend the day traipsing around a country estate with a bloke she barely knew.

But Calum had never given any indication that he was the jealous type. So why hadn't she just filled him in about the unexpected change of plan the previous day? He knew she wasn't able to find a flight back to see him in the evening, and that was one thing. But to spend the entire day gallivanting around and having a good time with Darren? When, ostensibly, she was *supposed* to be spending tomorrow filming? How might that be received, she wondered. And putting it off, waiting until some undetermined time at a later date to say something, would Calum then think she was hiding something from him? Would it upset him? Would he be offended? These were all concerns that had been bouncing around the inside of her head like a rubber ball.

She'd considered if she should just keep schtum, as after all it's not like anything untoward was happening. Still, keeping quiet about everything would be a form of lying, she reckoned, and she was utterly useless at lying and hated doing it anyway. For that reason, while wide awake in bed at about three a.m., she decided the best thing to do was to call and explain the situation in the morning. And really, there *was* no situation to speak of. She simply wished to keep him abreast of things so that there couldn't be any possible misunderstandings between them.

Unfortunately, after spending too much of the night tossing and turning, once she did manage to doze off in the comfortable hotel bed, she ended up sleeping right through her alarm, only waking twenty minutes or so before Darren was due to pick her up for their 'away' day. So rather than rushing a call to Calum, she'd settled on sending him a simple happy birthday text while promising herself to give him a proper phone call later that day.

And, presently, further compounding her overall feeling of guilt, Charlotte was irrationally annoyed with herself for having such an entirely splendid day, enjoying the lavish gardens at the historic country estate of Tatton Park as she was.

"My son Stan would adore it here," Charlotte suggested, holding her hands on her hips as she took in the majesty of the place. "Could you just imagine ever calling this place home?" she wondered aloud, feasting her eyes on the impressive mansion house. "But then again, I don't suppose I would enjoy the massive heating bill, or the cost of having to furnish a residence as enormous as this," she went on, talking herself out of the idea of ever moving in.

"At least you'd have plenty of storage capacity for all of your various crafting supplies?" Darren proposed, availing himself of a vacant seat in the nearby picnic area. "We could always bring your Stanley here for a visit if you like. You know, the next time you bring him over?"

"Absolutely. He'd love to see the herds of wild deer roaming about the place," Charlotte answered. "And I think he'd definitely be impressed with the number of ice cream vans dotted around the estate as well," she said with a laugh. "In fact..." she added, placing her things down onto the table. "In fact, after all that walking around we've just done, I—"

"The walking around pretending to know the names of all the flowers featured in the various displays?" Darren joked, holding his hands up to protect himself from any incoming assault.

"You cheeky sod! I can assure you, mister, that I *absolutely* know my chrysanthemum from my hydrangeas," Charlotte insisted. "Well, most of the time," she said with a laugh. "Oi, and there I was about to buy you an ice cream as a reward for bringing me to such a gorgeous place."

"In that case, please forgive me," Darren responded. "And I'd love a Whippy with raspberry sauce," he promptly added.

Charlotte gave him a scowl, but the grin that quickly emerged suggested she wasn't being entirely serious. "Coming right up," she said happily.

Fortunately, the queue at the nearby van wasn't as lengthy as some of the others they'd seen during their visit, so it shouldn't take too much time to get to the front, Charlotte reckoned. At least that's what she first believed, until she realised the woman ahead of her might be connected to the large group of primary-age schoolchildren in the immediate vicinity, some of whom were seated, some standing, but all of them with their eyes fixed lovingly on the ice cream van. And her concerns were only confirmed when the flustered lady unfolded an A4 sheet of paper with what appeared very much to be a rather lengthy list of ice cream requests written on it.

Charlotte turned around, glancing back over at Darren for a moment, wondering if they should perhaps give the frozen treat a swerve, when she felt a polite tap on the shoulder. "Would you like to go on ahead of me?" the lady in front of her kindly asked. "It's just that I might be some time, as you can see," she advised, looking over to her many young charges, along with a sigh.

"Oh, no," Charlotte replied. "No, I couldn't," she said, before taking another gander at the extent of the orders making up the woman's list. "Well, then again... I mean, if you're sure you don't mind?"

"It's fine," the woman assured her, graciously stepping to one side and waving Charlotte through. "You can warn the man behind the counter as to what's coming," she said, nodding again in the direction of the host of children watching on in excited anticipation.

Over at his and Charlotte's table, enjoying the melodic soundtrack of eager, enthusiastic children, Darren was grateful to take the weight off of his feet for a few minutes. Catching what he thought was the sound of a ringtone mixed in with the general din, he reached into his pocket to retrieve his phone, but then found the screen in darkness. Still able to hear something, Darren leaned in closer towards Charlotte's bag, where the source of the ringtone he'd heard was soon discovered, lying there beside it. He looked over to her, uncertain if he should sprint over with her phone, although suspecting that any of the kids standing nearby would pounce on their vacant table if he did. Instead, Darren held up the phone in the hopes of attracting Charlotte's attention, but that attention was presently being taken up by the ice cream vendor.

Unsure if he should answer the phone, especially as he could see the caller's identity being that of Calum, whom he knew to be Charlotte's fella, Darren hesitated.

"Hello?" Darren said after a moment, Charlotte's phone now pressed against his ear. "Calum, it's Darren here," he explained, assuming Calum would be aware of who he was, and also that he wouldn't mind him answering Charlotte's phone. "No, no, it's not a bad time to call at all," Darren said cordially. "Filming?" he said, responding to what Calum was saying on the other end. "No, filming doesn't actually start until tomorrow. Charlotte's away from her phone just now getting us both an ice cream as a reward for walking around a country park all day. Although, after all the food we packed away last night, you'd be amazed we have any room left to put it today."

The phone went quiet for a moment, just long enough that Darren briefly checked to see if the call was still connected. "Are you still there, Calum...?" he asked. "What's that? Tell Charlotte you called? Of course, that's not a problem."

With the call concluded, Darren placed the phone back where he'd found it, after which Charlotte made her return, shortly thereafter, a cone in each hand.

"I feel sorry for anyone in the queue behind me," Charlotte commented, handing over Darren's ice cream. "The poor chap behind the counter has just been given an order to prepare for forty kids."

"Well, I don't envy him, then. Or those waiting," Darren said, right before using his curled tongue to gather up some of the delightful raspberry sauce he'd asked for. "Oh, and don't forget your phone when we leave, Lotti," he added. "You wouldn't want to overlook it when we go," he said helpfully, although with no reference at all to the call she'd just missed.

❊ ❊ ❊

Charlotte politely resisted Daren's offer of another dinner date later in the day, opting instead for a quiet night in her five-star hotel, putting the complimentary fluffy slippers provided to her to maximum use. Along with some room service, Charlotte was looking forward to an evening with her knitting before getting a good night's sleep ahead of filming in the morning.

Although her relaxed agenda didn't quite go to plan as Mollie was first to phone, and then Joyce, then Beryl, and then Larry, with all of them wanting to know how her new adventure was going. With the phone still warm in her hand, she figured she ought to check in with Stanley as well. Which she did, with Stan sounding happy enough to hear from her though perhaps a bit preoccupied with the film he was watching with his dad. The other person she hoped to speak with was one she couldn't seem to reach, however. Calum, it would appear, was missing in action. Despite her trying several times, he remained elusive. But Charlotte wasn't overly concerned, as it wasn't terribly unusual for Calum to meet up with clients during the week for business dinners. Also, he could just as easily be out with his mates in celebration of his birthday. And so, mindful that she didn't want him returning home to find his voicemail loaded up with a pile of messages, giving the impression his girlfriend was a tad unhinged, she opted to leave him alone for now and simply try and catch him at another, more convenient time.

Thoroughly refreshed the next morning after a lovely night's sleep, Charlotte was showered, fed, and outside the hotel in advance of the driver coming to pick her up. And although full of nerves, she couldn't wait to arrive at the studio and get started.

Upon arrival, Phillipa from the production team was on hand to greet Charlotte in the reception area, what with it being her first day proper. "Oh, I feel like the new girl coming to school for the first time," Charlotte confessed, accepting the access lanyard she was given and slipping it over her head.

"You'll do amazing," Phillipa assured her, after which she led the way through a maze of tiled corridors, offering a running commentary as to which programmes were being filmed where, in reference to some of the various studios they passed by. "Oh, by the way, there have been a few last-minute tweaks to your show's format, Charlotte," Phillipa advised, as they walked. "It's nothing too major, but we've listened to viewer feedback from our focus group and swapped out a few features here and there that we think will improve the flow. But we'll run through all of that with you."

"Sounds good," Charlotte offered, looking through every window they passed, same as she did with the little cottages back home in Laxey. "Oh, and while I remember, thank you for sorting out my travel arrangements, Phillipa. My arrival a day early, before the start of shooting, was somewhat unexpected but rather pleasant as it turned out."

"It's all part of the service, Charlotte," Phillipa answered, soon drawing to a halt outside their destination, a sturdy wooden door with a printed *Crafternoon Showdown* sign affixed to it. "Although I thought you wanted to arrive a day early? At least that's what Darren informed me when I made the arrangements. He said you'd hoped to use the time to have a look around the area."

"Oh, okay?" Charlotte replied, confused by the explanation offered. Confused, as she knew it wasn't the case. Perhaps there'd been some kind of breakdown in communications, she considered, chalking it up to a simple misunderstanding.

Once inside the conference room and armed with a cup of coffee, Charlotte listened as Phillipa outlined the day's running order for both her benefit and that of the assorted members of the production team also seated around the table. Phillipa made clear that rather than filming footage that was eventually to air, today was merely a dry run, with the goal of making sure everybody was where they should be and, crucially, knew what they were doing.

The contestants in the two teams for today consisted of BBC staff with some crafting experience, under strict instructions, same as the film crew, to treat the experience as if they were filming for actual broadcast rather than just a rehearsal. The two teams, accompanied by their respective crafting captains, Charlotte and Darren, would set off in separate directions, each heading to a different charity shop in the area. There they'd be armed with a crisp fifty-pound note and given a maximum of one hour to forage for items they could use to upcycle. Then it would be back to the studio to get creative, producing an upcycled offering that would eventually go back on sale in the same charity shop.

The charity shop would be given a week to sell the item, at which point they'd report back. Of course, there would always be a delay between filming the show and the results being revealed, but with some clever editing all would appear seamless to the viewing public. The winning team would be the one whose item made the most profit. So, tactically, the teams ideally wanted to spend as little as possible and sell their finished article for as much as possible — assuming the item actually sold. If not, the team would score a big fat zero.

And just as Charlotte started to wonder if her co-host had settled on another hour in bed, Darren bounded through the office door, bursting with energy. "Sorry I'm late, troops!" he announced, placing the large box he was carrying down onto the nearest desk. "Fresh Danish pastries for all!" he declared, a statement which raised an immediate cheer.

With the pastries demolished in short order, the two crafting teams were soon on their way. And although it was a friendly contest, Charlotte's competitive spirit was bubbling up like a restless volcano. Making up her team were Kenny and Sophia, two enthusiastic interns working in the BBC's marketing department, from what she was told. With more than a passing interest in crochet and knitting between them, they'd both leapt at the opportunity to act as participants for the day. And keeping Charlotte's team in check and making sure they didn't veer too far off-piste was Gary, a shaggy-haired cameraman with a shockingly loud laugh. But according to Phillipa, Gary was as good as they came, with years of filming experience and, as Charlotte was relieved to hear, the patience of a saint.

With thirty or so charity shops in total on the filming roster, there were plenty of locations to offer a fresh backdrop without things becoming too repetitive. And, of course, the shops were thrilled to be involved, what with the potential for free publicity and the uptick in sales that would hopefully follow.

First up for Charlotte's team, today, was Aladdin's Cave, an unassuming little high-street shop tucked in between a kebab shop and a launderette. And it lived up to its name, as it was packed to the rafters with miscellaneous secondhand items, all laid out over the course of two floors. "Oh my goodness, I'm definitely going to like it in here," Charlotte remarked to her team, as Gary checked in with the owner.

"Remember, Lotti," Sophia reminded her, while trying to figure out where to start amongst the organised chaos. *"You're* supposed to be the one watching *us* spend money!"

With the camera soon rolling, Sophia and Kenny, looking resplendent in their red matching team jumpers, commenced rummaging through the miscellany. The contestants first had to settle on what crafting project they wanted to create, and then find the donor items that would be repurposed.

Watching on throughout the proceedings with a keen eye, Charlotte's role was twofold. Firstly, she was on hand to act as the voice of reason for the contestants, perhaps tempering aspirations if she thought they were biting off a bit more than they could chew (or were spending too much money). And secondly, Charlotte was tasked with helping to bring the viewer along for the journey, using her considerable experience in crafting to provide a running commentary as to the contestants' progress.

And, to be fair, the production team knew they weren't reinventing the wheel with this tried and tested format, as it was one that'd been adopted in, for instance, pottery shows, portrait painting, and even one about blowing glass. Quite simply, it was a formula the viewers at home were familiar with and one they seemed to warm to.

Charlotte resisted the overwhelming urge to expand her own already bulging crafting inventory while in the splendid Aladdin's Cave, focussing instead on providing pearls of wisdom to her intrepid team. Spotting a few pairs of denim jeans priced up at two pounds apiece, Kenny and Sophia had their hearts set on turning them into a pair of bespoke tote bags with their own unique flair. Having turned her hand to this same type of project more times than she could count, Charlotte was able to talk the team through the potential pitfalls, and crucially, how much work was involved bearing in mind the crafting time permitted. And from the moment Charlotte started speaking to them, she immediately forgot all about the camera and mic trailing her around and recording everything she did and every word she had to say. It felt to Charlotte just like she was back at home, helping out a couple of new Crafternoon Sewcial Club members, which served to directly put her at ease. And although it was her first time spent in front of the lens, Gary the director-slash-cameraman was delighted. In fact...

"Charlotte, that was terrific!" he said, packing away his camera equipment once their allotted time had elapsed. "You're a natural!"

"It was?" Charlotte asked. "I am?"

"You bet!" Gary insisted. "I've worked with seasoned professionals who weren't fit to, ehm... well, to thread your needle," he said, followed by one of his big, booming laughs that Phillipa had warned her about. "Honestly, I'm going to enjoy working with you."

Charlotte reflected on her debut for a moment. "I think I really enjoyed that," she said. "Although, I'm not sure how I'll be when we start recording the show for real, yeah?"

Gary looked over his shoulder, like he was making sure the coast was clear. Which, in fact, was precisely what he was doing. "Newsflash! Don't be telling them back at HQ that I've let the cat out of the bag!" he told her, followed by another one of his big, big laughs.

"The cat out of the bag?" Charlotte asked, confused. "What do you mean? What cat?"

"Your team, Kenny and Sophia, aren't really BBC interns, Charlotte. They're *actual* contestants," Gary revealed.

"They're what?" said Charlotte, stunned.

Gary nodded his head. "Yep," he told her. "Congratulations, you've just completed your first segment for the new show."

"That wasn't a rehearsal?" Charlotte asked, stating what was now obvious. "Ooh, how devious," she remarked, a crooked grin spread across her face. Then, thinking about how relaxed she'd been throughout the entire process, she added, "Ah, thank you, Gary. A sneaky way to settle me in, but an effective one."

"It worked, didn't it?"

"It absolutely did, Gary."

Charlotte felt the need for some fresh air, as the shop, without being unkind, was a touch fusty after spending an hour or so inside. And buzzing with excitement after her first stint on film, Charlotte wanted to share the news, reckoning it to be the perfect time to shoot Calum a quick text.

> Charlotte: Hi honey, the first part of filming just finished. All went well and I loved it! Looking forward to seeing you all soon XX

An ellipse appeared almost immediately on her screen, indicating that Calum was already busy typing a response.

> Calum: Ah, nice to hear from you stranger X
> I'm pleased it went well. How was your hot date in the park yesterday? 😊 PS why didn't you call me back?

Charlotte wasn't sure what he meant, as she'd already tried reaching him previously. And she didn't understand, either, how he could know about her day in the park when she hadn't had an opportunity to tell him about that yet.

> Charlotte: I did call, but it was you that didn't call me back? 😊 I'll ring later to fill you in XX

> Calum: I did! Your new friend Darren answered your phone. Told me all about your romantic stroll in the park 😊 ♥
> He said he'd tell you I'd phoned? Anyway, must dash. Speak soon. And well done, Lotti. We're all proud of you XXX

On the one hand, Charlotte breathed a sigh of relief, as Calum didn't appear at all upset about her not being able to connect with him the previous evening to convey her birthday wishes.

But this exchange with Calum also raised a concern. Namely, what on earth was Darren doing answering her phone the day before, and why hadn't he bothered telling her that he did? By itself, it might be dismissed as just a momentary lapse in recollection on his part. A simple brain fart, if you will.

But add to that Charlotte's earlier conversation with Phillipa, in which she'd learned of Darren's strange explanation for her arriving a day earlier than necessary, an explanation that very clearly stretched the truth, and Charlotte couldn't help but feel a little befuddled.

"That's definitely a bit weird," Charlotte said to herself aloud. "Darren, what are you playing at?"

Chapter Seventeen

The gutters struggled against the heavy downpour, the nearest downspout spewing water like a fireman's hose onto the sodden grass of the church lawn. Huddled together a safe distance away, taking shelter from the rain under a shared umbrella, Joyce and Beryl anxiously watched the cars arriving in the carpark.

"The rain's splashing my shoes," Beryl moaned, moving the brolly in her hand an inch to two in her direction.

Joyce reached for the handle of the brolly. "Yeah, but I don't want my hair ruined, do I?" she said, recapturing the coverage she'd just lost. "Besides, it's my umbrella."

"It bloody well isn't!" Beryl shot back, giving the brolly a tug in a repeated effort to protect her new shoes. "I'm sure I lent it to you last year, when we both went to that rugby match," she reminded her friend. "Although if memory serves, a good drenching might have cooled you down after being subjected to men in tight shorts for a couple of hours."

"Ah, that was a splendid day out," Joyce said, with her fond recollection emerging into a cheeky grin. "Although I'm still not sure the brolly was yours."

The two of them watched on as a car turned up the driveway towards the carpark. This did not go unnoticed by Larry, either. "Is that her?" Larry asked from his position of refuge beneath the nearby chestnut tree. "It's nearly ten past!" he shouted over. "And the others are starting to get restless!"

The others that Larry referred to were an additional group of Crafternooners who had all arrived on time and were currently keeping Larry company under the canopy of the tree, all likely assuming they'd be entering the church momentarily. But with that not happening, there was talk of ditching the tree and joining those who'd been smart enough to wait in their cars in the carpark.

Unfortunately, for the second week on the bounce, there had been some confusion amongst the keyholders as to who was responsible for opening up for the Crafternoon Sewcial Club's weekly meeting. The previous week, Bonnie and Abigail had an afterschool careers convention they needed to attend, forgetting, in the process, that they were supposed to be opening up at the church. Fortunately, it wasn't raining last week, and the inconvenienced club members weren't too frustrated as a result. However, this week was a different story. And with Bonnie and Abigail tied up again with school commitments, it was the understanding that Mollie had kindly offered her services in unlocking the doors. Although Joyce and the others were starting to wonder if Mollie was aware of that fact herself, if Larry's update of the time was anything to go by.

Larry waved in Joyce and Beryl's direction before cupping his hands around his mouth like a foghorn. "Are there any windows open?" he shouted over the noise of the falling rain.

"What?" Beryl shouted back.

"I asked if any windows were open!" Larry shouted over again, extending a finger towards the church windows. "Maybe we could climb in...?"

"Do I look like a cat burglar?" Beryl asked, with her patience levels waning and stray water droplets trickling down her chin.

"And if you think *I'm* climbing through a window with this skirt on, you've got another thing coming!" Joyce entered in.

Larry did his best to raise morale amongst the gang, slipping into an unscheduled performance of one of his finest comedy routines, in his opinion. But sadly, this selection from amongst his impressive repertoire was never going to succeed, especially when talk of an upcoming bingo session at a different location started to spread through the discontented troops.

THE CRAFTERNOON SEWCIAL CLUB: SHOWDOWN

And once the first few deserted their post it created a ripple effect, with the carpark soon emptying and anyone having arrived by bus piling into the collection of vehicles before being whisked away.

With most of the space under the chestnut tree now vacated, Joyce and Beryl braved the short jaunt over to join Larry under its sturdy branches.

"That was some of my best material," Larry lamented, lowering his head, disappointed his audience had abandoned him. But just when his ego could've used a much-needed tickle, Joyce and Beryl appeared somewhat anxious, as if the pair had somewhere else to be. "Wait, you two aren't thinking of trotting off to the bingo as well, are you?" Larry enquired.

"And why would we do that?" Joyce asked. "I mean, for what *possible* reason would we want to leave a flooded church lawn to go sit in a warm, cosy bingo hall with a large gin for company?"

Larry considered Joyce's response for a moment, weighing up the various pros and cons of such a proposition. "Yeah, that does sound quite appealing, actually," he had to admit, glancing up at the furious-looking dark grey clouds overhead. "Can I, erm... can I come with you...?"

Both Joyce and Beryl linked arms with their favourite comedian. "Of course you can," Joyce replied.

"After all, you're buying the first round," Beryl chipped in. "Oh," she added, a further thought occurring. "Do you think we should leave a sign on the church door?"

Joyce shook her head, freeing several droplets that had attached themselves to her new hairdo. "What's the point?" Joyce asked, her voice tinged with a certain sadness. "Nobody else is going to turn up now, and those that did have already gone."

But just as the three of them settled on making a mad dash for the nearby bus stop, all under the umbrella of questionable ownership, another vehicle turned off the main road at such a pace they feared it might strike the gatepost. They watched on as the car sped past them on its way to the carpark at the rear of the church.

"Was that...?" asked Larry.

"Yep," Beryl advised, as the three of them drew to a halt. "That was Mollie."

And she was correct because a moment later Mollie sprinted along the concrete path holding out a hand in apology. "Oh my God, I'm so sorry!" she said upon arrival, invoking the good Lord's name on church grounds, appropriately enough. "I was all set to leave work but found the farmer's tractor parked behind me, blocking me in," she explained. "I had to run over three fields to find him, falling over several times in the process, which will explain the sizeable mud patches on my knees," she added, motioning towards her soiled jeans. "Anyway, where is everybody?" she asked, although her defeated expression suggested that she already knew the answer. "They've already gone, haven't they?"

Larry, Joyce, and Beryl all nodded in unison.

"Aww, I don't believe this," Mollie offered, wiping the rain from her face. "Is there anything I can do?" she asked.

"There is one thing," Beryl replied.

"Anything. Just name it," Mollie answered.

"You couldn't drop us off at the bingo, could you?"

***

By his own admission, Larry wasn't the biggest fan of bingo, or the competitive, cutthroat attitudes it brought out in otherwise civilised folk, with proceedings even sometimes turning physical in the most serious of cases. Indeed, ever since he was threatened with having his "bingo balls" removed for talking during one session, he was now a reluctant and cautious visitor. However, as many of his dear friends — including Joyce and Beryl — were ardent enthusiasts, he was happy to take one for the team even if it meant a defensive posture to protect his family jewels.

"Two large gins, as requested," Larry announced, returning from the bar area during a short break in the proceedings. "I've also treated us all to some crisps," he added, placing the various items down before taking a seat.

"Munching crisps during the bingo?" Joyce asked, with a disapproving, raised eyebrow.

"Ah, duly noted," Larry replied, deciding it best to leave them for the bus ride home. Then, leaning across the table, "I was just talking to Esther and Susie," he whispered carefully, afraid of the repercussions of speaking too loudly.

"What? Speak up, man, I can't bloody hear you," Joyce replied, right before taking a noisy slurp of her drink.

"You don't need to whisper yet, Larry," Beryl advised, drawing his attention towards the electronic timer sat next to the bingo caller. "There's still three minutes until the next session."

"Ah. I said I was just talking to our Esther and Susie while I was waiting to be served at the bar," Larry tried again, only a little louder this time.

"Well it's no shock finding that pair of lushes taking up space at the bar," Joyce suggested. "Were they trying to tap you up for a drink?"

"No, we were talking about Crafternoon," Larry replied. "Although I did buy them both a drink. Anyway, it turns out they're having second thoughts about coming back next week, and apparently they're not alone, if what they've told me is accurate."

"What? They're leaving Crafternoon?" Beryl answered. "But they're amongst the founder members."

"Ah, there's a surprise," Joyce said with a scowl. "I've heard on the grapevine that there's another crafting group setting up. One that's apparently serving hot food each week."

"Hot food, you say?" Beryl asked, her interest suddenly raised.

"Oh, you're not going anywhere, you," Joyce admonished her friend. "Not like those rats deserting a sinking ship," she said, glancing about the bingo hall to direct her ire towards any such rebels in attendance. "Not that our ship is sinking, mind you. Because it bloody well isn't."

Larry raised his hand like a pupil wanting to ask a question in class. "No, it's not that," he stressed, hoping to prevent a possible battle. "It's just that for Esther and Susie, and several others as well, getting to Crafternoon often involves two, sometimes even three different bus journeys. And they're happy to make the effort, because they love going. But to go to all that trouble, and then find a locked door, two times in a row? Well, I can sort of understand where they're coming from, yeah?"

"Right, where are they now?" Joyce asked. "Are they still out lurking around the bar?"

Fearing he'd set her off, Larry's shoulders dropped. "Hold on there," he said softly, in calm, measured tones. "There's no need for any sort of unpleasantness, Joyce."

"Unpleasantness? Don't be silly, there isn't going to be any unpleasantness today," Joyce countered. "Because I completely understand their concerns."

"You do?" Larry asked, uncertain as to how sincere she was, and scanning her face for clues.

"Sure. And if they're sober enough, I'm going to go and assure them normal service will be resumed next week," Joyce advised, taking to her feet. "We're not letting all of Charlotte's hard work be destroyed so easily, Larry."

"No we're absolutely not," said Beryl, in steadfast agreement. "Business as usual will be restored next week even if we've got to break down the church door ourselves."

"We could just take ownership of the keys ourselves?" Larry helpfully suggested, not entirely on board with the whole breaking-down-of-doors approach.

"Well, it's either that, Larry, or I'm wearing my trousers next week so I can climb through the church window," Joyce insisted. "Now come on, let's go and convince our fellow club members that all is not lost."

"Yes!" an energised Larry said, jumping up from his seat. "You know, you two remind me of Mel Gibson rousing his warriors in that film Braveheart," he told them. *"Freeeedooom!"* he added, for no particular reason.

But poor Larry evidently hadn't been keeping an eye on the electronic timer next to the bingo caller, as his inspiring war cry was greeted by a collective and angry shushing from the bingo faithful hoping for improved fortunes in the next game.

Chapter Eighteen

There were times in Charlotte's life when the thought of relaxing in a five-star hotel, with a luxurious spa bath, sumptuous bedsheets, and delicious gourmet food only a phone call away, was something she could only dream of. But now, after staying in such a place amidst an unexpected schedule of unrelenting, prolonged back-to-back days of filming, the allure was starting to wear off a bit. It was the little things that started to grate, like the constant thud of footsteps from the corridor at all hours, or, say, the length of time the lift took to arrive, stopping at each and every floor on the way to the reception area. Of course, when you were in holiday mode, these minor annoyances would ordinarily pass by without notice. But when the hotel became your home away from home for any extended period of time, it was perhaps a different matter.

Originally, Charlotte was assured that being able to return home during the week was a given. However, due to a change in production to accommodate the broadcaster, it would seem, the team were requested to record footage for two episodes each day rather than the originally intended one. So what this meant for Charlotte in practical terms was two visits to the charity shops in the morning (with a change of outfit for each) and two lots of filming the actual crafting segment of the show. And the working day didn't end there. Once the shows were more or less completed, Charlotte and Darren's dulcet tones were still required for voiceover work that would be added during the post-production process, and with all of this making for very long days indeed. As such, any hopes of Charlotte making it home to her fair isle were dashed for at least another week.

But it wasn't like she didn't enjoy what she was doing. Because, aside from being stuck in the hotel a bit longer than she might've liked, she was having an absolute blast and loving every moment. Besides, she'd already been promised that the hectic work schedule wouldn't last forever, with things easing up in the next week or so.

All in all, the prolonged absence from home was far from ideal. But with Stanley's dad happy and willing to accommodate him for as long as required, plus FaceTime available to keep her in touch with everybody, Charlotte was just about able to put up with her luxury, five-star accommodation, fine dining, and spa facilities. For another few days, at least.

Charlotte found her new colleagues in the production crew were a delight to work with, providing support, guidance, and companionship. Darren, who she'd briefly harboured reservations about, was key among them. With the confusion about Calum's phone call long since forgotten, he'd proved himself to be a valued friend, often going well out of his way to ensure that Charlotte was as comfortable as she could possibly be during this new experience.

And working with the crafting teams was a particular thrill for Charlotte as well, getting to know them, and being a part of their creative process. And while some of their projects were absolutely inspired genius, others, it's fair to say, didn't quite go to plan, the crafting equivalent of opening the oven door and finding your soufflé had collapsed (and in front of the entire nation, no less). However, none of the contestants allowed the disasters to bother them too much, and in fact the complete calamities often provided for the most compelling footage anyway.

And speaking of calamities, today's filming, as it should happen, turned out to be a calamity of the highest order! Firstly, an overzealous charity shop employee — unaware that Charlotte was part of the filming crew — had mistaken her for a shoplifter, threatening to call the police. Fortunately, Gary was on hand with his inordinately loud laugh and camera rolling to capture the entire event for future posterity, only stepping in to clarify matters when Charlotte was in danger of being subjected to a citizen's arrest. And then, later, while back at the studio, Darren was talking to one of his contestants on camera, thus distracting them, when they managed to remove the tip of their finger with a rotary cutter. Needless to say, the cheery sundress the woman was working on didn't really lend itself to a generous spattering of blood, and Darren, for his part, promptly fainted at the sight of it. Fortunately, the ambulance crew who attended were able to patch up the wounded contestant, as well as apply a suture to the cut above Darren's eye caused by his unceremonious topple to the floor. Watching on, Charlotte joked that the paramedics should apply to be on their show, such was the expert workmanship of their stitching.

Later that day, with the last of the blood long since cleared away and filming having been concluded, Charlotte relaxed in the studio with a nice cup of tea. She turned to Darren, who'd joined her at her crafting workstation. "Well, I know your team technically retired..." she began.

"Technically retired?" Darren answered. "Ah, I see what's going on here, Newman," he added, a grin emerging. "That poor woman nearly loses an arm, and you're going to try and use that to claim victory, is that it?"

Charlotte shrugged. "Well, a bet is a bet, Darren," she said, in reference to a friendly wager they'd made earlier in the week. "And today's victory, if my maths are correct, means that I'm now in the lead in our little competition," she pointed out. "And what do you mean she nearly lost an arm? It was nothing of the sort, you silly thing. Though that didn't stop you from turning whiter than a... than a..." she said, searching for just the right illustrative comparison.

"Than a...?" Darren teased.

"Than a polar bear's bum!" Charlotte offered triumphantly, entirely pleased by her comedic genius.

Darren didn't appear quite as impressed with Charlotte's creative wit, playfully rolling his eyes in response. "Well, anyway, I've never been too good when it comes to blood," he confessed.

"Ah, that'll be why you were a community reporter working on bake sales and the like, rather than a war correspondent," Charlotte joked. "Anyhow, do you think they'll air that footage?"

Darren laughed, though not in an unkind way. "Oh, they'll air that footage, alright," he declared. "And not only that, but they're certain to take that clip of me keeling over, add some dramatic music over it, and use that snippet in the adverts for the show, I guarantee it. The producers love a bit of drama."

Darren glanced down at his watch and offered a lazy yawn. "Anyway, I have news for you," he told her.

"Does it involve detailing my winning score?"

"Nope, this is good news, I hope. How about I give you a lift back to your hotel and I can tell you all about it over an undersized and overpriced glass of wine?"

"You'll promise you won't faint again?"

"I'll see what I can do," Darren said, running a gentle finger over his bruised eye socket.

* * *

"So they were going to call the police?" Darren asked in response to Charlotte's recounting of her 'shoplifting' incident.

Charlotte took a sip from her wine glass, nodding in response. "It's true," she confirmed. "I was digging out some items for my team but ran out of hands to hold everything. So I dropped some of them into my bag, only temporarily, of course, to make things a bit easier. And that's right when I felt a firm hand land on my shoulder."

"The shame of it, being caught stealing from a charity shop," Darren replied with a chuckle, along with a playful tut-tut. "I can just see the newspaper headlines now. They'll probably call you... *The Crafting Klepto*," he suggested with a shake of the head, and then another laugh. "Another one?" he asked, noticing that both their wine glasses were nearly empty.

"Fine, go on, then."

"Two more of the same, if you'd be as kind?" he asked of the hotel bartender.

"So," Charlotte pressed, keen to hear what Darren had teased her about earlier. "This good news...?"

"Good news?" Darren replied, with a blank expression, like he didn't know what Charlotte was referring to.

"Darren, do you want a matching cut above your other eye?"

Darren ran a concerned finger under his shirt collar. "Theft and assault in one day, Lotti?" he joked. "Anyway, as to the news..." he said, stopping to build the tension before his big reveal. "I was in the ivory towers talking to the big bosses this morning."

"And?"

"And..." Darren said, pausing a moment to flash the returning barmaid a friendly smile, before then returning his attention to Charlotte. "And they're impressed with the footage that they've viewed so far."

"Impressed? That's it?" Charlotte replied, sounding a tad underwhelmed. "That's the news?"

"Oh, no, Lotti. Trust me on this, impressed is about as gushing as you'll get from the suits upstairs. And in fact, there's already talk about commissioning a second series."

"Oh, goodness, that's amazing, Darren," Charlotte answered, now suitably impressed. "And even before the first episode has aired?"

"Indeed," said Darren, raising his glass to toast their good fortune. "They must know a winning combination when they see one, Lotti," he remarked, gently chinking her glass. "And there's more."

"Oh? Spill it."

"What, the wine? It's far too expensive for that," he suggested. "Okay, okay," he quickly added in response to the disapproving stare being offered his way. "The powers that be have confirmed a four-day break in filming, starting on Friday."

Charlotte's mouth fell open on hearing this news. Of course, potentially having another series in the works was wonderful, but the thought of seeing Stanley, Calum, and all her friends again was a more immediate joy to consider. "Oh, that's brilliant,

Darren," she said, resisting the urge to cry out in delight. "Honestly, that's really made my day."

"I thought it would. Now how about we see if this restaurant of yours has room for two little ones, and us move to a table?"

"Why not?" Charlotte replied. "After all, we *are* celebrating."

"Splendid," said Darren, rising from his seat. "I'll go and make a reservation."

Charlotte immediately reached for her phone, unable to contain her excitement as she furiously typed away.

> Charlotte: Guess who's coming home on Friday? So clear your schedule, hot lips. Catch up on your sleep now as you won't be getting much this weekend 💚🖤

Sitting there, grinning madly, Charlotte couldn't wait to get back to her cosy cottage in Laxey. And while it certainly wasn't five-star glamour by any stretch, it was their little home in the village she loved. And regardless of what the weather was on Friday, she decided she was taking Stanley and Calum down to the beach, heading over to The Shed, her favourite artisan beachside eatery, for some of their scrumptious cake. That was her plan.

They say absence makes the heart grow fonder, and just now, she couldn't possibly be any fonder about the idea of returning home for a short break.

> Larry: I often nap during the day anyway, Lotti, so I'm all caught up. The 'hot lips' might be some sort of infection, so I'll have a word with the nursing staff 😊
>
> Joyce: Someone's getting lucky on Friday 😊
>
> Beryl: Not me, sadly ☹
>
> Mollie: Grrrr. Go get 'em, Lotti!

"Aww, crap," Charlotte said, reading the texts pinging up on her phone, realising she'd sent her intimate sexytime message to the entirety of the Larry's Lookout WhatsApp group, of which Calum was a member, rather than to Calum exclusively.

"Right. That's us booked in," Darren advised, retaking his seat. "Erm, everything okay, Lotti? You look a bit flustered."

"I'm fine," Charlotte said as she switched her phone to silent mode. "Just super excited about seeing everybody back home."

Charlotte limited herself to one more small glass of wine over dinner, that dinner being a steak so amazingly tender it melted in her mouth like butter. She didn't want to get too awfully carried away with the wine, as with a full day of filming on the morrow she wanted to maintain a clear head and complete control of her faculties. After all, she had witnessed firsthand just how easily accidents can happen and how things can go so unexpectedly awry in the wild and wacky world of crafting.

"You know, I've thoroughly enjoyed your company this evening, Darren. So, honestly, thank you for that," Charlotte offered, leaning back in her seat.

"I can't tempt you with the desserts menu?"

Charlotte puffed out her cheeks, indicating she was already stuffed. "No, I reckon I'm done. But don't let me stop you if you want something?"

Darren considered the menu for a moment, before deciding his belt was probably under enough strain already. "Yeah, I think I'll take a pass as well."

"I do appreciate you taking such good care of me," Charlotte went on, reiterating her thanks to him. "I'm not used to being away from home, alone like this. So I'm grateful for your friendship."

"Please. It's been my pleasure," Darren assured her. "Besides, you're going to be stuck with me for another series by the look of things."

Charlotte reached for her handbag, removing her purse from it. "Now, Darren, I know you'll want to put up a fight, but please don't."

"Charlotte..."

"It's my treat, Darren. My way of saying thank you for keeping an eye out for me."

Darren held up his hands, admitting defeat. "That's very kind of you. You didn't really need to do that," he told her. "And, em, not to be rude, but on that note, I'll just need a quick visit to the gents, if that's all right...?"

Charlotte caught the attention of the passing waiter by raising her hand and briefly wiggling it, as if writing something invisible in the air, the universally accepted way of requesting the bill. While she waited, she considered checking her phone to see what other responses she might have received in answer to her risqué message. But before she could do that, the bill promptly appeared, enclosed in a leather wallet and accompanied by a tiny plate of mints. "Oh, my," she whispered to herself, as the bill was larger than her weekly food budget at home. But she consoled herself in that she didn't do this too often, and at least the new job was providing a major boost to her once-paltry bank balance.

"All set?" Charlotte asked, once Darren made his return. "The tab is all squared up, so would you like me to escort you out?"

"Making sure I don't steal anything, is that it?"

"Well, you do look like a ruffian, what with that bruise coming up a treat," Charlotte suggested, as she began to lead the way from the restaurant and out through the colossal hotel foyer.

Once near the exit, Darren paused and turned to face her. "Thanks again for treating me to dinner, Lotti. You really didn't need to do that," he said, reiterating what he'd said earlier.

"It was my pleasure, Darren. And I'll see you tomorrow, bright and breezy, for another shift at the fun factory."

Darren smiled but didn't move, appearing as if his feet were glued to the spot.

"Ehm, everything okay?" Charlotte enquired, after an uncomfortable, protracted silence. "You've not forgotten anything, have you? Because if you have, we could—"

But before Charlotte could even finish her sentence, Darren moved in close, placing a gentle hand against her cheek. Then, without warning, and without speaking, he looked deep into her eyes and pressed his lips right against hers, kissing her softly.

Chapter Nineteen

Thanks to the seemingly constant schedule of roadworks in the island's capital of Douglas, traffic crawled along the streets at a snail's pace. And while the frustration was evident on the faces of those cooped up in their metal cans, foot traffic moved without too much delay.

Larry, with the day's newspaper tucked under his arm, spotted a gap in the now-stationary traffic. He made a dash for the other side of the road, taking advantage of the opening, appearing to offer up a quick little prayer to the traffic gods that this safe passage would hold. Once he'd made his way across, he then stopped for a moment, looking this way and that, taking stock of his present location.

"Ah," he said, sounding pleased with himself as he spotted the cashpoint on the corner of the street, not too far away. Whistling a happy tune, Larry proceeded to his destination, reaching inside his jacket pocket for his wallet.

"Oh, excuse me," a well-groomed man in a smart grey suit offered, having nearly collided with Larry. "Are you wanting the cashpoint?" the man asked, apparently having the same idea as Larry. "Please," said the man, stepping to one side by way of apology. "After you, sir. I'm in no rush, as I have plenty of time before heading back to work."

Larry graciously tipped his hat. "That's very kind," he said, before presenting himself in front of the cash machine. He'd never been too fond of these devices, from the looks of things, appearing confused as to how these new-fangled contraptions actually worked. But, no matter, he inserted his card, narrowing one eye as he struggled to initially recall his PIN. "Ah, that's it," Larry said out loud, quickly tapping the keypad before the numbers might elude him again. Then, waiting patiently for something to happen, Larry allowed his mind to wander off, daydreaming about the toasted teacake he fancied having along with his tea, not long from now, when this was all over.

In fact he didn't know how long he'd been thinking about the prospect of sweet, luscious, melted butter dripping down his chin when the fellow from behind cleared his throat in an *are-we-nearly-done?* manner, bringing Larry effectively back to the present. "Oh, how strange," Larry declared, as he stared down at the screen that was currently doing not much of anything.

The chap behind him stepped forward a bit, enough to look over Larry's shoulder. "My goodness, I think it's swallowed your card," he advised gravely. "It happened to me just last month as well. Modern technology, eh?" he added sympathetically. "Perhaps you should pop into the bank and order a replacement?"

Having no wish to hold up the queue, it would seem, Larry quickly stepped out of the way. "I think I'll pop into the bank," he said to the suited man, echoing the fine fellow's helpful suggestion. "Yes, I think I'll do just that."

Once Larry was thus out of the picture and a safe distance away, the man in the suit proceeded forth, stepping towards the device. But rather than reach for his own cash card as one might expect, he simply fiddled with the ATM slot, quickly retrieving Larry's card. "Bingo," he said, chuckling away to himself. And having secretly taken note of Larry's PIN just earlier, he deftly punched the numbers back in, a few moments later procuring a sizable portion of Larry's savings, by all appearances, as a host of banknotes promptly fluttered into a pile, the neat, tantalising wad of cash protruding from the machine and all lined up for stealing.

"Great work!" Ella advised, skipping forward to deliver a congratulatory slap on the smartly dressed fraudster's back.

"We're all done?" the man asked, holding Larry's card up triumphantly, along with the thick stack of bills he'd just successfully obtained with it.

THE CRAFTERNOON SEWCIAL CLUB: SHOWDOWN

"That, as they say, is a wrap," Ella confirmed, in her official capacity as director. Then, turning to one side, "Larry, we're all finished!" she reiterated, for his benefit, clapping her hands in satisfaction as Larry ambled back over to them. "All done in one take, gentlemen. You're both naturals at this," she told her two outstanding actors.

Larry was clearly delighted by her praise, proud of the performance he'd just put in. "Ella, do you think I need to buy a new suit for the Oscars?" he joked.

"Oh, absolutely, Larry. The red carpet awaits!" Ella answered, happy that Larry was happy.

The self-appointed award in the best actor category was for Larry's fifth and final performance appearing in the fraud prevention adverts commissioned by his bank. Highlighting some of the most common scams that people commonly fall victim to, the video spots would form a large part of the national campaign to be launched the following week. And as one of the stars of the adverts, Larry was cordially invited to the launch party, along with several of his distinguished guests who he'd already managed to secure an invite for.

Geoff, Larry's magnificent co-star throughout, was actually a bank employee who'd thrown his name into the hat for a chance to defraud innocent customers (or to pretend to, at least). "Larry, it's been a pleasure working with you," he proclaimed, offering a hearty handshake. "Although I'm not sure what the public will think of me when these things are actually broadcast?"

Larry chuckled. "You'll be like the panto villain," he suggested. "Look out, he's behind you!" Larry cried, acting out this panto-themed scenario.

"I'll see you in Liverpool for the launch?" Geoff asked.

"Oh, I wouldn't miss it for the world," Larry answered, before offering his farewells, the thought of that toasted teacake still fresh in his mind, and with him determined to make it a reality.

But before Larry could progress too far, Geoff called over to him. "Larry, you've forgotten something!"

"Oh no I've not!" Larry shouted back, assuming his partner to be continuing with the panto-based banter, and thus playing along with him. However, it was at that point he could see Geoff raising a hand to hold up his debit card, looking like a referee disciplining an unruly footballer.

"Ah. But that's not really my card," Larry advised, after walking back over.

"Hmm, I didn't think so," said Geoff. "But then... what about this?" he asked, pulling out the tidy wad of cash still in his possession, having somehow escaped Ella's notice.

"That– that seems like real cash. *Actual* cash, not prop money," Larry marvelled.

"I know, right?" Geoff answered. They were both whispering now. "And it's not yours?" he asked Larry.

"No, of course not. But if that's not Monopoly money, so to speak, won't you need to give it back?" Larry replied. "You don't want to defraud the bank, do you?" he asked with a cheeky wink, a bit irreverent given the nature of the adverts they'd just filmed.

"Or *do* I?" said Geoff, along with his best villainous laugh, playing up his part beautifully.

※ ※ ※

The issue of the money was of course sorted. And, as far as other matters were concerned, Larry hadn't been the only one thinking about cake and such, as it turned out...

Mollie took in a deep breath of the tantalising aroma found only in a coffee shop — a heady mix of roasted coffee beans and freshly baked cake — which brought a beaming smile as she returned to their table with a packed tray. "Yay!" she said, unloading her coffee, letting out little squeaks of excitement as she did.

"I know you like a bit of cake, Moll," an amused Charlotte observed. "But I don't think I've seen quite this degree of enthusiasm from you about it before."

Mollie parked herself down, happy to be alive if the look on her face was anything to go by. "I'm just so pleased to have my buddy back," she advised.

Charlotte reached across the table, taking hold of her friend's hand. "Me too, Moll," she said. "I've been gone hardly more than a fortnight, but it feels like an eternity."

Mollie gave Charlotte's hand a mild squeeze. "Once again, I just wanted to say I'm sorry for what happened at Crafternoon these past two weeks," she told Charlotte. "It shouldn't happen again. Like I said on the phone, we now have a plan in place to rectify the—"

But before Mollie could say anything more, Charlotte cut in. "Mollie, Darren kissed me," she revealed, wincing as if saying the words was causing her actual physical pain.

Mollie opened her mouth to speak but nothing came out at first. She took a quick sip of her coffee, in an effort to lubricate her vocal cords. "He did what, now? What do you mean he kissed you?" she asked, once she'd regained her voice.

"I'm sorry, I just needed to tell someone," Charlotte answered, apologising for dampening the mood.

"Did you... I mean, you didn't kiss him back, did you?" Mollie asked, unsure where this conversation was headed.

"What? No, of course not. I told him I already had a significant other, which he well knew, and then I walked off."

"Yikes, that sounds a bit awkward," Mollie commented. "Have you told Calum about it yet?"

"Not yet, no," Charlotte admitted, shaking her head. "Mollie, it's turning into an absolute nightmare."

"He did know beforehand that you already have a hunky boyfriend...?" Mollie asked, wanting to be clear on this.

"Well, not specifically the part about Calum being hunky," Charlotte said with a laugh, finding some humour in Mollie's remark. "But yeah, he absolutely knew I was with Calum, Moll, which is why I was so annoyed when he planted a bloody kiss on me. And to make matters even worse, Darren's being an absolute arse about the whole thing, making out like it was me that was leading him on or something. And now he's barely speaking to me as a result, and when he does, it's only to belittle me in front of the production team."

"Absolute arse," Mollie offered, in complete agreement with Charlotte's assessment of Darren's behaviour.

"I know. And he's so calculated, getting me over a day early to take me out for the afternoon," Charlotte continued. "And then the situation with him taking Calum's call on my phone, which I was telling you about before, and then him not even mentioning it to me. The more I think about it, Moll, the more I'm convinced that had to be deliberate on his part."

Charlotte was getting herself more and more worked up, gripping her cake fork like she was about to take someone's eye out with it. "You know, I wouldn't be at all surprised if he somehow arranged for the filming schedule to be adjusted as well, just so I couldn't get home."

"You think he'd do that? Would he go that far?"

Charlotte raised her hands, unsure of the answer. "I dunno, Moll. At this point, I'm not putting anything past him," she said. "Oh, look, I'm sorry. I've been so looking forward to seeing you, and there I go hitting you with all of my problems."

"Charlotte."

"Yes?"

"Shut up," Mollie said, smiling warmly. "That's what friends are for," she insisted. "But have you given any thought to what you're going to do, Lotti? Should you just throw in the towel?"

Charlotte considered her response, long enough for her to take a forkful of cake and a sip of her coffee. "I don't think I can, Moll," she said after a moment. "I've signed a contract, and now there's even talk of another series. Besides, how could I show my face back here, giving up so easily? After everybody sees me on the TV, and then there I am just up and quitting, throwing away a gift like that? I'd be a laughingstock."

"Just tell everybody Darren was a complete dirtbag, and that you couldn't work with him anymore. Or if you don't quit, then you could just punch Darren right in his stupid face. You'll probably get fired anyway, but even if you don't, you'll at least feel a whole hell of a lot better about the situation you're in."

"Thank you, Moll. You always know just the right thing to say to cheer me up. But do you think I should mention something to Calum?"

"Lotti, you know nothing's going on between you and Darren. So, on that basis, do you really need to elaborate other than saying you think he's a bit of a spanner?"

"A spanner. Duly noted," Charlotte said, taking her fork and having another go at the lovely chocolate cake she was enjoying. Then, after spotting her friend grinning at her, "What are you smiling at?" she asked.

"Oh, I was just thinking about your message to the WhatsApp group," Mollie recalled with a laugh. "Hot lips, indeed."

Charlotte's cheeks flushed at the mere thought of it. "Oh, God, don't. Honestly, I didn't know Larry had signed up so many members to his Larry's Lookout group. I must have received over thirty replies, including a particularly saucy one from somebody called Frank, who was delighted to receive my message. I've no idea who he is, but it seems he's now very, very keen on getting to know *me*. So there I am with yet *another* unwanted admirer."

"Frank? Hmm, I can't say I know who that is either," Mollie replied. "Best to nip this in the bud, though, before any trouble starts!"

"Yeah, I think you're right, Moll. I must remember to ask Larry which one of his frisky friends this Frank character is."

"You could ask right now," Mollie remarked, tipping her head towards the window. "Because someone's walking this way."

And she was right. Larry, who'd just finished his teacake at another coffee shop only two doors down, was on his merry way to the bus stop when Mollie's banging on the window got his attention, causing him to come to an abrupt halt just outside.

"Aww, it's Larry," Charlotte said, offering him a hearty wave, encouraging him to join them inside.

However, with a look of devilment in her eyes and minimal consideration for the relaxed quiet of her fellow coffee shop patrons — or Charlotte's embarrassed blushes, for that matter — Mollie rose to her feet so she could better communicate with

Larry. "Larry!" she shouted, hopeful that it was loud enough to be heard through the glass. "Charlotte..." she said, pointing out who Charlotte was, not just for Larry's benefit but for the benefit of everybody in the coffee shop as well. "Charlotte wants to know which of your friends in the nursing home was looking for a sleepless night with her!"

Chapter Twenty

From the moment Charlotte landed back at Ronaldsway Airport on the Isle of Man, she'd not stopped, desperate to pack as much as she could into her limited break from filming. Along with her earlier catch-up with Mollie (the first of several planned) a trip to Joan's Wools & Crafts was also in order for a much-needed top-up of supplies, as with so much time spent back in her hotel room, the crocheted granny square blanket she was working on there had grown to the extent that it could now cover several grannies. Indeed, she'd likely need to book the blanket a separate plane ticket for its eventual return to the isle as there was no chance of it fitting inside her suitcase.

Further, there was a good catch-up with Bonnie and Abigail to address any issues they may have had with Make It Sew. Although, being only a phone call away, they'd already spoken several times since she'd left, so really it was more of an excuse now to simply have a good natter. And the same with Joyce, Beryl, Larry, and the rest of her crafting fraternity, with whom she'd remained in regular contact thanks to the benefits of modern technology, but whom she still wished to see now in person.

And even though George, as Stanley's loving dad, was always delighted to spend as much time with the young sprout as he could, Charlotte still wanted to drop him a bottle of his favourite whisky to thank him for being so accommodating.

And all of this was without factoring in the abundance of snuggles she needed to catch up on with the two special men in her life, those being Stanley and Calum.

However, a nice challenge she also faced was that each and every person she ran into on the isle was intrigued to know what it was like filming a major TV show for the BBC. Being from a small island meant that a lot of people already knew Charlotte's business, and she was stopped at nearly every turn by well-wishers wanting to chat about her crafting adventure. But far from it being a chore to deal with, this was the kind of response she'd hoped from people, and was now happy to embrace. Because, as a consequence of raising her own profile, it meant that, in theory, the work they were doing at the crafting clubs would be known by a wider audience and then perhaps replicated in other communities as well (meaning other folks would be able to get just as much enjoyment from it as she did). And as she conveyed to anybody who wanted to listen, she really was having a whale of a time, for the most part, although spending time away from her friends and family was, of course, a bit of a challenge. But as she related, the double shifts weren't a forever feature and soon enough she'd be able to return home on a more frequent basis.

Unfortunately, there was one difficult subject she kept encountering in conversation, and that was in regard to Darren. With him being a rather smooth-talking, handsome chap on the television, she was constantly asked what he was like in person, and whether he was just as charming as he appeared onscreen. Ultimately, while she was tempted to reveal that he was, in reality, a bit of a scuzzball, he was still her co-host, and a positive public perception would have a significant bearing on the success of the show. For that reason, she opted to play it safe and simply tap her nose in a *wouldn't-you-like-to-know* sort of fashion, figuring this to be the most tactful way of handling things.

By the time Sunday morning arrived and she'd enjoyed a few days of normality, the thought of getting back in front of the cameras wasn't entirely unappealing. Charlotte had decided she was going to sit down with Darren upon her return and clear the air, as after all they had at least several more weeks filming in close proximity, and with the prospect of another series in the offing on top of that. Charlotte was comfortable chalking it all up as just one of those things, and she had to hope that Darren would as well.

But for now, all Charlotte had to concern herself with was simply making the most of her remaining time at home. And what better way to start today than bacon sarnies on the beach...

"You've used one of these stoves before?" Charlotte enquired gently, for fear of offending the chef.

"*Pfft*, of course!" Calum replied with confidence, though discreetly running his eyes over the gas bottle in hopes of finding some inspiration as to what he ought to be doing with it. "I used to do a lot of wild camping, you see, and these gas stoves are a staple when you're an experienced explorer," he explained.

"An experienced explorer, eh? I didn't know I had my very own Bear Grylls," Charlotte remarked, giving the appearance of being impressed. "And as an experienced explorer, then, you'll know you need to open the valve to release the gas...?"

Calum rolled his eyes, as if this was absolutely the next thing he was going to try. "Well I know that, obviously. I was just..." he began. "Oi, pass me the frying pan, will you?" he asked, quickly changing the subject.

Meanwhile, down by the water's edge, a shoeless Stanley was scampering about, a plastic bow and arrow set slung over his shoulder, looking like he didn't have a care in the world. "Just think," Charlotte said, fondly watching on. "In a few years, Stan will probably still be in bed at this time on a Sunday morning, nursing a hangover."

"After a night out on the tiles with me," Calum joked, finally managing to fire up his camping stove.

"Oh, I'd love that," Charlotte remarked. "My two boys out and about, bonding over a few pints."

Calum peeled off a slice of bacon, placing it on the frying pan with a satisfying sizzle, following that slice with another, and then another. "Oh, here comes Robin Hood," he observed. "The lad must have a sixth sense about bacon sandwiches, because the smell can't have travelled down the beach that quickly. Oh, and watch out, because as I learned at our archery session over in Center Parcs, he's a bit of a crack shot with that thing."

"I'm sure that bow and arrow's been stuffed in his wardrobe, untouched, for about three years," Charlotte answered. "Why he's decided to take it with us today to the beach, of all places, I've no idea."

"He's probably just excited about archery now. But best not to try and figure out how the mind of a kid works, as that way lies madness," Calum advised, to which Charlotte gave a gentle chuckle.

"You hungry?" Calum asked their returning archer. "Bacon sarnies shouldn't be long."

Stanley peered into the frying pan, enjoying a good whiff of the lovely aromatherapy this provided. "Hot chocolate to go along with?" he asked expectantly, as that's what he'd been promised.

"Yessir, bacon and hot chocolate, the breakfast of champions," Charlotte replied. "Anyway, Calum tells me you're a bit of a sharpshooter with that?" she said, pointing to Stanley's gear.

Sensing a chance to impress, Stanley rummaged through his satchel. Amongst his inventory were a couple of empty tin cans he'd repurposed as potential targets. "Here," he said to his mum, handing her one of the tins.

"What am I meant to do with this?" Charlotte asked.

"Put it on your head," Stanley advised, as if the answer should have been obvious.

"What? We've now gone from Robin Hood to William Tell?" she said, not liking the sound of this very much at all. "You can't be serious, Stanley. You'll take my eye out with—"

"No I won't," Stanley cut in, handing over a pair of plastic eyeglasses that'd been included with the set. "Safety comes first," he said, along with a cheeky wink. "Now come *on*, Mum," he wheedled, piling on the peer pressure. "I'll stand here, yeah?" he told her, after taking several steps back. "And don't forget, the arrows only have rubber suction cups at the end," he reminded her, wetting one of the rubber tips with his tongue for maximum adhesion. "So in other words, you'll be *fiiiiine*."

"You'll need to go further than that, Stan," Charlotte said, trying to rest the tin can on top of her head. "Ah!" she shouted, as

Stan, after repositioning himself, was getting ready to shoot. "No, no, further back than that, even!" she ordered, now having to balance the tin can all over again after twitching her head.

Stanley did as he was asked, even though he ended up so far away this time that he was in danger of putting his feet into the water again. "Ready?" he said.

With safety glasses already donned as instructed, Charlotte raised her thumb in confirmation, being careful to keep her head as motionless as possible. "Go ahead, fire away," she said. "But there's no chance you'll hit me from all the way back there, Stan."

"Which I'm sure was your plan," Calum entered in, from the corner of his mouth, along with a playful snicker.

Stan made some final adjustments to his stance before drawing back his bow, closing one eye as he took aim. Then, without further warning, he released the bowstring and loosed his arrow. And considering it was essentially a kid's toy, the arrow flew through the air at surprising speed, almost belying the kit's apparent cheap build quality.

Before his mum even had a chance to blink, the rubber sucker made contact with her forehead, sticking fast and holding tight thanks to Stanley's moistening it with his tongue and his deft, pinpoint accuracy.

"Bloody hell, Stanley!" Charlotte yelled, unsure whether she should laugh or just shout.

"Told you he'd be a good shot," Calum reminded her with a chuckle.

"A good shot?" Charlotte protested. "If he'd hit the *tin can*, he'd be a good shot!"

Following the initial shock, Charlotte realised she wasn't in any actual pain. "How could you do that to your poor mum?" she asked, but Stanley wasn't listening owing to the fact he was doubled over with tears of laughter running down his cheeks.

Charlotte glanced up, cross-eyed, at the arrow shaft protruding from her forehead. "Do I look like a Dalek?" she asked, setting herself off laughing as well. "EXTERMINATE," she said, presenting her best impression of Doctor Who's fearsome foe, and doing her darndest to imitate the distinctive sound of its voice. Although, in truth, it ended up sounding more like she simply had a sore throat.

"Uhm, you might want to promptly remove that," Calum advised, sounding like he was speaking from experience. "Because if you don't, you'll..."

But Calum's warning fell on deaf ears, with Charlotte shaking her head repeatedly from side to side to see just how stuck the arrow actually was. Fortunately, about twenty seconds later, the same time as Stanley had finally stopped laughing, the arrow unstuck itself, falling harmlessly to the sand.

Calum turned the sizzling bacon on the grill before looking back over to his beloved. "Uhm, Lotti?" he said with a pained expression, extending his BBQ tongs in her direction. "You might want to have a look at your forehead," he suggested.

Charlotte did as instructed, pulling out her compact mirror to inspect the damage. "Oh..."

Calum nodded. "I had a similar experience when I was a kid," he recalled. "Blood vessels burst, and I had to go to school with an angry red ring on my cheek."

"What? You mean this doesn't disappear?"

"Well, yes," Calum replied, hoping to put her mind at ease. "I mean, *eventually* it will disappear, sure."

Charlotte laughed, unsure of how serious he was being. "I've got filming tomorrow," she reminded him. "And you're saying I'm going to have this blinking great circle on my head?"

"You could maybe disguise it," Calum suggested.

"From a BBC HD camera?" Charlotte remarked. "Those things can zoom in on a dusty grain of sand on the moon."

"Just lash a load of foundation over it, Lotti. You'll be fine."

"Mum," Stanley weakly called over, struggling mightily to stifle his continued laughter, given the ramifications if he didn't. "Mum, did I tell you how awfully nice it was to have you back...?"

* * *

THE CRAFTERNOON SEWCIAL CLUB: SHOWDOWN

For Charlotte, like many, hearing the familiar intro theme to *Antiques Roadshow* on a Sunday evening heralded the imminent conclusion of the weekend. It was at this point that thoughts, unfortunately, might turn to one's job the following morning and another long and often arduous five days until the next weekend break from the workweek was finally ushered in.

Ordinarily, Charlotte escaped this sense of despondency on account of doing what she adored for a living, which was something she was eternally grateful for. Tonight, however, there was something of a glum cloud hanging over her.

Perhaps it was partly the thought of soon being away from home for at least another week, or the frosty relationship with Darren, or, as she suspected, the fact that she wasn't being entirely forthcoming with Calum about that whole Darren situation, even now as she was cuddled up next to Calum on the sofa.

In Calum, she had found her soulmate, a wonderful person who made her feel all warm and fuzzy each time she was with him. Bringing a new man into her and Stanley's tight-knit family dynamic was always a concern for Charlotte, yet Calum had slipped in so easily, without any issue at all, and with him they were the three amigos who made each other happy.

And while Charlotte had no doubt Calum would understand that she was the innocent party in the whole Darren debacle, she didn't want Calum to have to worry each and every time she'd find herself in Darren's company.

"Glass of vino?" Calum asked, after unwrapping his arm from around Charlotte's shoulders.

"No, I shouldn't," Charlotte replied, enjoying a nice stretch. "I need to get up early, bright and breezy, and..." she began.

"Yeah, actually, go on," she said, giving in to temptation almost immediately. "And there are some of those nice crisps in the cupboard by the fridge, by the way. Lamb and mint flavour, the ones you like," she added.

"Muuummm, are you opening those crisps?!" a voice shouted from up the stairs, with Stanley somehow able to hear the word "crisps" from some distance away, up on the next floor and all, and through several closed doors as well, astonishingly enough. One might almost call it a superpower.

"Yes, come and grab some before we gobble them all up!" she shouted back, and then spread herself out in order to claim the space on the sofa just vacated by Calum. But just as she was getting settled in, her phone vibrated over on the coffee table. "Now who's that?" she wondered aloud, stretching out her arm so that she wouldn't need to adjust her comfy position. Upon picking up her phone and having a gander, her face lit up in delight, not something normally to be expected when one gets an email from work on a Sunday night.

But this was an email Charlotte didn't mind receiving. It was something she was rather looking forward to, having expected it though forgetting about it until just now. Fortnightly, as she was told, the production team would be sending out a 'Meet the Contestants' memo, in which would be provided a summary of the show's participants set to appear in the coming two weeks. With headshots provided, it allowed the team to get a look at who they were working with, along with an overview of the contestants' motivations for applying to the show, what they hoped to achieve, what their crafting experience was to date, et cetera.

To Charlotte, meeting new crafters was one of the absolute highlights of working on the show. And getting to know the various contestants in advance enhanced Charlotte's ability to engage with them during filming. Also, by familiarising herself with their crafting CVs, Charlotte would be able to plan which of them might need some additional support, for instance, in their quest to secure victory.

Moreover, another reason she had been particularly looking forward to this specific email was to be able to see the inclusion of two very special contestants who, as she knew, were like a pair of giddy kippers over their upcoming appearance on the show.

"One glass of wine," Calum announced, placing it down in front of her as Charlotte sat back up, making room for him again on the sofa. "And thanks to Stanley, one much-lighter-than-expected packet of crisps," he added. "The way he ravaged them, like a bear snatching salmon from a stream, was actually rather impressive."

Calum sat back down, watching as a woman on the TV put on a brave face about the measly valuation she'd just received for some cherished family heirloom. "Oh, dear," Calum remarked. "She thought it was from the Ming Dynasty, and it's actually cheap tat sold to the tourists," he commented for the benefit of Charlotte, who was still engaged on her phone at the moment.

"I don't believe this," said Charlotte, sounding furious. "This cannot be happening."

"I know, right? She looks absolutely gutted," Calum replied, still watching the telly. But when Charlotte remained glued to her phone, Calum realised they were at cross purposes. "Everything okay, Lotti?" he enquired, concerned by the heavy breathing and flaring of nostrils he was witnessing.

"Joyce and Beryl are supposed to be on this," she replied by way of partial explanation, scrolling furiously. "Where are they?"

Calum was able to somewhat fill in the blanks. "On the show, you mean?"

"They were supposed to be on the schedule for next week," Charlotte answered, scowling at her phone.

And at that moment the reason for Beryl and Joyce's absence became clear to her. She knew precisely how and why her two dear friends were no longer on the filming calendar. She was certain of it. The difficulty would be in explaining this to Calum without giving him chapter and verse about her strained relationship with Darren.

"Maybe it's just a clerical error or something?"

"Sadly, I don't think it is," Charlotte replied, accompanied by a heavy sigh. "And Joyce and Beryl have both been so excited about appearing on the show, Calum. They've even been out to buy new outfits to wear," she advised. "How on earth am I going to let them down gently?"

Chapter Twenty-One

With about two dozen completed episodes of *The Crafternoon Showdown* safely under her belt, Charlotte was finally starting to get her bearings around her home away from home at the MediaCityUK production offices. Not only was she no longer getting lost in the maze of corridors, but she was even starting to become something of a familiar face to the others there as well. In fact, much to her immense delight, Charlie Stayt, one of the wonderful presenters of *BBC Breakfast*, had now held the door open for her on two separate occasions. In addition, one of her high points to date had to be sharing a lift with famous TV presenter Michael Portillo, all decked out in his trademark exotic colours, and who had been kind enough to offer her a mint humbug whilst they changed floors.

And now, after a temporary break from filming and having said her goodbyes at home, Charlotte was relishing the chance to get back into the thick of it. All except for that one pesky issue in need of attention, that is. And so...

"I know what you've done," Charlotte growled, thrusting an extended finger into the air. "In fact, ever since I declined your romantic advances, you've been nothing but a big– a big... well, a big meanie to me, yeah? Well that I can handle. But what really unravels my stitching, so to speak, is you getting my two friends kicked off the filming schedule when they've done absolutely nothing wrong." She left her pointer finger in the air, pointing, while offering a hard, steely gaze she hoped would aptly convey her displeasure. "What's wrong, mister man?" she asked, when no response was forthcoming. "You've got nothing to say to me? Not so unpleasant now, are you? Why, I'll bet you wish—"

"*Ahem,*" someone offered, diverting Charlotte away from her conversation.

Charlotte spun around in her modest-yet-comfortable dressing room, finding Imogen, the hair and makeup lady, standing in the doorway.

"Oh, heya!" Charlotte said brightly, as if she hadn't at all just been startled and taken completely unawares. "You're probably wondering why I'm having an argument with a coat stand?" she asked, pointing casually to the object of her seeming discontent.

"It did cross my mind, Lotti."

"Uhm, I'm taking an online acting class?" Charlotte began to explain, thinking fast. "And, ehm, what you just witnessed was a, erm... a module. Yes, that's it. A module I needed to practice ahead of my next class," she said.

"Well, the acting classes are working, Lotti, because I would not like to have been that coatstand, being on the receiving end of such a severe tongue-lashing," Imogen offered.

Charlotte was delighted to receive such positive critical feedback in indication that her non-existent acting classes were already producing such encouraging results. "Aww, thank you, Imogen, that's good to know," Charlotte replied, wondering if a career in acting might be something she ought to actually pursue. "Oh, darn it. Am I late, Imogen? Is that why you're here?"

"It's fine, Lotti. I'd just wondered where you were, and now I know," Imogen answered. "Now are you ready for me to make you look even more beautiful than you already are?"

Charlotte followed Imogen the Miracle Worker, as she was affectionately referred to by the rest of the staff, along with anyone else who'd had the pleasure of benefitting from her expert hand. With a flourish of her brushes, she was always able to quickly hide blemishes and disguise the tiring effects of a heavy weekend, leaving those under her care looking simply radiant.

Relaxing back in Imogen's makeup chair, Charlotte admired herself in the Hollywood-style mirror, the glass surrounded by a dozen or more LED bulbs, as the master worked her magic. "Honestly, If I had the money, Imogen, I'd employ you to follow me around wherever I go, all day long, with your makeup brush right there on standby," she remarked.

"You're too kind, Lotti," Imogen said, standing back to regard her work like an artist inspecting their canvas. "Right. That's you ready for the camera," Imogen suggested, happy to sign off on her latest work.

Charlotte took a moment to appreciate Imogen's efforts in the illuminated mirror. "You've worked around here for a while now, have you?" Charlotte asked, making conversation.

"Four years now. Give or take."

"And you've known Darren during that time?" Charlotte asked.

In an instant, Imogen's personable nature changed. "No. Not so much," she said, matter-of-factly. She wasn't exactly cold, but neither was she all that friendly just now.

"So he doesn't come and see you for a refurb before filming?"

Imogen shook her head in the negative. "Darren will look after himself when it comes to that."

"Ah, well I'm sure he doesn't know what he's missing out on," Charlotte offered with a gentle laugh. "But if you've worked with him for several years, I don't suppose you know if—"

"Charlotte," Imogen cut in, her expression firm. "If Darren is your thing, you should probably know that he's married. Or at least he was the last time I heard. A surprising fact when you consider the wandering nature of his busy hands."

"Eh? Darren's married?" Charlotte said, with the rest of Imogen's words still registering. "Wait, hang on, what do you mean, *if Darren's my thing?*" she asked, a moment or two later.

"So he's not?" Imogen asked, sounding relieved.

"Oh good lord, no," Charlotte assured her. "No, I was trying to gauge your thoughts on him, actually, because if I'm being honest, I think he's a bit of a—"

"Tosspot?" Imogen offered bluntly.

"Well, I was going to say creep, I think, but yeah, I think I like your description better," Charlotte was happy to concede. "So if your comment about wandering hands is anything for me to go by, might I assume Darren is something of a ladies' man?"

"Pest, more like, Lotti. Although he's harmless enough, I suppose, as long as you know enough to keep your distance," Imogen answered. "It's just his wife I feel a bit sorry for. And if you're asking me about him, can I assume that his wandering eye has wandered in your direction?"

Irrationally, Charlotte was slightly put out by the fact Darren appeared to be chasing anything in a skirt, instead of chasing her exclusively (meaning she wasn't anything that special). But she swiftly put that thought out of her mind.

"Yes, sadly, you could say that," Charlotte replied, answering Imogen's question. "Although I've made it abundantly clear to him that I'm not interested."

"But he won't take no for an answer?" Imogen ventured.

"No, it's not like that, fortunately. It's just that he's been really off with me since I'd spurned his advances. It's like he's a completely different person. And now he's also put me in a situation where I need to disappoint two dear friends of mine. Oh look at me, I'm sorry to bother you with my problems, Imogen."

"Hey, it's all part of the job. Hair, makeup, counselling, and whatever else you need," Imogen joked. "But seriously, Lotti, if you need to talk, you know where I am, yeah? Oh, and can I assume the coatstand you were dressing down earlier was a stand-in for Darren?"

"Yeah. The story about acting classes was a little bit of a white lie. Sorry."

"Well, you were still good at it, Lotti."

"What, lying?" Charlotte asked, uncertain if she should accept a compliment like that.

"No, I meant acting," Imogen clarified with a laugh.

"Ah, thanks, Imogen. That means a lot."

* * *

Charlotte wasn't someone who enjoyed any type of conflict, and as such, confrontations weren't something she was particularly good at handling. It was for this reason she figured some practice to be in order, hence the reason the poor coatstand had been on the receiving end of a scolding a bit earlier. She had no desire to fall out with her co-star, as after all, they needed to work together. But if the conversation did get heated, Charlotte wanted to make sure she was primed and ready for action.

Before proceeding to her shooting location for the morning, Charlotte first headed to the production office, where she hoped to have a word with her co-host. "Knock-knock," she said, opening the door, though only finding Phillipa on the other side. "Oh. Sorry to bother you, Phillipa. I was looking for Darren?"

"You've just missed him," Phillipa said, breaking her attention away from her computer screen. "If you're quick, you might catch up with him?"

"Ah, it's fine. Nothing important," Charlotte replied, hiding her frustration, knowing she'd have to mentally prepare herself all over again later that day.

"Can I help with anything?"

"Thanks, no. It's nothing that can't wait," Charlotte answered. "You're still good for lunch this week?"

"Anytime, Lotti."

Charlotte turned to leave when a thought presented itself. "In fact, there was one thing, Phillipa. You know the schedule you emailed around yesterday?"

"Oh, yes. You could say that we're well acquainted," Phillipa replied, along with a slight frown. "My husband now refers to it as the Sunday killer, on account of how long I spent preparing it over the course of the day."

"You spent your weekend working?" Charlotte asked, smiling sympathetically.

"No rest for the weary, I'm afraid," Phillipa said with a laugh.

"Well I can see how you did put a lot of time into it," Charlotte offered. "It was very good."

"But...?" Phillipa asked, suspecting there was a bit more to Charlotte's enquiry than this. "I didn't make a mistake, did I?"

Charlotte stepped closer, so that she was in front of Phillipa's desk and wouldn't have to keep speaking from across the room. "No, it's not that. Or maybe it is? I'm actually not sure," Charlotte answered. "You see, Darren arranged for two of my dearest crafting pals, Joyce and Beryl, to appear on the show as contestants," Charlotte explained. "But I couldn't see their names in the email you circulated, and I just wondered if that could have been some kind of oversight, perhaps?"

Phillipa appeared distressed that an error may have occurred on her watch. "Hmm, let me just have a look," she said, opening up the spreadsheet on her computer.

Charlotte anxiously waited, convinced her suspicions about Darren were about to be proven correct, although uncertain as to what information Phillipa could provide, exactly.

"Well, I can't see any contestants with those names," Phillipa informed her, scanning her spreadsheet again just to be sure.

"That lousy..." Charlotte muttered to herself.

"Wait," Phillipa said, providing Charlotte with what sounded like perhaps a glimmer of hope.

"Yeah?"

"Did you say *Darren* arranged for your friends to appear on the show?" Phillipa asked, appearing puzzled as she looked up from her screen.

"That's right. Darren phoned me up to say he'd sorted it all out for them."

"That's very odd, isn't it?" Phillipa offered.

"I know. Do you think it's possible that Darren had somehow, accidentally, removed them from the list?" Charlotte asked, not wanting to appear too accusatory if there was still a chance to remedy the situation.

"No, that's the thing, Lotti. It's not a matter of Darren possibly removing them. It's more that Darren has absolutely nothing to do with scheduling contestants in the first place."

"What? So my friends were never on the list at all?"

"I don't think so," Phillipa advised. "But I could give you a couple of application forms if they still wanted to apply?" she offered, rummaging in her desk drawer and finding some.

"Thanks," Charlotte said, taking hold of the forms, and knowing precisely whose throat she wanted to stuff them down.

Chapter Twenty-Two

Larry swivelled from side to side in the plush leather office chair, adjusting the microphone on his headset so it was positioned millimetres away from his mouth. "Do I look like a popstar with this thing on?" he asked of nobody in particular. But before he could receive any kind of response one way or another, Larry remembered his chair was equipped with castors. "Yee-haw!" he called out like a rodeo cowboy riding a bucking bronco, thrusting himself outward from his desk aboard his wild, wheeled steed. And fortunately for him, his headset was of the Bluetooth variety, meaning there were no wire cords which would garrotte him. "Come on, Beryl!" he said. "Let's race!"

But Beryl didn't appear overly keen on the invite. "If you think I'm racing office chairs at my age, you big dafty..." she said.

"Spoilsport!" Joyce entered in, careering past with her feet stretched out ahead of her.

"You know who'd love this?" Larry asked, preparing for another launch. "Young Stanley," he said, answering his own question. "I must remember to bring him here for a race."

Just then, the office door opened and Calum's head appeared into view. "I'm just checking you're all in one piece?" he asked rhetorically, in response to the noise emanating from within.

"Are we disturbing your colleagues?" Joyce asked, drawing to a halt. "Awfully sorry."

Calum waved away her concerns. "Not at all, Joyce. The guys were watching you through the window and were actually hoping to come and join you for a race when you're finished," he told them with a laugh.

"Tell them it's a date!" Larry advised, using his heels to drag himself back to his desk.

Calum couldn't help but smile. There was just something about the gang from Crafternoon that he found so invigorating when in their company, particularly that of his guests for the day, Larry, Joyce, and Beryl. And yes they could moan and grumble with the best of them, but their zest for life was almost childlike in its innocence. Indeed, Calum could completely understand why Charlotte so enjoyed spending time with them all, and he could appreciate why she missed them so much when they weren't near.

And it was their collective appreciation of Charlotte's Crafternoon Sewcial Club that brought Larry and the others along to Calum's business premises at Microcoding. Aware of the ongoing confusion and disruption stemming from Charlotte's absence, Calum had reached out to see if there was anything he might do to help restore some confidence in the membership. Among the suggestions to remedy the situation, Joyce had proposed to phone each of their members, knowing most of them liked nothing more than a good chinwag anyway. During the call, she would provide assurances that the club would be open for business so that there were no concerns about turning up and finding the doors locked like they had been before.

But with a membership list as long as your arm and only one good ear to press to a phone, it was clear Joyce would need some assistance to contact them all. As such, Calum was quick to offer the use of his offices (and his phone bill), as well as some of his staff, if required. And to sweeten the deal for the members they were calling, Calum also offered to supply a generous selection of bakery-sourced treats for their next few club meetings as a further incentive for them all to return. It could well be considered a bribe. But it was a tasty bribe, and so Larry and the girls were only too happy to relay the information to the others, as they would most certainly be enjoying the benefits of Calum's offer as well.

Unfortunately, once they'd set to work, their temporary call centre wasn't exactly getting off to an auspicious start, with poor Larry already on the receiving end of an apparent ear-bashing.

"What?" Larry protested, startled by the thunderous voice in his earpiece. "If I– if I could just... excuse me, if you'll let me explain..." he said, trying to get a word in. "How dare you, madam!" he said before ending the call, visibly shaken by the experience.

"Things going well, Larry?" Joyce enquired with a cackle.

"It was Helena. Helena Långström. She called me all sorts of nasty names, some of which I didn't even understand," a flustered Larry explained. "I tried to calm her down, but nothing worked."

Beryl peered over from the adjacent desk with an idea as to what might be going on. "You see that red light on your phone, Larry?"

"This one?" Larry asked.

Beryl nodded. "It means you're on mute, Larry."

"Mute?"

"Yes, mute. So whoever you called would have been greeted by silence."

"Oh. Oh, dear," Larry replied, realising the error he'd made. "I don't even know how I did that. But that will be why she hung up on me the first two times I called, and then finally let loose with both barrels on the third attempt. She thought I was a telemarketer at first, and then she accused me of being some kind of pervert stalker, claiming she could hear me breathing on the other end, even though that can't be true if I was on mute. Blimey, do you think I should phone her back to apologise?"

"Maybe later, once she's had a chance to cool off for a bit," Joyce offered with a chuckle. "Just move on to the next one for now," she advised.

Fortunately, after the initial setback, the trio's efforts were soon rewarded by the positive reaction to their calls. Indeed, the difficulty, as they soon discovered, was concluding each call, as most of the members they reached appeared perfectly happy to chat all morning. As such, progress through the list was slower than a snail swimming through treacle. But that didn't matter.

Not one iota. Because Joyce and the others knew a good portion of those they contacted lived alone, and that these calls might well be the only one they'd received that week. And if some of their friends wanted to chat for a bit longer than necessary, well that was just fine by them.

With progress made and with plenty of names scored out on their lists, the morning soon disappeared as did Beryl's voice. "Time for lunch?" she croaked, figuring a nice cuppa was just the ticket to rejuvenate her parched throat. She wandered over, first to Joyce and then Larry, tapping them both gently on the shoulder, indicating it was time to clock off for a bit, a suggestion the other two appeared to find agreeable.

"So?" Joyce asked as they made their way towards the staff canteen, what with them being honorary Microcoding staff for the day. "Folks were happy enough to talk, that's for sure. But what's the overall feedback?" she said, sounding like she had her own thoughts to share, but wanting to hear what the others had to say first.

Larry sucked in air through his teeth, like he was considering how to sugarcoat what he was about to relate. "Well, the people I spoke to?" he said, stopping to hold the door open for his two esteemed colleagues. "They do enjoy the club, and they want to come back, but..."

"But?" Beryl pressed.

"They miss Charlotte?" Joyce ventured. "Because that's what I was hearing."

Larry nodded his head wearily, like it was too heavy for his neck. "Yeah, that's what I was hearing as well. They said it's just not the same without her," he advised. Then, aware that Beryl had somehow fallen behind them, he turned to find out where she might suddenly have gone.

Beryl gradually caught up, appearing consumed in her own thoughts. "What's up with you?" Joyce enquired. "I'm usually the one trying to catch up with *you* when there's food on offer," she teased, though not in an unkind manner.

THE CRAFTERNOON SEWCIAL CLUB: SHOWDOWN

Beryl sighed the sigh of someone slightly sad. "It's not just them," Beryl offered. "The members we phoned, I mean."

Joyce flicked her eyes over to Larry for a moment, wondering if he knew what she meant. "What's not them?" Joyce eventually asked, when she received a blank expression in return.

With concern written all over her face, Beryl appeared conflicted. "It's not just them that feel that way," she said. "I really miss our Lotti," she admitted. "And as silly as it might sound, it's like the colour in my life is duller without her in it. You know what I mean?"

"Oh come here, you," Joyce said, spotting a tear welling up in Beryl's eye. She wrapped her arms around her friend, giving her a gentle squeeze. "It's not silly at all."

Larry, watching on, took a step towards them and then one back again, like he was dancing a solo tango. "Uhm, is there any room for—?"

"What are you waiting for? Get yourself over here," Joyce instructed, raising an arm to gather him into their embrace.

"I dearly miss her, too," Larry said, after positioning himself amidst the Joyce & Beryl sandwich, though unsure if he was the bread or if he was the cheese. "But we must remain resolute!" he advised, hoping to raise the spirits of his fellow call centre operatives. "We need to redouble our efforts," he said. "If our members are feeling despondent, we must convince them never to despair. We must be the friends they need us to be. We need to give them reason to leave their houses, their cottages, and their flats each week, for the very survival of the Crafternoon Sewcial Club is at stake!"

"Oi, did you nick that motivational speech from something Winston Churchill said?" Beryl enquired.

"What? No," Larry replied, wishing to dispel any suggestion of plagiarism, although sounding far from offended. "Why? Are you saying I'm an inspirational leader like the great man was?"

"I s'pose," Beryl supposed. "Anyway, you know what? You two don't half give a bloody good cuddle when a girl needs it most."

Chapter Twenty-Three

Working on a hectic TV show meant very little, if any, idle time for those involved. For anybody watching from the sidelines, it must have appeared very much like unorganised chaos, but that conclusion couldn't be further from the truth. As Charlotte had soon come to realise, everybody on set had their own individual roles to perform, often running around like headless chickens, but the end result was a collective team spirit with all involved working towards a common goal.

However, what this also meant for today, in particular, was that Charlotte was struggling to find just the right time to try and speak to Darren. Of course, she could always make contact with him after hours. But based on his previous behaviour, she decided this wouldn't have been the ideal approach.

Since she'd returned from her weekend break, Darren had continued with his rather snooty attitude. Where once he'd been a colleague whose counsel she valued, ready and willing to help her succeed in her new endeavour, now he was condescending to the point it started to feel to her like bullying. The frustration, however, was that he was rather adept at doing it while other people were distracted, or, saying it in such a way that it might appear Charlotte was being overly sensitive if she took offence. He was so good at doing this, in fact, that Charlotte even started to question herself, wondering if she was perhaps making more of the situation than she ought to. The only way she'd know for sure was to have it out with him.

Having both returned from morning filming with their respective teams, Charlotte reckoned this might be as good a time as any to pull him aside and have a word. Outside the production office and away from the rest of the crew, Darren and his crafters were presently having a little bit of a debrief before lunch.

"How was your morning foraging?" Charlotte enquired of the group, heading over and trying to sound pleasant.

"Oh, look out. The competition has come over to steal your ideas," Darren said with a laugh.

Charlotte smiled politely, aware that the contestants, Billy and Sandra, would have little idea of the friction between the two hosts. "I'm really not, Darren. I just wondered if—"

"Cover up your essays, because the school cheat is trying to catch a glimpse!" Darren added in, not quite finished, it would seem, and appearing quite happy with himself.

In response, Charlotte decided it best to give up any pretence of civility. "Darren, I need to speak with you. *Now*," she said, placing a firm hand on his arm.

"Ooh, sounds important," Darren said. "Are you fed up with being on the losing team?" he asked, in a mixture of sarcasm and what was meant to be some semblance of humour, Charlotte had to assume. And then, looking over his shoulder, "If I'm not back in five minutes, team, Charlotte has probably bored me to sleep," he joked, allowing Charlotte to lead the way.

Charlotte took several deep breaths to compose herself, and once a safe distance away from the others, finally turned to face him. "Darren, I've been trying to speak to you about something," she said, her voice partially breaking due to the build-up of frustration.

"Oh? How can I help?" her co-host asked.

Charlotte resisted the urge to raise her voice, knowing she'd weaken her position by doing so. "Darren," she said in her most forthright manner. "Darren, ever since you kissed me that day, I can't help but notice that—"

"What? *Kissed* you?" Darren scoffed. "I didn't *kiss* you," he insisted, briefly glancing over his shoulder as one of the sound engineers wandered past with some audio cables coiled up in each arm.

This denial caught Charlotte completely off-guard. "What, now?"

Darren grinned inanely, running his hand over his hair, until it was just the two of them again. "Kissing you was a mistake," he admitted, now speaking in hushed tones so no one else could overhear.

"Oh, so at least I didn't imagine it, then," Charlotte answered, crossing her arms. "So why are you now treating me like something you dragged in on your shoe?" she asked. "And why did you tell me my friends were scheduled to appear on the show when that was an out-and-out lie?" she scolded him.

Darren's smug grin from earlier was now mostly gone, but it was only because he appeared slightly confused by her question. "Your friends?" he asked.

"Yes. Joyce and Beryl. You met them over on the Isle of Man, remember? And then you phoned me later on, telling me you'd secured them a slot on the programme."

Darren's eyes rolled skyward, his tongue clicking against the roof of his mouth. "Oh, yeah, that," he replied with a chuckle. "You know, I'd completely forgotten about that."

"Well *they* haven't, Darren. Two lovely ladies, thrilled to be appearing on the show. They told all their friends, and even bought new outfits in preparation for being in front of the camera."

This information appeared to raise Darren's spirits, judging by his childish smirk. Charlotte watched on in disbelief, kicking herself for ever having respected this man.

"Darren, you're pathetic," she said, struggling to contain her emotions, desperate they didn't spill over, as she suspected he'd probably thrive on that.

In response, Darren gave his watch a casual glance, as if he were uninterested in all of this and had someplace else to be, which only infuriated Charlotte further.

"Oh relax," he said, now looking back up from his watch. "If anybody should be annoyed, Lotti, it's me, you know."

Charlotte stared at him, incredulous at what he was saying. "What the hell are you on about?"

"You, Lotti. Flirting with me in the Isle of Man like you did. It's the only reason I recommended you for this job in the first place."

"You recommended me for the job only because you expected me to jump into bed with you?" asked an astonished Charlotte. "And then you make my life a misery when I don't?"

"If you don't like it, then you can always quit," Darren suggested, sounding rather tired of this conversation. "Remember, there's a queue of women a mile long who'd do just about anything to be in your position. And I mean anything."

Charlotte's hands started trembling, as she couldn't believe what she was hearing. "Darren, you're a horrible, horrible person," she said, before turning her back on him, feeling like her legs were about to give way.

"Charlotte," Darren said from behind, once again checking to be sure that there was nobody within earshot. "Charlotte, what did that boyfriend of yours say about our lovely little smooch?" he asked. "You did tell him, right, Lotti? Lotti...?"

※ ※ ※

What troubled Charlotte most during the afternoon's in-studio portion of filming wasn't working metres away from Darren — although that was certainly no treat — but the feeling that she was letting the contestants on her team down. Still shaken from her earlier altercation, Charlotte's mind was elsewhere (and to the uninitiated, she may have appeared uninterested, which was most certainly not the case). As such, the director had to intervene on several occasions, pointing out that her team needed assistance and requesting a little more engagement on her part.

And her distraction was genuinely upsetting for Charlotte, because she knew that appearing on the show was likely a huge deal for her contestants, and if she wasn't performing at her very best then that meant she was failing them.

Further, also compounding Charlotte's less-than-stellar day, Darren seemed to take great delight in shaking his head in mock dismay and offering a noisy little tut-tut each time the director needed to step in like a schoolteacher chastising an uncooperative pupil.

"Good job today, Lotti," remarked Darren after filming had concluded. And for those standing in the vicinity, it may have sounded sincere, even though he was absolutely being sarcastic.

And if there had been any doubt, the flicker of a smile and a subtle wink conveyed its real meaning to Charlotte. She couldn't wait to get out of there. But rather than returning to loving family and friends, all she had to look forward to were a sterile hotel and an evening in her own company.

Later, sitting in her room, Charlotte had to resist the urge to deplete the contents of her minibar. How had this opportunity, a dream job, soured to such an extent that she was giving actual consideration to the idea of getting wasted from the large collection of miniature whisky bottles there in her fridge, she wondered.

Perched there on the edge of her bed, she placed her head in her hands, with Darren's words replaying in her mind, over and over, like some kind of horrible, broken soundtrack. "Do I just quit?" she asked herself, giving this option serious consideration. But then the prospect of returning home with her tail between her legs, feeling like a failure, consumed her.

"Aww," she moaned, gripping handfuls of hair like she was about to rip them clean out by the root, the realisation sinking in that she was going to have to subject herself to another round of torture the next day. Then, the familiar sound of Charlotte's vibrating mobile served to distract her from the thoughts that plagued her. And like a rainbow emerging on a stormy day, with skies clearing, Charlotte's mood immediately lifted upon seeing Larry's name on her phone's display screen.

"Hello, my lovely," Charlotte said. "It's wonderful to hear from you!"

"Isle of Man calling Manchester," Larry announced, sounding like a wartime radio operator. "Can you hear me loud and clear? Over."

"Loud and clear, Larry. Over," Charlotte replied.

"Brilliant," Larry answered. "Can we, uhm, switch to video? I wanted to show you something, assuming I can figure out how this thing works..."

Charlotte complied, dutifully switching over as requested. She was about to blow him a kiss as he came onscreen, but then held off as she presently found herself staring at his feet.

"I'm not calling at an inconvenient time?" said Larry's feet.

"Larry, I can honestly say that your timing couldn't be better," Charlotte answered.

"Splendid. So what do you think of this beauty, Lotti?" asked Larry's feet.

Charlotte moved in for a slightly closer look, scrutinising the video image before her. "Erm... yeah. Are they new shoes?" she asked, unsure of what beauty she was meant to be admiring, exactly, though there was little else onscreen to look at.

Larry went quiet for a moment. "Shoes...?" he asked, confused, before he must have realised what he'd done. "Oh, I think I've selected the wrong bloody camera on here," he informed her, something Charlotte already suspected to be the case. "I won't be a moment... flipping thing..." he moaned, humming and hawing as he mashed the screen to rectify the situation. "I know it's one of these... Oh, wait, there we go. I think I've got it."

And with that, Charlotte now had a worms-eye view directly up Larry's left nostril. "Uhm, you may want to move your phone away from your...?" she advised. "Yes, that's it, Larry," she added, once Larry had zoomed out enough that Charlotte could now see his entire head and shoulders. "Right. So what am I looking at?" she asked.

Larry didn't immediately speak, instead directing a finger towards his new bowtie. "Whaddya think?" he asked. "Bonnie and Abigail made it for me to wear on Friday night."

It took a second or two for Charlotte to register what she was seeing. "Is that a banknote pattern on the material?" she asked, squinting her eyes for a clearer view.

"Sure is, Lotti," Larry proudly confirmed. "Because we're all invited to the launch of the bank's fraud awareness campaign,

THE CRAFTERNOON SEWCIAL CLUB: SHOWDOWN

and the girls decided a dickie bow with banknotes on it would be just the ticket," he said. "I've also had the suit I bought for our Christmas Sewing Bee dry-cleaned, and Joyce and Beryl said I look like a real bobby-dazzler."

"I'm sure you'll be the belle of the ball, Larry."

"Did I tell you there's music and dancing once the formalities of the evening are over?" Larry asked.

The prospect of a boogie or two with her dear friend raised Charlotte's mood faster than anything the minibar could offer. "You did previously, Larry, yes. And I cannot wait to see you on Friday."

"It's in Liverpool, like I mentioned before. You can make it?" Larry asked. "You'll be off from filming in time?"

"I certainly hope so," Charlotte answered.

Larry moved his face closer to his phone for a moment, resulting in Charlotte briefly having a direct view into his *right* nostril this time. "Lotti, what's up?" he asked, after staring at her for several seconds.

"What's that? How do you mean?" Charlotte asked, unable, of course, to see what Larry was seeing.

"You're not yourself, Lotti," Larry suggested. "It's almost as if the twinkling bulbs in your eyes are fading and need to be replaced. And you look tired, if you don't mind me saying. So, I say again, Lotti. What's up?"

Poor Larry must have wondered what he'd unleashed when Charlotte proceeded to pour her heart out for the next twenty minutes unburdening herself on him (though with Charlotte choosing to omit any specific references to the unwanted kiss). But Larry didn't mind, not one bit. Indeed, in the nursing home, Larry was known by many as a wonderful shoulder to cry on, with several of the residents referring to him rather fondly as Listening Larry. And it was just the tonic Charlotte needed at just the right time.

"I'm so sorry for landing you with all this, Larry," Charlotte offered, once she'd eventually brought him up to date with her miserable day. "But I just don't know what to do."

Larry stewed on the information he'd just learned, building himself up into a bit of a lather. "I've a bleedin' great desire to fly straight over there and give this Darren scoundrel a seriously good walloping," he said, shaking his head in fury.

"As much as I appreciate that, Larry, I'm not too sure it'd end up solving much, even if it would be a definite joy to watch," Charlotte replied. "I dunno, maybe I only needed a chance to unload, Larry? Because after just talking to you, I now feel much better."

Larry looked at her, earnest and sympathetic. "Whatever you do, Lotti, you need to be happy," he instructed. "And always remember you've an army of friends and family who love and support you in whatever you do. And remember, as well, that quitting something that's making you sad isn't a sign of failure. But sticking around being miserable is a sure sign of madness."

"Larry, you're one of the very best friends a girl could have," Charlotte answered, placing her fingers to her lips and blowing him a kiss. "And please make sure I'm on your dance card on Friday, yeah?"

"Duly noted, Lotti. There will likely be a lot of competition, as always, but I'll see what I can do for you. And if you ever want me to bop that plonker on the nose at any point, you just say the word."

"I promise I will. And thanks for always being there for me, Listening Larry."

Chapter Twenty-Four

One aspect of hotel life that endeared itself to Charlotte was the ability to enjoy a dip in the pool before breakfast. She suspected, sadly, that her modest cottage back home in Laxey wouldn't quite lend itself to a swimming pool no matter how creative she was in rearranging her garden.

And so, revitalised after her morning swim and a good night's sleep (thanks to Larry's fine counselling session) Charlotte made her way to work with a refreshed perspective, a certain clarity of mind if you will. No longer would she act like a shrinking violet around Darren, walking on eggshells for fear of incurring his wrath. Because it was now apparent to her that Darren thrived on that sort of reaction, and so she simply wouldn't give him the satisfaction. In fact, now, rather than tiptoeing around him, she would do the exact opposite, making out like she was his best friend on earth and being as sickly sweet as humanly possible.

In the lift at the office, Charlotte hummed along to the Spice Girls song being pumped out the overhead speakers. Knowing Darren was partial to Danish pastries, she'd made a short detour to a local bakery on the way there to buy some treats for the entire crew, Darren included. "I'm going to be so darned nice to him he won't know what's bloody hit him!" Charlotte chuntered to herself, causing the lady standing beside her to take a cautionary step to her left.

Walking into the studio, Charlotte flashed her warmest of smiles. "I hope we're hungry?" she asked, holding up her bulging box of goodies, after which she resumed humming the tune she'd just heard in the elevator, the song still fresh in her head.

"You're in fine spirits this morning, Lotti," Phillipa remarked, first in the queue for something to keep her coffee company.

"I'm living the dream, Phillipa. Living the dream!" Charlotte replied merrily, and she meant it. For someone ordinarily so positive, a glass-half-full kind of girl, Charlotte was acutely aware of how pessimistic she'd been of late. It was an attitude she didn't particularly enjoy witnessing make an appearance. Sure, she was working away from those she loved, but many others did the same and got on with it just fine. Plus, she knew this was only a temporary inconvenience, with filming not lasting forever. Also, she was being put up in what was a rather swanky hotel, she had to remind herself, and she was getting paid handsomely to do the two things she adored more than anything else — crafting, and teaching crafting to others. So all things considered, and despite the unpleasantness from Darren, she really was living the dream. It was just a case of stopping once in a while to remember that.

"Ah, back for more abuse?" the newly arrived Darren joked, before noticing the pastries now laid out on one of the worktops. But with the amiable way he spoke to Charlotte when others were around, it was easy to believe the two of them were old pals and that this was just some harmless, playful banter. "If you need any more help from me today, just shout," he suggested, planting his gnashers into one of the pastries.

"Oh, I'll make sure to do that," Charlotte said, choosing to take no offence to the sarcastic undertones that only she was able to clearly detect. "And I appreciate it, Darren. I know I can really learn a lot from you," she said, sounding completely sincere.

Darren cocked his head, eyeing Charlotte suspiciously, which she didn't mind admitting she rather enjoyed.

"Savour that pastry!" she said, offering him a hearty, double thumbs-up. "And thanks again for being such a supportive colleague," she added, laying it on especially thick.

And that approach was the order of the day, and for the next few days, in fact. Indeed, anytime that Darren had a little snipe or threw a barbed comment in her direction, Charlotte simply took it on the chin and offered her gratitude for his generous assistance. While Darren didn't say anything in response, she could see it was annoying the heck out of him, knowing he was unable to get a rise out of her. So much so that soon enough he gave up on being an arse to her for the most part, as there became little point to it, it apparently no longer feeding his ego. And without that distraction to be had, Charlotte's natural charm and charisma shone through in front of the camera and she was rapidly cementing her position as a genuine star of the show. Much to Darren's clear and obvious displeasure.

Later that week, with her crafting team having scored a clean sweep of victories so far, Charlotte was counting down the days until filming finished for the weekend. But rather than returning straight home as she ordinarily might, she was looking forward to taking a shortish train trip across to Liverpool to celebrate Larry's second small-screen debut. There, she'd meet up with Calum, Stanley, Joyce, and Beryl, plus anybody else Larry had extended an invite to, and Charlotte couldn't wait.

On Thursday, as was the norm, the BBC reception area was teeming with people. With so many folks standing about, or sitting and waiting, it was easy to imagine how many dreams of a career working for the iconic organisation had been made, and conversely, how many hopes may have been dashed, both in this very building. And among those in the queue, waiting patiently to be attended to by the reception team, was a certain fellow new to the building.

"Can I help, sir?" Sanjeev, the smiley receptionist asked.

"Oh, yes, please. I don't have an appointment, but I'm here to see Charlotte Newman, if that's not too much trouble?"

"Not a problem, sir. Do you know which department she's in?"

"Oh, well she's a presenter, actually, from a show called *The Crafternoon Showdown*," came the proud response.

"Ah. Being a bit of an amateur crafter myself, I'm looking forward to that programme," Sanjeev revealed, tapping away on his keyboard. "And may I say who is looking for her, sir?"

"Well, the thing is, I'm here to surprise her. If that's possible, of course?" the visitor said, flashing his pearly whites. "Don't worry, she knows me well. I'm her boyfriend.," he quickly added, lest the receptionist get the wrong idea.

"Say no more, sir. How about I phone her production office and ask them to send her down? I can say she's had a parcel delivered just now, and it's in need of her signature in order to be released."

"Perfect. If you wouldn't mind?"

"But I'll still need your name to issue a visitor's pass."

"Of course. My name is Calum. Calum Whitlock."

Meanwhile, as this was happening, Darren was parked on the corner of a desk in the production office. He was clutching a small handful of paper receipts, fanning his face with them. "I wouldn't mind being reimbursed something this decade," he said jovially, but it was clear from his expression that he was being serious. "The last payment took three months to land in my bank account."

Phillipa eased back in her chair, smiling gently as she shook her head from side to side, unbothered by Darren's seeming impatience. "Uh-huh. So they're more expenses directly related to the promotion of the show, are they? Like the last lot were?"

"Hey, I'm out there socialising, getting the word out about our show with the movers and shakers, I'll have you know," he offered with a smirk. "If only other hosts on the show were as willing to put the hard yards in as I am."

"Hmm, well I'm not sure Charlotte, your co-host, has much use for taking attractive blondes out to expensive restaurants," Phillipa suggested, skimming through the receipts Darren had just handed over to her.

Open-mouthed, Darren shot her a look. "I'll have you know they were all business meetings. And that's just the small sacrifices I make for this show. Unlike others."

Phillipa laughed. She'd worked with him for long enough to know what he was like. "You're just bitter with Lotti because you're no longer the golden boy around here," she observed. And judging by his pained expression, it was clear that Phillipa had struck a nerve. "Make yourself useful, Darren, and grab that call that's coming through while I do this for you?"

Darren appeared mortally wounded by Phillipa's remark as he reached for the ringing phone. "Yes, hello?" he answered. "This is Mr Sacrifice," he added, sneering in Phillipa's direction. "Charlotte?" he then said to the caller. "No, she's not here," he replied, knowing full well he'd seen her just a moment before.

"Darren!" Phillipa chastised him. "She's right outside!"

"Of course I'll take a message," Darren offered helpfully, with no actual intention of doing so, only pretending to reach for a pen and paper. "Calum Whitlock?" he said, listening on. "Oh, but it's a surprise, is it? Yes, I see," Darren answered.

And then Calum's name suddenly clicked, as one Darren recognised.

"Wait, Mr Whitlock is down in reception waiting for her?" he asked, still listening to what he was being told. "Oh, don't worry about pretending she has a parcel," he advised to Sanjeev. "How about I come down personally and show the fellow up? I'll make sure Charlotte doesn't know a thing."

"What kind of mischief are you planning?" Phillipa asked, arching an eyebrow as Darren concluded the call.

"*Moi?*" Darren asked, sliding himself off the desk. "I'm just being a helpful colleague," he assured her. "I'll show you who the golden boy is."

Shortly, down at the reception desk, Darren cast his eye over the name badges until he located Sanjeev. There were a number of receptionists, after all, and he couldn't be expected to remember each one of them by sight (or that was his opinion, at least).

"Hello, mate," said Darren. "You just phoned. I'm here for—"

"Yes, over there, sir. It's the well-dressed fellow in the smart suit. The one with the closely trimmed beard," Sanjeev directed, pointing to the seats by the window. "Oh, and I hope your colleague likes her surprise," he cheerfully added.

"I've no doubt she will," Darren said, adopting his friendliest of smiles as he strolled across the marbled tiles. "Hi, is it Calum?"

he asked upon arrival, holding out his hand and hoping he'd got it right, as there was more than one visitor presently sitting there that matched Sanjeev's description.

"Yes, that's me," Calum said, accepting the handshake as he pushed himself out of his chair.

"I'm Darren. It's a pleasure to meet you."

Having listened to some of Charlotte's complaints about the man, Calum was surprised to find Darren so amiable.

"So, you're here to surprise our Lotti, I believe?" Darren asked, leading the way towards the lifts.

"That's the plan, yes. You see we're both attending a function in Liverpool tomorrow, so I thought I'd come over a day early and surprise her," Calum explained. "I believe there are a few wonderful restaurants to try in Manchester?"

"Oh, you'll eat like a king," Darren advised. "I know for a fact that Charlotte is keen on some of our local eateries."

During the brief journey in the lift, Calum elaborated a bit on their function in Liverpool, explaining how it was the launch party for the advertising campaign that Charlotte's good friend Larry was featured in.

"Fraud awareness is such a very important topic," Darren offered, sounding as if he cared, as the doors opened. Then, after a short walk, "This is the sweatshop," he joked, leading Calum through to the studio. "Why don't you take a seat here and I'll go and fetch Charlotte for you."

"I appreciate that, Darren. Thank you for helping me out."

"*Pfft*," Darren said in answer, waving his hand as if it were his enormous pleasure. "Not a problem, Calum. And there was me thinking you were here to beat me up," he added with a laugh.

Calum smiled politely. "Beat you up?" he asked, responding to what seemed to him like a rather bizarre statement. He knew Darren and Charlotte may have had their differences, but still, as far as he was aware, there was certainly no need for fisticuffs, surely? "Sorry. Why would I beat you up?" Calum asked, slightly confused.

Darren cleared his throat, grinning like he was enjoying himself. "Why?" he asked, as if this had been something of a stupid question. "Well because Charlotte and I kissed, of course," he whispered, just before setting off to find Charlotte. "Did she not tell you?" he called over his shoulder.

"Wait!" Calum called after him. "What do you mean you and Charlotte kissed!"

Chapter Twenty-Five

"Oh, would you just look at this place," Joyce said, running her hand across one of the crisp white tablecloths in the colossal hotel function room. "You know, this is a touch of luxury right here. Right up my street, it is, what with me being such a classy lady."

"Classy lady?" Beryl replied. "Is this the same classy lady who managed to tuck a bit of her skirt into her knickers on the boat journey over, giving the entire lounge an unexpected glimpse of her backside?"

"Well, that'll be the fault of that large gin you forced me to drink during the sailing."

"Always blaming the gin," Beryl responded, along with a sad shake of her head. "I've had a gin as well," she had to remind her friend. "But you don't see me making a spectacle of myself."

Larry, for his part, wandered over to the raised stage at the far end of the room, staring wide-eyed in awe. It was daunting to know that in only a few short hours, the venue would be completely heaving at the seams with, from what he understood, well over four hundred guests. And, as the leading man in the adverts, Larry was to be featured prominently in the proceedings, due to be interviewed right there, centre stage, which did nothing to calm his heightened anxiety levels. Furthermore, it wasn't just those turning up in person that Larry had to worry about. In addition, the bank's PR machine had arranged for the entire evening to be live-streamed, such was the desire to bring the subject of fraud prevention to as wide an audience as possible.

"You're going to be standing onstage?" Stanley asked, taking up a position next to his old buddy. "On your own?"

"I don't think so, Stan. I hope the other empty chairs arranged up there will mean I'll at least have some company."

"So they'll ask you a few questions and then show the adverts you starred in? Is that the plan?"

"I think so," Larry replied, swallowing hard as he ran through, in his mind, the events to come.

"Are you nervous at all?" Stanley enquired.

Larry nodded. "A little bit, yes."

"Ah. You know what you need to do to stop feeling nervous?" Stanley offered. "It's what I did when I played a donkey in the Christmas panto at school."

Larry looked down at his wise companion. "Yeah? Go on," he said, happy to hear whatever young Stanley might have to say.

"You need to imagine yourself naked," Stanley insisted, presenting one particular, salient pearl of wisdom gleaned from his time on the earth.

Larry smiled. "Are you not supposed to imagine the audience naked rather than yourself...?" he asked.

"Are you? Oh. Herm, that might make more sense, actually," Stanley admitted, realising he just may have been getting it wrong all these years. Then, with his eyes still fixed on the stage, Stanley reached out, taking Larry's hand in his. "Anyway, you don't have anything to worry about. You'll be brilliant."

"I will?"

"Of course," Stanley said, giving Larry's hand a little squeeze. "So relax, 'cause you'll be fine."

"In that case, Stan, I think I'll let everybody keep their clothes on. Because knowing my good buddy has the utmost confidence in me is all I'll need to help get me through it."

But Larry also took some comfort in knowing he'd have his cheerleading section present, with Joyce, Beryl, and Mollie having already arrived earlier along with Stanley, and Charlotte and Calum due to join them a bit later on. (Sadly, Carole could not attend, as her sciatica had been acting up.) And it was nice to spend some quality time in each other's company again. He did see the others periodically, such as at their weekly Crafternoon sessions. But after their action-packed adventure to Center Parcs, it was nice to have much of the same gang back together for another special outing. Of course he had his friends in the nursing home to keep him company, but it just wasn't the same. Not like the current crew. As such, he was determined to make the most of their time together, savouring each and every single moment as best he could. It seemed the same, however, could not be said for all of the others, as…

"Joyce and Beryl have fallen asleep."

"What? How's that again?" Larry responded, asking Stanley to repeat himself.

Stan, having returned to the function room after a short tour of the hotel lobby, had just rejoined Larry. "Joyce and Beryl have fallen asleep," he repeated. "They told me they wanted to take a load off, and they did, parking themselves down on a sofa in the reception area. But then they both promptly fell asleep."

"Oh, dear. Is that my cue that I've spent a bit too long in here?" Larry replied.

"No, it's not that, Larry. It's just that Beryl and Joyce are snoring really loud, you see, and I didn't know what to do with them."

"How loudly?" Larry asked.

"Hmm," said Stanley, thinking for a moment. "Well, I reckon they sound like mum's old car when the exhaust pipe had a hole in it," Stanley put forth. "Anyway, I pretended like I didn't know them, because everybody in the check-in queue was staring."

"I'd have probably done the same," Larry said with a laugh, placing an arm across Stanley's shoulders. "Come on. We don't want the police called, so let's go and give the noisy pair a good nudge before they disturb the entire hotel."

"It's probably because of the long journey over here," Stanley suggested, yawning at the very thought of it.

"You're probably correct, Stan. That and the copious amounts of gin they've had over the course of the day so far."

* * *

"Right! I can't work with that odious, obnoxious oaf a moment longer," Charlotte growled, quickly closing the door of the production office behind her.

She'd tried her best, of course, but her plan to kill Darren with kindness was now in tatters. Now, it seemed, she wanted simply to kill him.

Phillipa slowly lowered her pen, surprised to see an ordinarily even-keeled Charlotte so clearly out of sorts first thing in the morning. "We're talking about your co-star?" Phillipa ventured. "Please, take a seat."

Charlotte did as instructed, placing her palms on the surface of Phillipa's desk to brace herself. "I just..." she started to say, but the anger blocked anything else from emerging.

"I'll get us a coffee," Phillipa suggested, making her way over to her percolator. "I've noticed a wee bit of tension this week. As much as Darren tried to hide it," she said over her shoulder. "But I figured it was sour grapes on his part because your team has been wiping the floor with his?"

Charlotte took several deep breaths, digging her fingernails into Phillipa's desktop. She was grateful the desk was made of hardwood, as otherwise she might have damaged it.

"It's sour grapes all around, at this point," she was finally able to reveal. "In fact, the grapes are now..." Charlotte said, searching for just the right words.

"Raisins?" Phillipa suggested, placing a coffee down for each of them.

"Raisins," Charlotte agreed. "Big, fat, nasty raisins."

Phillipa sat herself down, leaning forward, her elbows on the desk. "What's Darren done, Lotti?" she asked, adopting her finest *I'm-here-to-listen* expression.

"Done? Well, for starters, his bloody mischief nearly got me dumped by my boyfriend! That's what he's done."

Encouraged to take a moment to compose herself, Charlotte was soon able to elaborate further. She spoke again about Darren's initial deceit in getting her to travel over to Manchester a day early. Which, in itself, wasn't too dreadful, she had to admit, but it was the deception that bothered her, plus missing her boyfriend's birthday because of it. She also complained about that whole business with Darren promising her friends a slot on the show, even though that turned out to be complete bollocks because Darren never even had the power to do that. And then, of course, there was that issue of the unwanted kiss he stole, and his subsequent rotten attitude, ever since, after she'd rebuffed his advances, making all sorts of snide remarks to her every chance he got when nobody else was around to hear.

"And then to top it all off," Charlotte continued, nearing the end of her report. "Then, he then goes and tells my boyfriend, who'd travelled all the way over here to surprise me, that it was me that instigated the kiss! It took some doing last night to convince Calum that Darren's claims were a load of rubbish. And fortunately, I have a wonderful boyfriend. So I suppose he didn't really need all *that* much convincing, to be honest. But still, it's the idea that Darren would even do that. I think he's trying to get me to quit the bloody show."

Phillipa set her cup of coffee down, realising she hadn't taken even a single sip from it. She nodded sympathetically, as it appeared that Charlotte had finished. "Calum Whitlock? Is that your boyfriend?" she said. "Ah, so that'll be what Darren was up to yesterday," she remarked.

"You knew about this?"

"No, no, of course not, Lotti," Phillipa assured her. "No, I'd simply overheard Darren's conversation on the phone. I had absolutely no idea what he was up to, but it all makes sense now. I wondered why he was so... giddy, I guess you could say, when he went down to reception."

"*Grrr*," Charlotte answered, grinding her teeth at the thought of Darren making trouble for her like that.

"You say you think Darren wants you to quit the show?" Phillipa asked.

"I don't think, Phillipa, I know it. He told me as much, saying there was a long queue of girls behind me who'd be happy to do anything for him to get the job, all of them just waiting to take my place," Charlotte explained. "But aside from having to deal with Darren's nonsense, I adore this job, Phillipa, and the last thing I want to do is quit."

Phillipa took a moment to digest what was, after all, a lot of information to process. "They're some serious allegations, Lotti. Are you wanting to make a formal complaint against him?"

Charlotte considered this course of action for a moment before shaking her head. "No," she decided. "No, I'm not sure I want to take things that far. All I want is for him to tell Calum the truth about the kissing incident, and for him to just be civil to me, Phillipa. If I do something wrong during filming, then I'm more than happy to take criticism, of course, as I'll learn from it. But what I don't like is when it feels like I'm being constantly browbeaten by him, and all because his fragile ego can't seem to handle rejection."

"Okay," Phillipa said, formulating a plan. "Why don't we all get together later. I'll be there with another member of the production team for support, and we'll bring Darren along and we can talk about the best way of moving forward."

Similar to her talk with Larry, Charlotte now felt like a weight had been lifted from her shoulders. Only this time around she was speaking with somebody who might actually be able to do something about the situation beyond lending a helpful ear. "Thanks, Phillipa," Charlotte told her. "And I'm sorry for dumping all my problems on you."

"It's absolutely fine, Charlotte. And from what you've told me, Darren's behaviour is the furthest thing from acceptable. It's in all of our interests, the show included, to reach a workable solution. So, I'll arrange a meeting for us at the end of today's filming, all right?"

Charlotte pushed her chair back, ready to get to work, and relieved that any unpleasantness she might suffer from Darren would soon come to a hopeful end. "Oh, darn," she said, upon realising what Phillipa had just said. "Unfortunately, I can't do it today," she realised. "Do you remember me telling you about my friend Larry, in the television adverts? Well, it's the fancy launch party this evening in Liverpool, hence the surprise visit from Calum, as the two of us will be going together. I'll need to leave promptly, right after work, in order to make it over there in time."

"Oh," Phillipa said. "That's... tonight?"

Charlotte wondered why Phillipa suddenly had a funny look on her face. "We can just postpone until Monday...?" Charlotte proposed, but she could tell from Phillipa's worried expression that there was somehow more to it than that.

"Darren left a message this morning," Phillipa revealed. "In fact I was just about to gather up the troops to inform everyone, right before you came in."

"A message?" Charlotte asked, unclear as to how this might affect everyone.

"Yes. Apparently he's woken up with a toothache, and has made an emergency appointment with the dentist," Phillipa explained. "Which means he won't be in until later."

"Uhm, okay?" Charlotte said, still not sure what the problem was, exactly. Because a Darren-free morning, as far as she was concerned, could only be considered a good thing.

"He'll be coming in at noon. Which means we'll have to push the filming schedule back to accommodate," Phillipa clarified. "Charlotte, we've already got all of the contestants lined up and ready, so I couldn't really say no."

"If we push it back, that means a late day, and I won't be able to get to Liverpool in time," Charlotte answered, the full gravity of the situation now presenting itself to her as the penny finally dropped. "Darn it, Phillipa, Darren knew I was leaving straight after filming! I told him yesterday when I was making an extra effort to be nice to him. And then all of a sudden he develops a toothache? I'm just not buying it, Phillipa. I have to believe he's made this up, and he's done this to me on purpose."

"I'm so sorry, Lotti. Truly I am."

Chapter Twenty-Six

"You know, kiddo, you're just about the handsomest fella I've ever had hanging off my arm," Mollie suggested, extending her elbow in Stanley's direction.

"You don't scrub up too badly yourself, Auntie Mollie," Stanley offered, linking the arm thrust before him.

"Scrub up, indeed?" Mollie answered, happy enough to accept such an interesting compliment. "You've been listening to your father too much, I think," she said with a laugh.

Stanley escorted his date down the sweeping staircase towards the spacious hotel lobby, with Mollie treading carefully, cautious she didn't put one of her heels through the hem of her super-expensive rented ballgown.

"Am I even more handsome than your Sam?" Stanley asked.

"Hmm," said Mollie. "Well, it's a tough call, but I suppose you just edge it, Stan."

At the foot of the stairs, the pre-event drinks reception was already well underway, with the waiting staff dashing around dispensing glasses of fizz. "Is all that free?" Stanley asked, once they'd safely arrived with Mollie's dress still intact.

"Sure is," Mollie was happy to advise, as she was immediately approached by an attentive server.

"Can I offer you a glass of champagne?" asked the waitress.

"I s'pose it'd be rude to refuse," Stanley said with a giggle, reaching up for one of the fancy glasses.

"Oi!" Mollie said, playfully slapping Stanley's hand away. "Yes, thank you," she responded to the woman kindly attending them, availing herself of one of the crystal flutes on offer.

"Would sir like a glass of sparkling grape juice instead?" the waitress offered Stanley, as a non-alcoholic alternative.

"Yes, please," Stanley agreed politely, reluctantly adjusting the trajectory of his hand towards the opposite side of the tray.

"A-ha," said Mollie, waving her free, unladen hand. "There's Larry and the others."

Fresh from their afternoon nap on the reception sofa, Joyce and Beryl were standing on either side of Larry like they were his glamorous security detail for the evening. "The champagne is free," Beryl whispered to Mollie upon their arrival. *"Free."*

"I know," Mollie answered with a chuckle. "It also goes to your head quickly," she cautioned, sounding like she was speaking from personal experience. "Oh, we'll need to make sure we get a group photograph at some point, looking as smart as we all do," she remarked, observing their happy little group.

"Ladies and gentlemen!" a well-tailored fellow called out, his large, booming voice effectively bringing the bustling lobby to a gentle hush just then. "If you'd like to take your drinks and make your way through to the function room, the evening's festivities will commence in approximately fifteen minutes!"

Immediately, folks began advancing through the set of large chestnut doors leading to the function room where Larry and the others had been exploring a bit earlier in the day.

"I hope we're not sitting too far from the loo," Joyce remarked. "I've a feeling this champagne is going to run straight through my bladder."

Larry allowed those closer to the function hall doors to enter first. In fact he held back, not moving from his position in the lobby, and causing the others in his small group to follow suit, as they likely had the same concern as he did. Larry shifted his weight from one foot to the other, anxiously fidgeting with his new banknote-themed bowtie as he lingered there.

"Are you okay there, Larry?" Mollie enquired. "You're not feeling too nervous, I hope? Or is it the fact that—"

"Charlotte and Calum aren't here yet," Larry interjected, finishing Mollie's words for her. "Yeah," he said, flicking his arm forward to look down at his watch. "I thought they'd be here by now...?"

Mollie reached into her handbag, removing her phone. "Let me check," she said, attempting to unlock her mobile. "Cheese and crackers, the bloody thing has died," she advised, for some reason giving her phone a little shake as if this would imbue restorative powers to a drained battery.

"Didn't Mum say they were coming by train?" Stanley asked. "Does anyone know what time it should've reached the station?"

"Forty-five minutes ago. So they ought to have been here by now," a concerned Larry replied, directing his attention to the revolving glass doors at the hotel's entrance, hoping to see their two missing friends making their way through.

"They'll be here soon enough, I expect," Beryl said with confidence, reaching for more fizz from one of the remaining servers, swapping old glass for new. "Much obliged," she told the waiter.

But they couldn't tarry forever, as food was being served and the proceedings were set to begin in not too long a time. Hopeful that Calum and Charlotte would soon join them inside, they had no choice but to make their way in.

With the room fully seated, a portly chap in a smart dinner jacket appeared on stage, sporting a smile as wide as his middle. "Ladies and gentlemen," he said, tapping a finger on his microphone to ensure all eyes were upon him. "Ladies and gentlemen, I'm Barry Sincott, your host for the evening, and National Savings Bank is honoured to welcome you for what's certain to be a most enlightening evening, culminating in the debut screening of our national advertising campaign showcasing our fraud prevention efforts. As well as hearing what we're doing to protect our customers, we'll also be inviting some special guests on stage to share their experiences with us. And then, finally, the band will be out to play and delight us with some music so we can dance our way into the early hours," he told those assembled. "But on the subject of fraud prevention, please don't let me *steal* too much of your time just now, as I believe the first course is about to be served," he added, putting a huge emphasis on the word "steal." It was meant to be a joke. And everyone in attendance could tell it was meant to be a joke, based on the *aren't-I-terribly-clever* look on Barry's face that told them he was fully expecting a laugh.

But even Stanley, young as he was, couldn't help but notice what a rubbish attempt at humour it was. "Is that the best he can do?" he whispered to his Auntie Mollie. "I mean, he's probably had weeks to prepare, right? And that's the best he could come up with?"

Looking around the room, it was quickly evident that Stanley was the youngest by a considerable margin. And, for many, corporate bank events were often considered to be stuffy, formal affairs, only made bearable by the consumption of any free booze that might be available. A luxury that Stanley was, of course, too young to avail himself of on this fine occasion.

Still, the food was bloomin' good, in Stanley's expert culinary opinion, with prawns of some sort for starters, and a serving of beef that was the best he'd ever eaten. Not so fortunate, however, was that their table continued to have a pair of gaping big holes around it on account of the two seats that remained empty.

Conscious of the frown lines on Larry's face, as well as her own worry in regard to what was causing them, Mollie leaned over to him. "How about I pop up to my room and give the old phone a quick charge?" she suggested. "Hopefully we'll find out where the late twins are."

But before any response could be given, Barry reappeared on stage, once again tapping his microphone to bring order to the room.

"Ah. Maybe in just a few minutes," Mollie advised Larry, before leaning back in her chair, not wishing to get up and leave just as the announcer was about to announce something, as she thought it might appear rude.

"Oh, here we go. He's going to come out with another rubbish joke, isn't he?" Stanley said to Mollie, with one eye on the stage.

"I don't know about you," Barry said, patting his tum. "But I'm fit to burst after that wonderful meal. How about a good round of applause for the hard-working kitchen staff," he said, clapping one hand against his microphone. Then, once the appreciation subsided, he continued. "Now, just before the desserts are served, we'll have a team of helpers moving through the room selling charity raffle tickets, with some marvellous prizes on offer." Barry then turned, making as if he was going to exit the stage, but then spun around like he'd just remembered something important. "Oh, and on the subject of desserts," he said with a deadpan expression. "Did you hear about the reporter who investigated the ice cream shop owner for fraud?" he asked, pausing for a moment or two. "Apparently he had the inside scoop," he revealed, giving the answer to a smattering of pained groans, but sadly for Barry, no laughs to speak of.

Stanley shot Mollie a look. "I told you, Auntie Mollie, didn't I? This man's jokes are *horrible*," he said. "They're like something from a Christmas cracker."

Mollie placed a finger up to her lips. "Stan," she admonished him, although she couldn't really disagree with his assessment.

With twenty pounds burning a hole in his pocket courtesy of his dad for just such an occasion, Stanley was generous with his money, purchasing several strips of tickets for a good cause, that cause being a whopping great wicker gift basket, the largest of the prizes. "Are you eying up that giant hamper filled with lovely chocolates, by any chance?" Joyce asked, having checked out the items herself before committing.

"You've got to be in it to win," Stanley replied, fanning out his raffle tickets like he was playing a hand of poker.

With pudding soon dispatched, poor Larry didn't even have time to loosen his belt a notch or two before being whisked away by one of the organisers for the brief walk to the stage. And heading up there to keep him company was Geoff, who'd ably portrayed the bad guy in their little series of adverts. In addition, several of the bank's head honchos were apparently going to join them also, to talk about all things fraud.

And the audience was generous with their appreciation, welcoming their guests on stage with rapturous applause (thankful as they were, amongst other considerations, that this would mean an end to Barry's dreadful jokes). And the most rapturous among the rapturous was Joyce and the gang, still cheering their friend long after the rest of the room had quietened down.

"That's some fan club you've brought along with you!" Barry remarked, as he directed Larry towards his seat.

In response, Larry smiled politely, straining his eyes due to the powerful spotlight presently trained on him. "I pay them by the hour," came Larry's wry response, as a stagehand attached a microphone to his jacket.

With all of the panel guests shortly mic'd up, Stanley watched on with his eyelids soon starting to feel like lead weights. It wasn't that he was bored, necessarily. It's just that, other than a few snippets here and there, he didn't really understand what they were going on about, especially the bits where they were talking about legal mumbo jumbo. And he didn't appear to be alone, he observed, as some of the other people at nearby tables seemed to watch on with glazed eyes also.

But as soon as the panel started talking about real-life scams, frauds, and swindles, Stanley's ears quickly perked up, same as the rest of the audience, as this was now much more interesting. There were audible gasps, in fact, as representatives from the bank detailed case studies of customers who'd been duped, with some losing upwards of a million pounds simply for being a bit too trusting. And the speakers were at pains to explain how it wasn't just the elderly among the population who fell victim to callous criminals, as they cited several recent investigations involving young people taken advantage of on social media and popular gaming sites.

Indeed, Stanley would be returning to school the following week as something of a guru on the subject. And that was the entire point of both the evening and the campaign — to educate by highlighting the devious nature of certain factions, demonstrating just how easy it was to be caught out if you didn't maintain your wits about you.

"Wow," Barry said, puffing out his pudgy cheeks in response to what he'd just heard. "How about that, folks?" he said, along with a grave shake of the head. "After that insight, we all know what an internet scammer's favourite sport is, don't we?" he asked. "That's right..." he said, answering his own question. "It's *phishing*."

With the response to this latest pun being tepid at best, Barry moved things along to tonight's preview of the television adverts that were due to start airing the following week. As such, all eyes were now focused on two colossal monitors positioned on either side of the stage. Well, not all eyes, as Larry's at this pivotal moment were currently directed towards his and his friends' table, and in particular the two seats that still remained vacant.

However, just as Barry was about to give the instruction to proceed with the first of the clips, Larry noticed a sliver of light pierce through the darkness at the rear of the room, indicating somebody had briefly opened the doors to the hall and had just stepped inside. Hopeful, he watched as a lone figure came into view, moving at pace and weaving its way through the maze of tables. Larry was delighted when he realised it was Calum, attempting to find his seat with as minimal disruption as possible. The only negative, however, was the fact that as far as Larry could tell, Calum appeared to be unaccompanied.

Over at the table, a flustered Calum fiddled nervously with a cufflink as he greeted Mollie and the others with an apologetic smile.

"Would you look what the cat dragged in!" Joyce remarked in welcome.

"Hmm? What's that? There's a cat?" Beryl entered in, having just been roused from a brief nap induced by too much fizz. "I love the little devils, but I'm deathly allergic..." she offered, before nodding off again.

"Nice of you to join us," Mollie said to their new arrival as he took the open seat beside her, giving him a friendly pat on his arm once he'd settled in.

"Oh, Moll. What a nightmare that was," Calum answered. "I didn't think I'd make it here at all because of the bloody traffic."

"Is Lotti following?" Mollie asked, glancing towards the doors to see if Calum's other half was on her way behind him.

"Ugh, about that," Calum said, rolling his eyes while releasing a pained groan. "No, she's not coming, Moll," he advised. "But it's not her fault," he quickly added, wishing to make clear that his exasperation about the whole situation had nothing at all to do with her. "I tried phoning you to let you know, but your phone wasn't—"

"Wasn't receiving calls, because it's dead as a doornail," Mollie stated. "I was going to recharge the battery but I haven't yet had a chance. Sorry."

"Charlotte's had a bit of a situation at work," Calum revealed, being careful to whisper, as the first of the commercials had just started playing up on the monitors. He leaned in closer, so that he wouldn't disturb those around them. "She's had a bit of a situation at work, Moll," he said again. "She's had to work very late. I waited as long as I could, right until the last minute. Well, *past* the last minute, actually. Hence, me missing the train, and having to make a mad dash in an Uber to get here. Alone, unfortunately, as there was no chance she was going to get away soon enough to join me."

"Oh, no," Mollie said, flicking her attention towards the stage, as she knew poor Larry would be heartbroken, along with the rest of them.

"Do you think Larry will be terribly offended she's not here?" Calum asked.

"No, not offended, Calum, because he's such a lovely person," Mollie answered. "But sadly, I don't suppose that will stop him from being gutted his best mate isn't present to share this extra special evening with him."

Chapter Twenty-Seven

Coronation Street was one of those divisive programmes in the nursing home (and, quite possibly, further afield). It was divisive in that, for some, it was compulsive viewing, while others would find themselves reaching for the remote control the instant the iconic introduction tune kicked into life.

But tonight, even those at the nursing home who'd normally turn up their nose at the thought of wasting another half hour of their life on the show were glued to the TV set in the recreation room. And it wasn't solely the residents who had their eyes presently fixed on the screen either, as Emma, their home manager, had extended the invite to a wider, select audience as well.

And the reason for everyone's collective interest in what was a staple of living rooms across the UK for over sixty years? Well, it wasn't the show, precisely, but rather a certain advert that was due to be aired during the commercial break.

"Here, Larry!" Godfrey, one of Larry's mates, called over. "How's about I get your autograph now, and when you're famous, which you will be very soon, I reckon, I can stick it on that eBay website thingy and make a fortune!"

"You'd probably get more for the blank sheet of paper," Larry answered with a laugh, though reaching inside his blazer pocket for a pen anyway, happy to oblige. "As long as you aren't asking me to sign your wotsits, like that one lady did, who shall remain nameless," Larry advised, which produced a raised eyebrow from Godfrey, who appeared to want to know more about this intriguing story. But it was, perhaps, an anecdote to be shared at another time.

Keeping Larry company, in addition to his nursing home cohabitants, was a healthy contingent from the Crafternoon crew. And while Stanley didn't need asking twice to come along and support his friend Larry, the promise of a buffet after the programme aired was a most welcome bonus.

Unfortunately, in Charlotte's case, she was a notable absence once again. Already devastated at missing the launch party, her busy filming commitments during the week meant that, sadly, she would be unable to join them this time as well. But Larry certainly wasn't one to hold grudges, assuring Charlotte that he completely understood, but couldn't wait to catch up with her on her return. She was also left with strict instructions to watch *Coronation Street* which, of course, she was delighted to agree to.

Meanwhile, back on the island, one of the soap opera characters on the show had just been witnessed having a drink thrown in their face. A nervous anticipation started to build in the recreation room as those assembled sensed this might be the sort of cliffhanger moment that would lead directly into a commercial break. And they were correct. A shared cheer rang out, rising in volume as the adverts commenced. But when it became clear this first advert was just a boring spot for some rubbish washing machine cleaner, the cheer quickly fizzled out. Then, when the next advert started, the hopeful cheer erupted again, like football supporters shouting on their favourite team.

"This is it!" cried one of the residents, when Larry's character was spotted near a cash machine, with another well-dressed but rather sketchy-looking fellow lurking behind. But any hopes of actually hearing Larry's acting skills in action were soon quashed on account of all the whooping and hollering going on amidst the room.

Larry didn't really need to watch his performance, as after all, he knew what was going to happen in it. Instead, smiling away to himself, he ran his eyes around the room, honoured that so many of his precious friends were there with him, supporting him all the way. He'd watched enough harrowing news reports of pensioners, like him, holed up on their own all day with barely a soul to speak to. Too many, in fact, a reality which deeply saddened him. All the more reason he was so grateful to boast such a wild and wonderful group of friends around him now.

"This autograph is going on eBay!" Godfrey yelled once the advert concluded, holding the procured signature up like a racetrack punter waving his betting slip. "Right, then! Now let's go and get stuck into that buffet..."

※ ※ ※

Having received a broadly encouraging response to their Crafternoon call centre efforts the previous week, Joyce, Beryl, and Larry were confident of a bumper turnout at the next Sewcial Club meeting. And so, when Thursday afternoon arrived, they were first on the scene to ensure that the doors would be opened, the tea urn bubbling, and a warmest of receptions extended to each arrival. And they weren't alone, as it should happen. Sharing a sense of collective guilt for the previous confusion, Mollie, Abigail, and Bonnie were also early arrivals, eager to make sure everything went without a hitch.

Also on hand, appearing right on cue, was quite possibly one of the most welcome visitors they'd ever had grace the property, at least as far as young Stanley was concerned.

"They're here!" Stanley called out, sprinting up the exterior steps, through the modest church foyer, and into the main hall. "They're here!" he shouted again, barely able to contain his glee.

"Well what are you doing in here? Go and help them, then," Mollie suggested playfully.

"I just thought I should tell you!" Stanley responded, before spinning round on his heels and heading back out the way he'd come.

Now parked up was a white van, manoeuvred up to the rear entrance of the church via the carpark. But this wasn't just any white van, nosiree — a fact of which Stanley was acutely aware, having been expecting the vehicle and keeping a careful eye out for it. No, this white van sported the impressive image of an oversized doughnut on either side, with a bit of delectable jam bursting forth from each. "You're from the bakery?" Stan asked the moment the driver climbed out, though it was more of a comment than a question.

"Whatever gave you that idea?" the fellow replied, standing directly next to one of the giant doughnut illustrations with a smile on his face.

As promised, Calum had come good on his offer to provide an array of baked goods (and, in the case of doughnuts, deep-fried delights) to welcome the happy hordes back to their beloved Crafternoon Sewcial Club. And as the van doors opened, Stanley was immediately struck by an aroma so divine that it was like he'd been transported to heaven, sitting on a cloud.

"Do you want to help me get this lot inside?" the driver asked, amused but not surprised by Stanley's reaction.

"Oh, I do. I really *do*," Stanley immediately agreed, apparently having just discovered his dream vocation.

With a feast fit for a king or queen (minus some lost inventory, mysteriously going missing during the short journey from the carpark to inside the church) the Crafternoon Sewcial Club was fully staffed, open for business, and raring to go. All that was missing now were the members to fill all of the seats they'd laid out.

Indeed, as they waited in the empty hall for those soon to arrive, Mollie reflected to the others on how this sort of giddy, hopeful anticipation was what Charlotte must have felt in the early days of the club. And it was in contemplating this point that made them all realise just what a marvellous job Charlotte had done, growing the membership to the numbers it currently enjoyed. Conversely, there was the awful thought that, in only a short few weeks, Charlotte's positive work had all very nearly come unravelled like the stitching in a cheap jumper. But, with some due diligence on their part, that had fortunately been sorted. Or so they hoped.

"What if nobody turns up?" Stanley asked, breaking their lingering moment of reflection. "I mean, what would happen to *that* lot?" he said, gesturing to the table of doughnuts and assorted cakes. "I'd hate to see all those lovelies go to waste."

"Hmm," Larry answered, thoughtfully caressing his chin. "I suppose if that were to happen, we'd have no option but to throw them all out for the seagulls."

"Seagulls?" a horrified Stanley asked, but the smile on his old pal's face set him at ease, realising his friend was only teasing him. Quickly recovering from the shock, Stanley thought of a pun he reckoned Larry might enjoy. "If that were to happen..." he said, pausing for dramatic effect.

"Yes?" Larry asked.

"If that were to happen, Larry, then I'd say things had taken a tern for the worse," Stanley replied, grinning madly. "Get it, Larry? A *TERN* for the worse?"

"Aye, lad. That's very good," Larry answered, chuckling away, as he couldn't help but be impressed by young Stan's wordplay.

As had happened in the past, Stanley was soon dispatched to keep an eye out for the bus that would deliver many of the club's members, with him ready and willing to help those who needed an extra pair of hands.

But today, Stanley wasn't alone, because one by one, Larry and the others slowly filtered out onto the front steps of the church, all of them anxious as to how many people might actually be arriving on that bus. Of course, not everybody came by public transport, but, like an exit poll in a local election, it would offer an early indicator as to the final numbers.

So, outside the church in the sleepy village of Union Mills, a small handful of people with a collective interest in crafting had never been so interested to see a bus turn into Strang Road with its precious cargo of Crafternoon members onboard.

"Oh! I think... Is that...?" Larry offered, craning his neck, the first to catch a glimpse of what very much appeared to be the front of a bus.

"Yes! This is it!" Stanley was quick to confirm, poised and ready for action.

As the bus drew nearer, Stan rushed down the steps. But he didn't get too far at all before realising his services wouldn't be very much in demand. "It's... pretty empty?" he said, calling over to the others. "I think... I think I only see one person," he added, sounding confused and very much disappointed.

"Besides the driver, you mean? Or is it including the driver?" Larry asked, sounding disappointed as well.

"In addition to the driver," Stan clarified. "It looks like just some kid on the back seat, as near as I can tell from here. Unless there's someone else I can't see...?"

But there wasn't. In fact, the nearly empty bus didn't even bother to come to a halt at the designated stop, as there was no need. Instead, it continued on its route, trundling along with one lone child enjoying the bus all to himself, it would appear.

"Oh," said Stanley, lowering his head in despair. And even the thought of the entire refreshments table to himself wasn't enough to raise his spirits.

Bonnie wandered down to where he was, placing a gentle hand on Stanley's back. "Come on, mister," she said sympathetically, ushering him back towards the steps.

"We might still get some people arriving by car, or even on foot?" Stanley suggested, brightening up a bit, trying his best to sound optimistic. "There's still a good ten minutes before the start time, so there's hope, yeah?"

"I reckon you might be right, Stan," Bonnie was happy to agree.

Ever the gentleman, Larry held the door for the others, offering his stiffest of stiff upper lips as they were about to enter the church. "Wait! Hold on!" he shouted, scaring them half to death, and stopping them instantly in their tracks. "Over there. *Look*," he advised, with some urgency.

And with elevated heart rates, they all did as instructed. "It's another bus," Beryl pointed out, relating what they could all see.

A knowing expression washed over Stanley's face. "Oh, what a great dafty I am!" he chided himself, slapping a hand against his forehead. "That other bus must have been the school bus making its final drop-off. But this one's *our* bus. The one we're waiting for!"

"Don't feel so bad, I made the same mistake as you," Larry offered, feeling a bit daft himself for the confusion.

"So...?" Joyce said, turning to Stanley. She said this pleasantly but expectantly, as there was now work for the boy to do once more.

Stanley didn't need asking twice, however. "On it!" he said, tearing back down the stairs at a pace his mother likely wouldn't approve of.

And then, standing out on the pavement beside the street, Stanley chewed on one of his knuckles as the bus slowed down in preparation for the stop. He didn't want to jump the gun this time and make any assumptions. But as the bus drew near, it became exceedingly obvious that this was indeed the bus they were looking for. Stanley punched the air, never so happy to see a busload of wonderful crafters. "They're here!" Stanley hollered, for the benefit of the others. "And there's flippin' loads of them!"

Several minutes and multiple shuttle runs later, poor Stanley was well and truly earning his non-existent wages, humping a selection of bags from the bus stop over to the church. And as his aching arms were able to testify, serious crafters rarely travelled light.

But he didn't mind at all. Not one iota, as it should happen. Not even a smidge. Further, another thing he didn't mind, much to his surprise, was seeing the refreshments table soon attacked, the assortment of goodies quickly dwindling. For he knew that the Crafternoon Sewcial Club was back in business, not only with most of the existing members present but also a batch of new ones as well.

"Thank the stars," Larry whispered to Joyce and Beryl from the corner of his mouth, once he'd managed to conclude his initial round of tea-dispensing duties. "I think we may actually have pulled this one off, ladies, snatching victory from the jaws of defeat, as it were. Looks like a success, yeah?"

"I hear that," Joyce said, taking a noisy slurp of her tea as she appreciated the flurry of activity happening in the church hall, both creative and otherwise.

Beryl put her hands together, as if about to pray. Instead, she linked her fingers, stretching out her arms as she inverted her hands, giving her knuckles a good crack. "Right," she said, ready for action, while cracking her neck as well. "Stanley, pass me my crafting bag, will you?" she instructed. "I'm going in."

But before Beryl could set her crochet hook in motion, they were interrupted by a thunderous knock on the hardwood entrance door of the church, sounding very much like the good Lord himself wanted to attend their gathering.

"Flippin' heck," Joyce remarked. "Stan, will you be a dear and go let them in before they bloody put their fist straight through the door?" she asked, along with an audible tut-tut.

Stanley, ever diligent, was off like a whippet. But before he'd reached the other side of the hall, the metal latch raised and the heavy door began to creak open.

"Do you have room for one more?" someone asked, a moment before a smiling face appeared in the gap.

"Mum?" said Stanley, confused but delighted.

"Lotti?" Larry asked, looking over.

"Lotti?" Mollie asked, thrilled but also confused.

Stepping inside, a beaming Charlotte appeared, with Calum, who'd been close behind, soon by her side.

"Yay, Charlotte's back!" Bonnie shouted, serving to alert the rest of the room for anyone who wasn't already aware.

Charlotte threw her hands around Stanley, scooping him up in her arms. "Oh, it's so good to see you all," she said, planting a kiss on his cheek.

"What are you doing back?" Larry called out.

"Good to see you too, Larry!" Charlotte said with a laugh.

"You know what I mean!" Larry answered, skipping over for a cuddle. "We thought you were tied up filming for the next few weeks. We didn't expect you here!"

Charlotte released her grip on Stanley, now giving Larry a turn. "Nope, filming is done," she told him, pulling him in. "I quit," she advised simply, to both him and the others.

"Quit?" Mollie asked. "What do you mean quit?"

"Just what I said, Moll. I've quit the show," Charlotte admitted, sounding like a relieved woman. "I guess I was just missing you all too much," she said with a grin.

"So you're back?" Larry asked, cuddle now complete, pulling himself away from Charlotte, but continuing to rub her arm as if he was still checking to see if she was really there and not just a figment of his imagination.

"I sure am, Larry. I'm back for good."

Chapter Twenty-Eight

One week later...

"You're absolutely certain you didn't fancy something a little... well, warmer? And with, I don't know, cutlery and maybe a candle or two?" Calum enquired, taking a seat beside her on the slatted hardwood bench on Peel Promenade, overlooking the sea.

Charlotte wiped away a salt-induced tear, her hair rollicking about in the stiff sea breeze. "And miss that view?" she asked, appreciating the waves breaking against the sandy beach. "Not on your nelly, mister. Besides, if you're eating fish and chips, you should see where it's being sourced," she remarked. "The fish, I mean. Not the chips, obviously," she clarified.

"Well, unless they start farming sea potatoes," Calum said with a laugh. Calum then turned his attention to Stanley, who was presently being buffeted by the wind atop the long sea wall that separated the promenade from the beach, with him moving along the length of it like a drunk highwire act. "Stan, that's dinner!" he advised, holding up the large bag of food items with a giant fish printed on the side.

"Hmm, is it dinner or tea?" Charlotte pondered aloud. "Some people call it tea, even if there's no tea involved," she mused.

Charlotte ruminated a bit further about the subject of dinner and tea, the possible differences between the two, and how folks from various regions might generally refer to it. Eventually, she felt she was in danger of boring Calum, and even herself. As far as Calum, she needn't have worried, however, as pretty much any conversation with Charlotte was a pleasant one as far as he was concerned.

"You know," she said, shifting direction. "It's so nice doing things like this with you and Stan." At this, she couldn't resist staring down at the silver bracelet on her wrist that'd caught her eye for the umpteenth time. "And speaking of Stan, I can't believe my little boy gave me this," she said, chewing down on her lower lip in an exaggerated fashion.

"I didn't tell you this, Lotti. But he bought the raffle tickets at the launch party with his own money," Calum revealed. "And when his numbers were called, you'd honestly have thought he'd won a million-pound lottery by the look on his face. Although the poor lad was a touch intimidated when the spotlight caught up with him and all eyes in the room were upon him. But he was determined, and as I watched him walk on stage, I could see him making a beeline for this enormous chocolate hamper he'd been praying the earlier winners wouldn't snaffle. Then, at the last minute, he changed course and chose the bracelet for you."

"This tear isn't from the wind," Charlotte advised, wiping her cheek with the back of her hand. "Isn't he just the sweetest little boy?"

"Yeah, he's a good lad. You and his dad have done a wonderful job raising him."

Having worked up an appetite climbing this and jumping over that, Stanley finally joined them back at the bench, ready to get stuck into his double sausage & chips with pickled onion on the side.

"Plastic fork?" Calum offered, as Charlotte unwrapped her order of lovely fish & chips.

"*Pfft*," she said, waving away the offer. "If you use a fork then you're cheating," she insisted, ripping off an impressive chunk of battered cod with her bare hands. Or it could have been haddock. She wasn't sure. But before she could engage in any possible musings on the subject, Calum responded.

THE CRAFTERNOON SEWCIAL CLUB: SHOWDOWN

"I'll have to take your word for that," he said, deciding a more dainty approach to be in order, jabbing his little blue fork into a portion of his own dinner.

Stanley looked up, surveying the skies like he was looking for signs of alien aircraft. "You've got to watch out for the seagulls," he warned them. "If you're not too careful, then *whoosh*, they've swooped down on you and your tea is flying away, right before your eyes."

"Is it tea or dinner, Stan?" Charlotte asked with a smirk. But he was too engrossed in eating to care either way.

In the blink of an eye, Stan's polystyrene tray was empty apart from a small pool of vinegar. "Back in a bit!" he announced, before running and vaulting over the sea wall, landing on the soft golden sand on the other side, just beyond.

As Charlotte stuffed her empty food wrapper back inside the carrier bag it came from, her phone vibrated in her pocket. "Oh, which one is this going to be?" she asked herself aloud. Having earlier challenged the gang at Make It Sew with a particularly complex crochet project, she'd already received several calls asking for assistance, which she was of course more than happy to provide.

"It's not Larry again, is it?" Calum said with a laugh. "Honestly, he's openly admitted several times he's not really a crafter. But I suppose you have to give him ten out of ten for effort."

But Charlotte's cheery demeanour evaporated in an instant. "It's Phillipa," she said, panic lines forming on her face as she sat there staring at her mobile. "Darn it, if I wait too long to answer, I'll miss the call," she remarked, dithering. "What do you suppose she wants? Do you think they're going to ask for the clothes back that I bought on their credit card...?"

"Just answer it," Calum encouraged. "Don't worry, she likely just wants to check in with you or something."

In response, Charlotte placed her bag of trash down on the bench, rose to her feet, and then began pacing up the promenade with her phone pressed to her ear.

All alone now, Calum decided to join Stanley down on the beach, taking a short detour by way of the nearby bin. "Right, Stan!" he shouted along the way. "We've not got long, but I need your help with something urgent!" he decided.

Peel Promenade wasn't particularly long, maybe a mile or so, and it's not like Charlotte strolled the entire length of it. But by walking at a snail's pace as she spoke, it took Charlotte a good half hour before she returned to her original starting position after concluding her call. And when she did reappear, she had the most peculiar look on her face.

"Uhm, everything okay, Lotti?" Calum asked, having returned to the bench by this time in anticipation of her arrival. From Charlotte's expression, he couldn't tell if it was good news she'd received or bad.

"That was Phillipa," Charlotte answered.

"Yeah, you told me that earlier," Calum gently pointed out. "She doesn't want your clothes back?" he added, half joking.

But Charlotte didn't respond to his comment. It wasn't out of rudeness, but more that she was just coming out of a daze. "Do you remember I told you about that conversation with Darren?" she asked. "The one where he admitted to kissing me, and also about him having a queue of women lined up to do whatever he wanted if he gave them jobs on the show or helped them with their TV career?"

"Yep. Where he also confessed to lying about getting Joyce and Beryl on the show," Calum replied, confirming that he was a good listener.

"Exactly," Charlotte said, her eyes now becoming clear and focused. "Well, it wasn't just me that was privy to that conversation," she added cryptically, not immediately providing any additional information.

"Oh?" Calum asked, pressing her to elaborate.

"It appears that my old friend Darren has had his wandering hands all over the wife of one of the show's sound engineers," Charlotte continued. "And apparently, the engineer didn't take too kindly to that."

"Well, you wouldn't, would you," Calum agreed.

Charlotte broke into a smile as she relayed the further details of her recent call. "So this sound engineer, yeah? Apparently, he had access to everything that was recorded through the microphones, and not just the stuff from when we were filming the show, either. According to Phillipa, our voices are still being recorded until we either physically remove the microphone or they flick some sort of switch in the sound booth. So, Mr Sound Engineer, wanting to rip Darren's throat out, had gone through hours and hours of recordings in the hope of finding something incriminating about him. Something to corroborate what his wife was saying, yeah? So it wouldn't be just a case of he-said-she-said and that sort of thing. He really wanted to be able to nail Darren to the wall."

"And he found the recording of your little tête-à-tête?" Calum asked, quickly putting two and two together. "Jayzus, that dirty old sod," he remarked, in clear reference to Darren.

Charlotte's expression turned serious for a moment. "Calum, you know I can get you a copy of that conversation if you like. You know, if you want definitive proof that it was Darren who kissed me and not the other way around? And that I didn't want him to?"

"Charlotte. You know I love you dearly."

"Yes?"

"So shut up," Calum said playfully. "I never for a moment suspected anything, I was just so bloody angry with him when you told me before. Anyway, back to Darren, as I'm liking the sound of where this little tale is going."

"He's been fired," Charlotte was thrilled to reveal, dancing a happy little jig. "Gone. *Adiós. Arrivederci.* See ya later!"

"What about the show?" Calum enquired. "If you've gone, and now him?"

"They're going to air what's been filmed, as they've got plenty in the can at this point. And then they're on the lookout for a host for series two."

Calum scanned Charlotte's face, looking for signs that there might be more to this news. "And?" he said, suspecting there was indeed more.

"They want me to host the second series on my own, and with complete creative input!" she told him.

"And no arsehole Darren?"

"And no arsehole Darren," Charlotte was pleased to report.

Calum pulled Charlotte in, placing a long, lingering smacker square on her lips, and to which Charlotte offered no objection. "But what about the travel and time away?" Calum asked, once they'd both had a chance to come up for air.

Charlotte appeared fit to burst from excitement. "Well, from what I've been told, the plan is to turn it from an afternoon show into a weekly one-hour programme, to be shown in the evening. And if that happens, the filming schedule will be *much* less demanding," Charlotte explained. "Phillipa also said they're willing to work around my schedule, as she knows how important it is to me that my other crafting projects aren't neglected. And I can absolutely have Joyce and Beryl on as contestants as well!"

"That's amazing," Calum said, genuinely very happy for her. "Hmm, there is one problem, though," he said, thinking aloud. "If the show won't be aired in the afternoons, won't they have to change the name from Crafternoon Showdown?"

"Ah, good point. I hadn't really thought of that," Charlotte responded. "But since they're allowing me a great deal of creative control, perhaps you could help me come up with a new name," she proposed.

"So you're going to go for it?" Calum asked.

"As long as you don't mind?" Charlotte replied. "You do think it's a good idea, don't you?"

"Of course! And why would I mind! If you're happy, then I'm happy."

"I feel like this is all a dream," Charlotte remarked, still trying to wrap her head around everything. "Oh! Should we go and tell Stanley?" she added, nearly forgetting about her son.

"Good idea, as I wanted to show you something there anyway," Calum offered, taking her hand as they strolled over to the sea wall. There, Calum deftly jumped up, before turning to extend his hand to Charlotte. "Up you come," he said.

"Stan, guess what!" Charlotte shouted, while she was still adjusting her position on the wall. Then, looking down onto the beach below, she could now see what had been occupying her son's time. "Ah, so this is what you've been doing," she remarked, about the neat set of rocks he'd meticulously laid out, forming some kind of pattern or artwork.

"The both of us have been working on it," Calum was pleased to advise. "With Stanley at my direction, helpful lad that he is. I believe he was just finishing things up for me, in fact, as you were returning."

Charlotte smiled, unsure of what was going on. She hopped down from the wall, taking care not to fall face-first into the sand. Then, she looked behind her to Calum, who had remained up on the wall to survey the scene, inspecting his and Stanley's fine handiwork.

"Read what it says," Calum prompted, his face contorting with strange paroxysms as he struggled mightily to suppress a grin.

Returning her attention to the beach, Charlotte could now see that the array of rocks formed large letters which spelt out a collection of words. "Uhm," she said, struggling to decipher the message. It was made difficult by the fact that the boys had apparently been unable to find enough rocks at hand, with seashells, kelp, and whatever else Calum and Stanley could find sometimes being substituted in their place. Also, a seagull had swooped down, as they were talking, and demolished one of the letters.

"Erm, what's it supposed to say? Will... you... carry... me?" she said, certain she must be getting it wrong, as that made little sense. "Sorry, but who am I meant to carry?" she asked, confused. "You, or Stan? Either way, how would I—"

"Stanley?" Calum gently cut in. "Stanley, we need to shift our fine feathered friend," he instructed, from his elevated position.

"On it," replied Stanley, attempting to shoo away their avian interloper. He flapped his arms, trying his best to imitate a much larger bird. An osprey? An eagle? An albatross? He wasn't sure what other kind of bird might frighten the gull away, as seagulls didn't seem to generally be afraid of anything.

And in fact, the seagull seemed entirely unmoved by Stanley's performance, only buggering off, in the end, when it became clear there were no chips to be had or any other type of food to pilfer or purloin.

"Give me a minute," Stan said, setting to work, reconstructing the one key letter in the arrangement in need of repair. "There! Done!" he confirmed a moment later, stepping out of the way so Calum and his mum could view the results.

"Try again, Lotti," Calum suggested.

"Will... you... marry... me," Charlotte said, reading the message aloud. "Will you marry me?" she asked, a bit puzzled. And then...

"Oh my God, it says will you marry me!" Charlotte shouted, once the full meaning of the words finally clicked into place and sunk in. Then, she turned back to Calum, where she found him down on one knee, still up there on the sea wall, with something in his hands at eye level to her.

"Well?" he said, holding out a ring with a stone shimmering in the sunlight. "Are you going to refuse the stones?"

"Oh, Calum," Charlotte said, scarcely able to speak. "I would never refuse the stones! Nor the seashells! Nor the kelp!"

"What did she say?" Stanley shouted over, unable to clearly hear over the firm breeze.

"She said yes!" Charlotte advised, responding on Calum's behalf. "She was utterly thrilled, honoured, and delighted to say a BIG... FAT... YES!"

The End

But you can find more of the author's books via his website:
www.authorjcwilliams.com

If you had a moment to leave feedback on Amazon,
the author would be thrilled.